To my boundless optimism,
to the one from whom I inherited it,
·ho saw in me what I myself could not see.

Fabio Ranieri

KALIMERA LEFKADA

A year as an islander

FIRST EDITION

Traslation by Trish Cooper and Pietro Giordano

PROLOGUE

As I was driving all alone, in my carefree youth, savouring the pleasure of the journey and the beauty of the landscape, I was enchanted by a beautiful sight. I slowed to a stop and pulled over to the side of the road.

An expanse of still water lit by the red of sunset opened up before my eyes.

The coots and herons paced lazily, dipping their heads into the shallow water from time to time to get their dinner.

In the magical stillness, that I admired and in the total silence that enveloped the place, a small house floated in the middle of the lagoon.

I took my SLR, mounted the telephoto lens and got a better shot of the pretty little building with the sloping roof.

There was a veranda at the front to enjoy some shade on long, hot summer days, something that looked like a well, and finally a bell tower.

Only then did I realise that it was a small church.

Only some time later did I discover that it was dedicated to St Nicholas, the same patron saint of my home town.

Countless are the times I have returned to this place to admire it from the most diverse angles.

On mistral days, you can see the midnight-blue waves crashing against a rock barrier defending a lagoon of crystal-clear water.

Years later I had a feeling of déjà-vu.

This time, I was on the other side of the Atlantic on a remote islet in the Tobago Cays.

Instead of olive trees there were palm trees and instead of a church there was a fisherman's hut. Corals replaced the rocks in a beautiful reef, but the beauty and feeling of absolute peace as well as the conviction of being as close to Paradise as one can get was the same.

Continuing on of my usual wanderings here and there, I first came across a little place that is now very famous but at the time of my first visit it was still quite unknown.

I was this time with Alina and our little dogs.

Before arriving at the Lefkada causeway bridge, you can see a lagoon and a hill with the ancient fortress of Griva.

Continuing towards the island, there is an unmarked junction on the right that gives access to a dirt road.

After a few hundred metres through potholes and bumps, you come to a small car park. If you miss it, don't worry, the road is closed.

From that point, walking in a north-westerly direction leads to a small, long, shabby wooden bridge.

"I won't cross it," Ali said.

Bibi and Pepi nodded in support of Alina, while Tarallo did not even come close, more interested as he was, in the aquatic organisms of the marshy slime in which the half-rotten wooden pillars of the bridge sank.

Venturing ahead, I took my reflex camera and, being careful not to walk in the middle of the planks, many of which were and still are missing, I traversed the swamp one step at a time.

Reaching the other side, I had the distinct feeling that I was in another world.

A sand wedge divided the marsh from the lagoon.

Past the dune, one of the most beautiful beaches I have ever seen stretched as far as the eye could see left and right.

There was no one there.

My first thought was to turn back and let the rest of the troop cross the bridge, which we would later do countless times over the course of the years.

But on this occasion, I wanted to keep that moment to myself.

I began to stroll along, enchanted by the gentle roar of the waves breaking on the shoreline, accentuated by that of their big sisters breaking over the reef.

There are not too many trees down there, only fragrant maquis bushes that sing along with the wind blowing through their slender branches.

In the background, tiny and almost invisible, is the small church of St Nicholas.

I walked on that tongue of sand in a north-easterly direction and the little church got bigger and bigger as I got closer.

I was out of my earthly dimension, I remember that I did not even take pictures so as not to violate the bliss of the moment.

I was in a place where time no longer mattered, as if the bridge was the point of access to a space-time dimension.

I could almost detach myself from my body and see myself walking on the beach, alone on a spit of sand between a marsh and a pristine lagoon.

The feeling was that of living inside a bubble where the spirit of the place tells you its story.

Then a blurred figure appeared, becoming more and more real as she approached. She was beautiful and resembled an ancient Greek goddess.

She had red hair and rode a fast Serbian horse.

She did not speak, but her gaze was stern and almost seemed to say "what are you doing on my land?"

She paused, turned her gaze to the island, then turned towards Acarnania and disappeared, galloping fast.

I continued on and reached the end of the sand spit.

From there, the island seems within reach, all you have to do is cross the shallow, crystal-clear water.

I heard a rustling behind me. I turned around and a splendid Serbian horse similar to the first one was grazing there.

Then from the island I heard the laughter of a child, and sharpening my eyesight I saw him running naked and happy splashing about next to a larger figure, a man lying blissfully in the shallow water.

He was the epitome of happiness and almost seemed to radiate an aura of peace around him.

He noticed my presence, and from a distance waved to me.

I responded to the greeting and then heard Alina's voice say, "But who are you greeting?"

It was like waking up from a beautiful dream and begin in the same place as the dream.

I must have looked like a complete idiot as even the dogs looked at me turning their heads from side to side as they do when they hear an unknown sound.

"Ah here I... nothing, I thought..." and found myself looking towards the island again.

Only there was no one there, not even the horse that had been behind me.

"You didn't happen to notice a horse on the way here did you?"

"A horse?"

"Yes one of those... you know with four legs nice and fast."

"No, I didn't notice any horses, I only noticed that you had been missing for two hours and I had to come and find you! You don't know the trouble it was to get the dogs across the bridge, Tarallo didn't want to know and went straight across the marsh."

Tarallo was nowhere to be seen.

"Nice place eh?" I said.

"Yes, splendid indeed, to stay for some time."

"Yeah... but Gypsy I don't think she would be able to cross the bridge." (Gypsy is our camper van.)

"No I don't think so, but we could take a shower, come back, pitch our tent here and stay the night."

"Eh, that wouldn't be a bad idea, we certainly wouldn't be the first ones to do it."

"No of course not, while you were who knows where I had time to read a bit of history about this place," said Alina.

"And...?" I urged her.

"It seems that in the past a hermit lived there on St Nicholas Island."

"Is it dedicated to St Nicholas?"

"Yes... it used to be a temple dedicated to Aphrodite.

I read that one T. Mamaloukas wrote about a man who lived there with his wife, Eva Palmer, and his son, Glaucus, who learned to swim before he learned to walk."

"Ah..."

"Yes from what I read he was naked most of the time."

"And... how did this happy family live?"

"By fishing and hunting. His wife Eva liked to dress like an ancient Greek and ride her beautiful Serbian horses and they often went hunting together across the river in Acarnania.

"She must have been a beautiful woman, with her thick, red hair."

"Oh… that's it."

"What? You usually like these stories" Ali asked.

"Yes indeed I do. And the man: what was his name?"

"Angelos Sikelianos, and he was a poet."

I inhaled deeply, then said, "yes, you would not lack inspiration here..."

"Yeah... so? Shall we pitch the tent?"

"Another time, today let's leave them alone. We just met them...

...Another time..."

THE FORGOTTEN VILLAGE

We happened upon Vafkeri by chance.

The season had just ended and it had been truly terrible, as the 2020 season had been for everyone.

In August there were so few tourists on the streets of Nydri that it felt like April. We had decided to return to Italy for the winter, then Ali, thanks to her title of social worker and her mastery of English, found a job with a British family who needed a person specialised in dealing with a 'special' child; we were not allowed to know more.

"What do you say? Shall I try?" She asked.

"I don't know. If we want to stay here even in winter we can discuss it, but that doesn't take away from the fact that we are leaving this house."

"I'm sorry, it didn't seem so bad when I first saw it: a stone's throw from the sea, with a private dock and looking so pretty."

"Yes that was before we saw it from the inside, since then I have not liked it, excluding seeing Nitroglicerina moored by the kitchen window."

"And does that seem little to you?"

Nitroglicerina is my rabid little racing catamaran.

Alina called the number they had left her and made an appointment to meet the child.

Their home was located on a huge plot on the peninsula that closes Dessimi Bay to the south.

We arrived there with a rented moped because a week earlier Gypsy, our beloved camper van, quit us until I replaced a valve that regulates the air-fuel mixture entering the engine.

The road was and still is a disaster.

"I'm not putting Gypsy's wheels up here, let's also make arrangements for a ride from the asphalted point onwards, if they don't like it, worse for them, we're going home."

My mind was already back in my lovely Puglia, in the Murge, frolicking with the dogs on the rolling karst hills admiring some of the most beautiful views in the world.

Alina did not share my opinion.

After a few hours, she called me:

"Hey, it's OK, they'll take me."

"OK, see you there."

"But are you home?"

"No I'm fishing, the less I'm in there the better."

We met in the evening and she updated me on the latest developments.

"The child is beautiful, he just doesn't speak; he's closed in on himself in such an introverted way that I haven't seen since I visited an orphanage in Romania."

"So much?"

"Yes... he clearly has some problems but by working on them they could solved. I think I can do it."

Alina was radiant, she loves her job and dealing with children is what she enjoys most in the world.

"So what do we do?"

"Ah, nothing, they thought I wouldn't accept. The mother almost in a gesture of defiance asked me will you come back tomorrow?"

"And what did you say to her?"

"I'll see you tomorrow at 8 o'clock!"

We started to look for a more comfortable house to spend the winter in, since Geni's dive bar was "watery" in the sense that, when it rained and there was a north wind, the water physically seeped through the doors as if they were made of sponge, especially that oak kitchen door, which consequently flooded.

This was how we found the cottage.

"Hey look at this" Alina said to me, reviewing advertisements of houses for rent.

"Beautiful, I wonder how much they ask..."

"Less than three hundred."

"No way..."

"So it is written."

It was a stone cottage and looked quite nice from the pictures, the amount was not too high and so we called the attached number.

We were answered by a guy who fortunately spoke English and we made an appointment to go and have a look at the place.

"Perfect," I said to Alina, "tomorrow at 5pm in... Vafkeri."

"Where?"

"Vafkeri... at least that's what he said."

"And where is it?"

"I've no idea... I'll look it up on the map now."

We arrived at the village early. We stopped in a car park that could have accommodated three cars at most, but that would have been better for two.

There were two natives leaning against a small stone wall speaking to each other and they asked why we were stopping. With gesture we understood what they wanted because they spoke nothing but Greek.

We tried to understand each other somehow but there was no way. We did not speak Greek and they spoke only that. After several attempts, I think we managed to make it clear that we were waiting for a guy called Vangelis.

"Ah Vangelis, ne ne Tanassis."

Whereupon they started calling him on the phone, I don't know why.

Considering that everyone around here is called Vassili, Dimitri or Vangelis, we didn't know for sure who they were calling.

In any case the matter was soon resolved when our Vangelis called me back a few moments later and told me he was on his way.

So to pass the time we let the doggies out of Gypsy and started walking down the street trying to figure out which of the countless uninhabited houses was the one seen on the advertisement.

There were a couple of secluded ones at the entrance to the village; very nice, a little too close to the road maybe, but free-standing, made of stone with a sloping roof and a nice chimney stack.

From the car park, a road descends to the lower part of the village where the houses are all close together. As I walked along it, I noticed the sign of a tavern that is no longer in business; there are left only the tables with the logos, a faded and weather-worn sticker of an award from a tourist guide and many cobwebs fluttering among the dust.

"Everything seems abandoned around here" said Alina.

"Yes, I'm starting to like it."

A feline colony still inhabits the old tavern, who knows maybe the cats in their memories still smell the odours of those foods with which the tourists fed them.

We got back up in time to see a car pull up, from which a not-so-bright-looking guy got out, looking around in bewilderment.

"I think it's that one there" I said.

We greeted him and after introductions he asked us to follow him in the car, as if we needed a car to get from one point to another in Vafkeri.

We climbed into Gypsy and started to drive in the direction of Karya, but after not even two-hundred metres he engaged the left arrow and climbed a stone-paved road at a prohibitive gradient.

After a bend to the right we began to see a couple of houses.

We came to a crossroads with a tiny and incredibly pretty square: the famous wine square.

Vangelis turned right and after ten metres stopped in the shade of a tree in front of which stands a small church, which we later discovered to be dedicated to St Marina.

Opposite the church is our Devonshire-style cottage.

"This must be it, at least from the pictures" Alina told me, smiling.

"Nice."

It is actually quite beautiful: a fence wraps around the entrance: a wooden door surmounted by a stone and iron arch, two symmetrical windows in the classic Greek blue colour are framed by a living stone wall with a sloping tiled roof.

It is not only beautiful, it is a fairytale cottage.

Vangelis opened the door and we stood before a warm and cosy environment once the lights illuminating the wooden counter-roof were switched on.

A sofa, two armchairs, a wood-burning stove and a fireplace were part of the essential and spartan furniture.

Behind us, we noticed a garden with an olive tree in the middle and a panoramic view of the spring whose roar can be heard during the long winter days.

Alina immediately fell in love with it, and so did I. She smiled at me and made a gesture as if asking me to move forward. I was hooked as soon as I saw the fireplace.

I love them, they remind me of my childhood - I always lived in houses with fireplaces.

Alina took me by the hand and we began to explore the little house with those eyes that see something that you know is already yours to the extent that you imagine yourself mentally decorating it.

The lady accompanying Vangelis understood Italian so we tried not to reveal too much, but we already knew we would say yes; it seemed so cosy, so isolated, so similar to our little house in Cassano delle Murge...

The next day we went to the bakery of Tanassis, Vangelis' father, and a man with a benevolent, round face, a nice moustache and a seemingly affectionate smile greeted us with a coffee.

The day before, Vangelis had made the grave mistake of informing me that Tanassis is madly in love with the Italian language and I artfully used this information.

"Tanassis dearest! Vangelis told me more about you than about the cottage yesterday and we finally got to know each other" I tell him in Italian.

"Oh Mr Fabio what a pleasure and what an honour to be able to speak Italian with you."

"Come on Tanassis please, call me by my first name."

"Oh but only if you do the same."

"Alright let's skip the pleasantries then."

"Do you like the cottage?"

"Very nice, very nice indeed, a little bit far from the nerve centres of the island and with what petrol costs... but come on, if we agree on the price it can be done."

Alina whitened instantly; if it were up to her, she would have accepted even double what they were asking.

But the game worked, we agreed in a few minutes and Tanassis even left us the keys on the same day, a week ahead of the agreed date for the first payment.

"That went well, huh?" I said.

"I mean, did he even give you a lower price? But where did you Italians learn to haggle?"

"As children, we swapped football stickers; we do it more for fun than anything else but you see... it also has its advantages."

"Yes I can see that," Ali replied, shaking her head. "What is to be done?"

"Well let's go buy something to clean it up and from tomorrow we can start the transfer."

"But what if we buy two blankets and sleep in them from tonight?"

We did it. We liked it so much that we slept there from day one, instantly forgetting about Geni.

The next morning when we woke up, the silence was surreal.

I opened the window and the valley flooded us with colours and scents.

I never speak when I'm happy, I breathe life in and savour every single moment.

"It feels like a dream," Alina told me.

I nodded.

We started the transfer and the next day or so as we unloaded Gypsy a lady with an unmistakable British accent stopped at our door and in perfect English asked us:

"Ehy good morning! Are you moving here?"

"Yes..."

"Wow new neighbours! Two more people in Vafkeri very good!"

"OK... thanks..." I replied uncertainly.

"I will introduce you all! I am Ann Edwards and this is my husband John."

A nice blue-eyed gentleman greeted us from inside the car.

"There is another Ann who looks after stray cats, her husband's name is Dave, and there is a German couple who live in a house further up the road. Ah, you will love this village."

Alina and I looked at each other shocked.

We were coming from a less than idyllic period considering expectations, and this welcome was exactly what we needed to caulk a financially bad and humanly disappointing season.

On the adjacent property lives an elderly gentleman who laughs all the time. He has a wonderful hunting dog called Atina but he can never get her on a leash because he is too old and she is too impetuous, so as soon as we moved in I offered to take her around and from then on our walks became threesomes.

Bibi and Pepi immediately accepted their new hiking companion, only to regret it a couple of days later when they discovered the impetuousness of her character – only due to the happiness of leaving that chain for a few minutes a day.

Atina is disarmingly sweet.

And Vafkeri is a fantastic, beautiful, fairy-tale village – where the demons of the past live hand in hand with the magic of the present.

It stands exactly in the centre of the island, as if it were its pivot.

The streets are all paved in stone, the same material used for the houses.

No supermarket, no shop, just a tavern: O' Platanos, an 1807 building with stone walls and wooden beams still bearing the axe marks made by the shipwright who fashioned them.

A cast-iron wood-burning cooker doubles as a kitchen when needed, and hanging on the wall there are ancient keys and old utensils, oil lamps, and pots and pans from the last century called *casani*, so large that one of them would be enough to cook for the entire village.

Nothing is square in there: the walls, the beams, the windows, not even the door leading into the pantry, which also serves as a cellar.

The kitchen can be mistaken for that of a small house from which delicacies of yesteryear come out.

To be fair, it is like stepping back into a place from another era.

It is the meeting point of the Vafkeritis, where the spirit of the ancient Lefkadians still lives on, convinced 100% that they are the true heirs of Odysseus.

"Mario Draghi cuckold!" shouted Dionissis in Italian.

Vafkeri like all mountain villages has a chairman, a kind of councillor.

Dionissis, *Gnogno* to his friends, looks after the village and does so with love, getting his hands dirty himself if there is something to be repaired, be it a water pipe or an electricity pole.

At the end of each job you see him return to the tavern clutching a cigarette between his lips: 'I fix it', he says as he crosses the threshold.

He loves Italian and the Italians, except for our former leader whom he never fails to call a cuckold... And with good reason I would say given how he reduced Greece when he was president of the EU.

But what he loves most is our language. He likes its musicality.

He always tells me of his grandparents, they lived in Vafkeri and like many other elders in the mountain villages spoke fluent Italian.

Winter in Vafkeri flows by slowly and quietly.

The air is so pure that breathing it almost hurts your lungs if you're not used to it, especially after a gust of Mistral.

There is not much to do, to be fair, but it is situations like these that bring me back in touch with the true essence of things.

It is not that difficult: reading a good book in front of the wood-burning stove, walking in the woods admiring the clouds that enter the valley as they climb up the slopes, contemplating the panorama that changes every second, clandestinely gathering in the tavern in the evenings to drink a tsipuro together and try to learn a few words in Greek, inebriating oneself with the scent of wood burning in the fireplaces mixed with that of moss and wet grass.

There is something mystical and inexplicable about it.

It has been the wine country for years.

In the small square near our house there is a huge old wine press, and at the entrance to the village there is a smaller one that has been used by island families every October for two centuries.

As in a ritual, the scent of pressed grapes wafts through the alleys of the village, tickling the lucky nostrils of its inhabitants.

Vafkeri is the ideal place to enjoy and understand the mountainous part of Lefkada, the real part.

In summer it is much cooler than the coast, in winter it becomes magical.

Around the hill on which the village stands there is a bucolic path that we never tire of walking.

Climbing up to the summit, dubbed the Australian's Peak, one climbs through bushes and follows a goat path between karst rock and a small overhang towering above a valley planted with vine saplings.

You come out of the grove and again cross a field of small trees before reaching the asphalt road.

Following it, you arrive at a beautiful, abandoned monastery.

The ruins are not well maintained except for the central church, but the place is full of energy.

A solitary bench overlooks a well in the middle of a garden surmounted by the shady foliage of an immense plane tree.

You can stay there for hours meditating and recharging your soul.

Every time we go there the dogs disappear for a while recovering their hunter instincts; there is no one to disturb.

Silence, in its best expression, is the only sound to keep you company: the wind whistling softly and lightly through the branches of the trees, the last leaves fluttering and gliding the ground, then the scents of the grass and undergrowth.

Every time we leave the monastery we say goodbye, certain that we will return soon to enjoy the spirituality and aura of magic it conveys.

The path continues downhill to the springs.

In winter, it is possible to see the water gush out of the living rock and get lost in the valley below.

Here too, two immense plane trees tower over the rocks as guardians of an ancient fountain system that collects some of that water, used in the past to quench the thirst of the island's countless goats and a few wild vagabonds.

From the spring it is a moment's walk up to the cottage, enjoying the view of the valley below.

At the end of one of these walks I happened to notice a shape over there among the trees.

It was Lakis, the brother of our neighbour Theodoric.

He smiled as always, his big blue eyes framed by a cheerful, wrinkled smile from life.

Vafkeri is the kind of village where, as you walk by, you can see an elderly gentleman carrying a small pile of wood from the forest to his house, where at dusk you hear the echo of cowbells on the necks of goats returning from their pastures at the bottom of the valley, where as you go out to fetch wood from the porch you find a family of foxes drinking from the bowls of your dogs, and as you try to be quiet to admire them you hear the sound of hooves on the pavement, which in the mystic glow of the street lamps, blurred by the floating fog, takes the form of two or three cows walking down the only street in the village.

Vafkeri is like that, a place from another era: hopefully no one will ever repair the clock.

NEW LIFE

At the end of any of our walks, the dogs ran as if they had just left home, except for Pepi, the tiniest and oldest, who was beginning to feel a little tired.

"We should try it the other way around this path, finishing uphill is a drag," I told Alina.

"Yes, we can go down and then up again, we would come down from the Australian's peak."

Every time Theodoric saw us pass by with his dog, he gave us one of his beautiful smiles.

Perhaps he was simply happy that someone was walking Atina around.

We returned home and threw ourselves exhausted on the sofas.

"What shall we eat?" I asked hungrily as if I had walked the Camino de Santiago.

"You had breakfast two hours ago."

"And yes indeed."

"It's still early, I'll see what's cooking."

"Yes, but I am hungry."

"And have a snack before lunch."

I opened the fridge and a sandwich with Lefkada salami and smoked goat cheese took shape, all washed down with a Mamoz.

"There's not much point in walking miles if you then have a beer and a sandwich as an aperitif."

"So let's skip lunch and go to Platanos tonight."

"That's... even worse."

"Are we on a diet?"

"No not yet, but if you keep this up you will be soon."

"Buongiorno!" A voice echoed from the window, it was Dave who in his marked British accent was trying not to mispronounce too much one of the few Italian words in his vocabulary.

"Hey Dave!" I replied, opening the door.

"Hi Fabio, we are going for a bike ride tomorrow, would you like to join us?"

"OK but we only have one bicycle."

"Oh no, no, don't worry, I'll lend you the bikes."

"Ah thank you, all right then."

"OK tomorrow morning at ten o'clock."

"OK bye."

"Tomorrow we go cycling," I said to Alina as we returned to the house.

"Yes, I heard."

"You up for it?"

"You already said yes I think."

"Eh, so you don't put me on a diet."

A bike ride was just what was needed after an evening at the Platanos.

There were never too many people in the tavern, apart from Iorgos and the president, who were almost always present.

Maria, a nice and fantastic cook, lived upstairs.

"Ela Fabbioooo" shouted Iorgo as soon as he saw me cross the threshold.

"Olympiakos!" Iorgo's sympathy and laughter are infectious.

The President, on the other hand, when he saw us he was a bit aloof; he is the kind of person who does not give confidence right away but once you become his friend he would give you his soul.

"Ela Fabio," said Sotiris Santa, the *manager*.

"Something to drink?"

"Yes thank you Sot, a tsipuro for me and an ouzo for Alina."

"Tsipuro huh? Iiihihih," Iorgo echoed, waving his hand.

Now when I ordered drinks at Platanos, regardless of what was being drunk, I would get a plate of olives, one of cheese, one of tomatoes dressed with oil and oregano, and then something hot: stew or roast.

And this was repeated with every order of each new drink.

The ambience was warm, smoky and cosy, a bit like being at a friend's house: you watched something on TV, swore at a politician's joke, whistled at the pretty valet on some talk show, while eating and drinking all the time.

Of course, following the speeches was not easy, despite Santas' efforts to translate for me as much as possible of the avalanche of words that were spoken every second into English.

A quarrel was going on between Iorgo and the President, great friends but from opposite political sides. You never know when a Greek is talking or arguing, they are always shouting; except for Santas: thin and with an old-fashioned look, with his medium-long straight hair, his always groomed moustache and his aloof manner.

He would dismiss political speeches with just a light wave of his hand.

One of his maxims was: "politicians always pretend to argue, then eat together laughing at people taking their sides."

The morning always comes too early for Alina.

"Is it time to get up already?" she said, slurring her words and crinkling her eyes.

"If you want to come by bike, yes."

"You say it's bad if I don't come?"

"Considering it's the first time we've been invited, yes."

"Mmm that's not fair!"

"And I know... life is unfair... come on get up."

After a quick breakfast and a little walk to let the dogs stretch their legs, we all met up in Dessimi, at Andrew's beautiful villa.

Dave and Ann were there with a couple of friends: Peter and *Little Ann,* his wife.

"Good morning, this is your bike Fabio," Dave said, introducing me to a beautiful white Specialized.

"For Alina, on the other hand, we have a more comfortable and quiet mountain bike."

We began our ride by skirting the bay of Vliho with the few boats moored for the winter, continuing to the Nydri waterfalls.

The group was anything but slow.

Dave and Peter years earlier had been on a rather peculiar adventure: *From London 2 Lefkada.*

That is, cycling from England to Greece, supported by their ladies who followed them in their cars.

I couldn't keep up with the first group, Alina on the other hand was much further behind.

At the end of the trip, we – who were the youngest in the group – were the most tired.

"I guess we'll have to train more if we want to keep up with them" I told Alina once we were back at the villa.

"Speak for yourself, this is my first and last time."

"You didn't like it?"

"It's not that I didn't enjoy it, it's just that I thought I'd go for a quiet ride, take a few pictures, not get caught up in a race!"

"Yes, they are very fast."

"I don't like speed."

"That's fine, it means we will do more walking."

"It's already better, a quiet walk, with the dogs, taking pictures and admiring the landscape."

"So? Shall we go for coffee?" asked Dave, coming towards me.

"It's a bit of a ritual, after every ride an invigorating coffee is what you need."

We stopped at the Tea bar on the way to Dessimi: a quiet, floral-themed bar where Alina would wait for me after work, and which would become one of her favourite places on the island.

It is very pretty and from its terrace one has a breathtaking view of Vliho bay.

As soon as they arrived, Ali immediately took possession of the swing chair, her favourite spot, anticipating the others and flashing that beautiful, boyish smile of hers to the rhythm of its rocking.

Sometimes she really looks like a child.

"Nice ride guys. Thanks!" I said.

"Whenever you want Fabio, today was a bit like that, easy-peasy, but if you take the training you'll come with us when we do more challenging laps."

"More challenging? Like?"

"Well I don't say we go around the island, but we go to the valley of Vassiliki, for example, or around the lagoon, or even mountain biking around the oldest forest of Lefkada."

"Beautiful, I have heard that the ancient forest is inhabited by spirits."

"Yeah, I've heard that too," Dave replied, laughing, "I think the local people put these stories out there for who knows what reason."

At a small table sat a lady, standing there on her own, not old but not young either. She was a bit overdressed for that hot day and looked old-fashioned, with her wide-brimmed hat framed by a light lace veil.

Her skin was quite whitish, as if there was no blood flowing inside.

She was sipping a cup of something and when she heard Dave laughing she froze.

It was as if time stopped with her.

Not a gust of wind, not a leaf moved. A surreal silence enveloped the tea bar and we were all a little intimidated by it.

With a calculated slowness the lady turned to Dave and with watery eyes of a different colour stared at him with a look that was meant to be reproachful.

Now you have to know that Dave is a gentle soul, one of the nicest people you could meet on the island, and those two eyes, one blue the other grey, made him a little uneasy.

We looked at each other slightly disturbed, not understanding what that frail lady wanted from us, nor why she was looking so insistently at Dave.

Then she spoke.

"These are no stories" she said in a voice as light as a hiss and as vibrant as a tuning fork.

"The spirits of our ancestors live in the ancient forest, you do not perceive them because you are *foreigners,*" she said, accentuating the sense of contempt on the word foreigners.

"You should not go up there, and you should show more respect."

Then as she turned around, picked up her cup and sipped its contents, a gust of wind blew from the bay up the hill, caressing the leaves of the trees on the terrace of the Tea bar.

"OK" Dave said in a whisper more to himself than to others.

Ann, his wife, smiled shaking her head in amusement.

Alina, on the other hand, was still trying to look the lady in the eyes, but she was protected by her hat.

A bit puzzled, we finished our coffees chatting in low voices and then left.

Driving along the road that climbs up to Vafkeri, you can enjoy a fantastic panorama: the view of the small islands on the east coast is something that captivates anyone who sees it for the first time.

Scorpio, Scorpidi, Xeloni, Madouri, Sparti and further on Meganissi; small strips of land rising from the sea.

Then the road goes deep into a valley and climbs around the hilltop on which Vafkeri stands.

The most beautiful way is to drive it downhill.

We went down that road every day in the early morning, and the colours of the sunrise over the bay were always different, depending on the weather, the temperature, and the clouds.

One particular morning, after leaving Alina at work, I was returning to the bay to check on my boat *Nitroglicerina,* and a very thin layer of fog had formed on the water, enveloping boats and birds.

Meanwhile the sun was rising, giving everything a surreal aspect.

Silence enveloped the bay and mist drifted over the surface of the water, changing its colour from pink to gold as the sun rose.

This show lasted less than an hour and only a lucky few of us were able to admire it.

Those are moments of purity that the island gives and if you are not there, ready to grasp its beauty and authenticity, that mystical aura disappears and the island no longer reveals itself.

Only a few can enjoy it – only the deserving.

"That child is an angel, if only…"

"What..."

"Oh... nothing..."

"Come on, stop talking about work" I told her.

I had spent the day fishing, using a fixed rod and breadcrumbs soaked in feta liquid, the old-fashioned way.

I was on the beautiful bay of Dessimi, the sun was shining and the temperature was perfect.

The summer season was long over, but the temperatures remained high and pleasant despite it being late November.

"What shall we do?" Alina asked.

"Whatever you want."

"Do you still have to fish?"

"It's almost sunset, that's the best time, but if you want we'll go up to the cottage."

"No we can stay a little longer, I'll lie in the sun, but let's not be late – the doggies are waiting for us."

We stayed another half an hour, then before sunset, I dismantled the rod and put it back in the car. I had a nice basket of fish, it would make a great fry-up.

Returning home, we did not meet a soul, the island was deserted.

It had emptied out completely.

The season had been very meagre and local people complained about the lack of tourist income.

Added to this was the ban on hunting for the entire winter, so there was hardly anyone around.

The island breathed tranquillity.

It was not even allowed to fish, but down in Dessimi it was difficult for anyone to go down and check.

Greek islands are a world apart and Lefkada was no exception.

There are Greek laws, laws of Lefkada, then laws of the mountain.

That is also why I love living up here.

That evening I went down to the taverna for a tsipouro, as always it was "closed" but open to friends.

You arrived, knocked, the red curtain was drawn aside, and Santas' slender face looked at you with those beady eyes and a cigarette between his lips barely hidden by his moustache.

Then the curtain closed again and the door opened. "Ela Fabio pame come inside."

The usual ones were always there: Iorgo, the President, Maria...

The ambience was as always warm, smoky and cosy.

The feeling was that of being out of time, in an era decades away from that two thousand and twenty, that glass of tsipouro that warmed your soul and those goat cheeses made from ancient recipes.

"Are you OK Fabio?" asked Santas.

"Yeah I'm OK, I've been fishing."

"Did it go well?"

"Only small fish."

"Well better than nothing."

"Ah sure... yamas."

"Yamas."

"If you want to catch bigger fish you have to go to two places" he told me between puffs on his cigarette.

"At the salt pans, and at the mouth of the Dimossari. Today there is much less of it, but years ago, before the water was channelled towards Scorpio and Meganissi, the mouth of the Dimossari was a freshwater lake in the sea; it reached as far as Madouri."

"Man, that was real fishing back then."

"Ah! Some sea bass... enormous."

"I was in the Dimossari Gorge yesterday, we went cycling with Dave."

"Nice place! Now there is little water, but you will see as rains start how it swells."

"Yeah I guess... listen Santas, can I ask you a question?"

"Sure, tell me."

"What about the ancient forest? Can it be visited?"

Sot lowered his gaze, inhaled from his cigarette and exhaled, enveloping his head in a cloud of bluish smoke, like his eyes.

"Yes of course, you can visit..."

"And why is there so much mystery around this forest?"

At my question, the President and Iorgo stopped talking and again a feeling of absolute silence enveloped the air as if in a vice.

"Because it is easy to get lost up there, the trees are immense and all look alike."

"Are there no paths?"

"There is a path from the Red Church that climbs into the forest but be careful, it is not well marked and is often hidden by vegetation."

"It must be beautiful to walk up there."

"Yes..." said Sot sighing "it is beautiful, but do it in silence, to fully enjoy the beauty of the place."

"And to not disturb the spirits" I added.

At that line, the silence became palpable.

Iorgo, usually very talkative, twirled his rosary beads in his hands, then said something in Greek to Sotiris, who replied in a raised voice.

A discussion ensued that also involved the President.

He told me in Italian: "Don't go alone the first time. Go with someone who knows the way." The tone was serious and peremptory.

"OK, thank you President."

He replied nodding.

Iorgo seemed to calm down, then turned his attention back to the TV and his Olympiacos. "Ela malaka pame!" He railed at a player, opening the five fingers of his hand.

"How do you get there Sot?"

Sotiris looked up, staring at me with his blue eyes tending to grey.

You have to take the road to Karya, then right to Platystoma, and from there you have two roads, one going downhill to a junction that takes you to the Red Church, but it is not indicated and the road is unpaved.

"And the other one?"

"From Platystoma goes towards Alexandros. You park your car there and then take a path that gets lost in the forest. From that point you have to get your bearings because the path disappears as you go deeper into the forest. First keep to the south, then after a while turn south-west; at this point you should arrive at the Red Church.

From there, you can head for the main road and return to Playstoma on foot, or you can get picked up."

"I'll bring my surveying compass."

"Eheh... you don't need a compass up there" he told me putting out his cigarette and tilting his head to the side.

"Yes, but as a precaution."

"You don't need it because up there the compasses doesn't work."

"What do you mean?"

"There must be a magnetic field or something driving them crazy, the fact is they don't point north. You can bring it if you want, so you can see it for yourself, but don't rely on it OK?"

"OK, thanks Santas. My dogs will guide me on the right path."

"Yes, dogs are much more useful, they can connect better with... Nature."

The days passed in tranquility, all the same but always a little different.

I would engage in fishing and sometimes I would come home with bigger fish than I used to catch with bread.

I followed Sotiris' advice and went to the salt pans.

A fabulous, surreal environment, especially at dawn.

I left Alina at work and drove almost twenty kilometres to the east coast.

The old salt pans date back as far as the time of Alexander the Great.

They remained in operation until a few decades ago, before the tourist boom changed the island forever.

The capital city expanded more and more and the European Community financed a project to channel the sewage that still flowed into the canal.

The money arrived – and disappeared.

No work was carried out and the sewage from the increasingly populous capital continued to flow into the canal to this day.

On Mistral days they are pushed southwards, lapping the edge of the salt pans.

When the sea succeeded in breaching the embankment, the salt marshes were dirtied forever and after millennia of activity, this was the end.

This is the dark side of the island, *una faccia – una razza*... even the mafia.

Nowdays the place is a fantastic site for fishing and bird watching.

The fish that come from Preveza to Lefkada pass through the channel and if you are patient you can catch a lot of them and they are very good.

December arrived and temperatures began to fall.

Smoke came out of the chimneys of the houses, drawing spirals in the sky.

The air was permeated with the scent of burning wood.

From the salt pans it is a stone's throw to the mainland. You can watch herds grazing, and when the wind blows towards the island you can feel the bittersweet smell of stables and manure.

At that time I used to watch out for any car coming from the access road, it was still forbidden to fish and that was a well-known place, every now and then police cars would come to have a look and so I and the fishermen would hide in the abandoned cottage on the shore.

No policeman ever bothered to get out of the car to check the inside, after all those rules were stupid and not even they were happy to enforce them, not to mention that on the island people know each other.

From the west came not only the road and the control cars, but also the winter storms.

The stormy wind pushed dark clouds up to 1176 metres with heavy rain falls; spectacular to watch!

The sky turns a sombre grey, bright red if they arrive at sunset, with the sun backlit; swollen with water, they climb over the mountains and roll down the opposite slope.

That is the signal to dismantle the equipment and take refuge in the car.

If they last a short time you can continue fishing, but sometimes they last for hours and there is nothing to do but return home to the warmth of the hearth.

It is always nice return to Vafkeri, the stone cottage is a cosy gem and spending the winter up there gives a sense of protection and security.

Out there, the wind howls through the trees, and doors and window shutters start vibrating.

But inside you are sheltered, with a cup of hot chocolate in your hand, watching the flames dance in the wood stove.

Christmas was approaching and Sotiris had a great idea:

"You know Fabio, I was thinking that for Christmas instead of each of us spending it at home we could organise something here at the tavern."

"Yes why not, it's a good idea."

"Yes, I think so too. I thought I would invite all the villagers."

"All of them?"

"Yes... all eight of them!"

CHRISTMAS AT THE TAVERN

Christmas came quickly.

It was a wonderful experience and Santa's idea turned out to be really good.

Eventually, we became a dozen and each brought something from home, a typical Christmas dish to share with the others.

And so the tavern welcomed a cheerful, smoky and rowdy company of Lefkadians, or rather as they like to call themselves: people from Vafkeri - Vafkerit!

In fact, only the residents of the village were invited, partly because of the ridiculous restrictive rules imposed by the Greek government on the pandemic, rules that may have been fine for a big city but not for an island, and partly because they are like that: proud of their pretty little village.

Being considered Vafkerit made us proud.

That invitation was worth as much as an honorary citizenship.

Wood crackled in the oven and on its cooker meals were kept warm.

As always, these people had overdone and most of the food was left over for the next days.

In the mountains of Lefkada, the food is excellent and always plentiful, strictly prepared with local ingredients, from vegetables to meat.

From outside the island they use only soices and flours for the bread.

The main reason why those dishes are so tasty, is because they are cooked with love following traditional recipes and cooking methods – handed down over generations.

There was no exchange of gifts, but just the pleasure to spend time together.

Iorgo's laughter echoed in the air, he finds the comic side in everything, even in some idiotic phrase on TV.

"I'm full" Alina said after the first round of appetisers.

"Look, we haven't even started as far as I can see."

"Yes but I want to leave myself some room for sweets, hihi" she said with her adorable childish smile.

Alina and sweets have a relationship of their own, best not to judge.

"I guess they won't let you do it this time, you'll have to taste a bit of everything or they'll be disappointed."

"Look, you take small portions, I'll just taste and then I'll pass you mine as well."

The problem was that after the main course even I could not eat anymore, and when the platter of local cheeses accompanied by sweet village wine arrived, the effort became bigger, but those goat cheeses so tasty, some spicy, others smoked, that we just couldn't resist.

"OK..." I proposed, "I'll do the cheeses and you do the desserts."

"Deal."

"Eeeela Fabio bravo!" shouted Iorgo.

Everyone smiled to see that the dishes had been enjoyed by the new Lefkadians, or rather Vafkeritis.

"Fabio kala?" asked Maria motherly, "are you OK?" translated the president.

"Everything is delicious, only I'm overfilled; what I ate today I usually eat in three days."

Maria burst into laughter, "and parties are like that, but also in Italy, right?"

"Yes not much changes, just the menu."

"Ah! You don't eat meat at Christmas?"

"No at Christmas it's all fish at our place, at least on Christmas Eve, then on the 25th—"

"You don't eat meat at Christmas?" the President interrupted me.

"Mmm... no a lot of raw seafood, some cooked, then fish."

"Oh... no here in the mountains always meat, you can't go hunting otherwise I would have let you taste the wild boar of Lefkada, very good... but sooner or later I will bring it to you."

A dish for wolves, to be enjoyed in the middle of winter, when it is snowing outside and the wind whistles between the wooden joints of the Taverna, with the stove on and the tsipuro flowing.

Instead we tasted it in the summer, in the heat, as a welcome for my family: spiced with cinnamon and accompanied by bucatini passed off as spaghetti that had been floating in the boar cooking sauce since the early hours of the afternoon

But that is another story.

At dusk, after several hands of a kind of *scopa* played with poker cards, the guests began to thin out.

"Kai tora? How do we get home now?" I said.

"Eh... don't let it show if you don't get a ride, let's walk a bit so we can at least start the digestion."

"Digestion? I hibernate after tonight."

The uphill walk to the cottage was slow, zig-zagging, but permeated with the damp scent of the Mountain.

The spring gushed into the valley, its roar could be heard all the way up to the village.

December rains had filled the karstic subsoil of Lefkada and from there, the centre of the island, spring water poured into the Vafkeri valley following a path traced by centuries.

The village was shrouded in cloud and the light of the yellowish street lamps hovered ghostly in the air.

The pavement of the streets was damp and eternal, nothing could scratch it.

Generations of Lefkadians had trod those stones, shepherds and hunters.

You could almost see them in the strange, spirited shapes that swirled in the moisture-saturated air. They drove their flocks to the green mountain pastures, rich in fresh, nutritious grass.

Not much has changed since those days, only the candles in the shepherds' houses are no longer there, and instead of using donkeys they now have rickety, noisy, unhinged mopeds.

On balance better for donkeys, in fact if there is one thing I do not forgive the local people it is the way they treat animals.

Apart from Maria and the President, most of them keep their dogs on the chain, out in the cold, the most cared-for under a makeshift shelter.

"Atina is crying," said Alina.

"Yes, she must have heard us, now I'm going to stroke her and bring her some kibble."

"You say we don't take her in for the night?"

"If we show her how comfortable it is to stay warm and then leave her out the next day it will be worse."

"We can ask Theodoric to let us keep it in."

"It's bad enough that he makes us carry his dog around with ours. Then if we leave one day, what do we do with it, tie it to the chain?"

"No if we leave one day we will take her with us." ...Simply Alina...

Atina was in her kennel, huddled up to fight the cold.

A sweet hound, her funny and always cheerful face was sad that day.

I climbed over the low wall dividing the two properties and she came out of her cold shelter to meet me.

"Hi Tinuzza."

She cuddled close to me, taking all the caresses she could.

"If you didn't maul every mattress I put you in here you'd be warmer you know?"

The dog gave a whine of disapproval, then started sniffing me and when she realised I was hiding some kibble behind my back, the rhythm of her wagging increased.

"Merry Christmas to you too, don't get used to these because they cost a fortune and they normally are for veterinary use for Pepi, he can't eat any more."

I poured the contents of the bag into the aluminium bowl and tucked it into the kennel to protect it from rain and humidity.

Ati dived into it with her whole muzzle wagging her tail happily.

The rumbling of the spring could be heard even louder from the garden, it was as if the island was breathing, a continuous guttural gasp amidst the icy, pure streams of water gushing just below.

Back in the cottage, Alina was rekindling the fire, Bibi and Pepi were next to her enjoying the renewed warmth.

"Tomorrow, in order to digest everything we've eaten we'll take a trip to the spring, then see where the path up the hill leads. What do you say?"

"If it doesn't rain..." replied Alina.

"It's not supposed to rain tomorrow, by the way: I have to write the weather forecast."

To this day I still write the daily weather forecast of the island and share it with my friends.

At first I only wrote it in summer, but it gradually became a much-awaited appointment and the compliments I received on the way I write it convinced me to publish it in the winter as well.

"Dave said that the path leads to an old abandoned monastery, I would like to see it" Alina said.

"Let's go find him tomorrow, did he say anything else?"

"No just that it's a ruin shrouded in vegetation, on foot you can see it but doing the route by bike you run the risk of not noticing it because you get there downhill and on a bend; so the way they go I think they pay more attention to the road than to the landscape.

I nodded.

"I'm going to have a cigarette and go to bed."

"Yeah me too... I'm wiped out, I am exhausted, sometimes eating is more tiring than cycling."

"Yes but you are disgusting, you ate for two!"

" I couldn't offend them, then it was all delicious."

We slept happy, in the absolute silence that reigns in the Vafkeri valley.

Few sounds can be heard up there, especially in winter.

And those few conciliate sleep: the lapping of water, the wind whistling through the branches of the trees and a deep, barely perceptible, indefinable sound: a guttural breath that does not let you sleep if you are not used to it, but relaxes your soul once you make it your own; some call it the sound of silence, others do not even hear it.

It was that sound that we heard loud the first night, so loud that it was almost noisy and we couldn't sleep a wink.

Then out of exhaustion sleep comes and that sound lulls and cuddles you like a purring cat, so that you look forward to the next night.

THE MONASTERY

Morning came sweet and colourful.

Pure air enveloped the cottage and clouds caressed the valley slopes, tickling the branches of the trees.

Waking up early in the morning, opening the door and looking out while inhaling fresh mountain air is as rejuvenating as one could wish for without having to move a muscle.

"Good morning love," said Alina.

"Did you fall out of bed?"

Alina answered me with that grim expression of someone who does not want to be criticised, with the addition of a half-smile just to make her non-belligerent intentions clear.

"I want to go to the monastery."

"It really calls you if you woke up only half an hour after me... breakfast is ready."

"Thanks cicci."

"We are taking Atina, yes?"

"Yes, yes."

We called her and she came out of her kennel, wearing Bibi's leash for the occasion.

We still didn't trust leaving her free.

Actually, we don't even trust her now... Once she ran away for a whole afternoon, then when all hope was lost we heard the door scraping, and once it was open she was there with her tongue hanging out asking for asylum.

We went down to the spring where the water gushed freely onto the road to the point that we had to be careful where we stepped.

It is beautiful to see it emerge pure and clear from the rocks.

Atina without missing a beat stuck her snout into it, drinking greedily.

Our two little dogs, smaller and more timid, tried to imitate her.

Pepi got all wet, the jet was too strong and he started to sneeze, shaking the water off.

"I want to try it too," I said.

I lowered myself onto the jet of water and took a long sip, "fucking cold! Very good though."

Alina shook her head, smiling as she climbed up the path.

The road rises steeply, earth-moving equipment that once should have widened it lies lifeless in the woods, exposed to rust and the elements.

As we progressed, the path narrowed with the tree tops hugging you, closing off the view of the sky.

"Did you hear that?" asked Alina.

"What?"

"No, nothing..."

"There are no bears like in Romania up here, go easy."

"No it wasn't that kind of noise, it was like... but nothing – I must have imagined."

After several hundred metres the path became a small goat track, winding along the ridge of a hill with the karst rocks exposed in plain sight.

The landscape is beautiful and fairytale-like; the smell of humus, mushrooms and undergrowth intoxicated our nostrils and even more so those of our hypersensitive dogs happily trotting alongside us.

Only Pepi was a little restless.

Suddenly a huge tree appeared in front of us, massive with a trunk so wide that not even two people could have encircled it.

The branches rose up into the sky, almost falling back onto the asphalt.

"No one has passed through here for a while."

"Look..." Alina said to me, remaining open-mouthed.

Behind the thicket, stone ruins could be glimpsed.

We approached the tree with reverential awe.

Alina stroked its trunk. Then she embraced it and, closing her eyes, lowered her head.

"Try."

I embraced the giant and relaxed instantly.

"Trees talk to you," Alina said almost in a whisper, "you just don't listen to them with your ears."

It was true.

That tree, that old guardian, infused an immense energy and just by resting your palms on it you could sense it flowing through your body, coming into harmony with the place.

I only managed to tear myself away after a few minutes to continue towards the ruins of the monastery.

There was a meadow that looked as if it had been groomed recently, in the middle there was another tree just smaller than the guardhouse with a bench and a stone well at the foot of the trunk.

"There is water down there," I told Alina.

We wandered around the ruins, the central church was closed and intact while what had been the monks' cells had collapsed, but we could still make out its shape and sober ambience.

Small niches can still be seen in some walls, used in the past to place candles or relics.

"How can the lawn be so manicured... who lives up here?"

"I don't know," I replied, "but it certainly doesn't mown itself."

Behind it, the meadow widened again, and was perfectly mown.

The place is bucolic, winter flowers bloom near the walls among the grass.

"You think I can take some pictures?"

"What's stopping you?" I replied.

"I don't know, I don't want to be disrespectful."

"I don't think it's a problem," I said, looking up at the ancient bell tower, with the bell still in place.

"Look at that, that's left standing," I said, pointing at it.

Alina started taking pictures with her SLR camera, while I went back to the well and sat on the bench.

Atina was itching to go exploring as were Bibi and Pepi who were rather restless.

"Stay here you two, and you stop, I can't let you free or I'll have to explain to Theodoric why I lost you in the woods and I don't feel like it at all."

A gentle gust of wind moved the branches of the elm next to us, a few leaves that had resisted strenuously until then fell twirling in the air, dying where they had been born.

A couple of them ended up in the well.

The silence was perfect. I closed my eyes, inhaled and connected with the place.

I went back in time and saw a monk in front of me tinkering with a pulley and a rope to pull a bucket full of pure water out of the bowels of the mountain.

I turned around and saw the monastery in all its splendour, two monks were walking on the freshly mown lawn with their hands folded, further up others were picking fruit from the trees.

A sheaf of straw could be glimpsed just beyond the boundary wall.

I could hover and fly over the place, within the walls figures could be seen moving gracefully, each of them performing a task with a calculated calm and slowness.

There were those who ploughed a vegetable garden, those who came out of a room with a jar full of some kind of liquid, those who read sitting on a bench, those who were leaning on a shovel smiling and perhaps discussing the best way to manage the land around them, there were farmyard animals: geese and chickens, goats.

All around the monastery there were fields planted with vine saplings.

"Hey" I heard calling.

"Hey everything OK up there?"

What the... it was the monk leaning on the shovel, he was waving at me looking up.

The dogs started barking like mad.

I felt myself tugging as I realised I had fallen off the bench and lost my grip on Atina's leash.

I opened my eyes as if waking from a deep sleep and was stupefied.

"Where the fuck did these come from!"

"Hey!" shouted Alina. "what's going on?!"

"Nothing, don't worry, we have visitors."

"What visitors?!"

"The gardeners..." I replied.

Two wild cows had appeared from behind the boundary wall and dogs were barking at them.

The mystery of the freshly cut grass had been unravelled.

JANUARY

The long-awaited New Year arrived without fuss. No silly bangs to celebrate it, no parades or mega parties as usually happens in big cities.

With the New Year, Alina left her job.

We tightened our belts a little, but in light of the facts it was a good thing.

The previous season had been rather stingy, tourism had not come and so we were almost broke.

With the limitations imposed, it was also difficult to find other jobs; therefore, we set out to create something different, and this materialised in a digital guide dedicated to Lefkada, which could be downloaded at no cost and where the island's tourist activities could be advertised.

This new venture took a lot of my time: time taken away from fishing, from caring for Nitroglicerina, from maintaining Gypsy and more generally from living quietly and relaxed.

In the long run we would have paid the price, but at the time that was the only option, so we jumped right in.

A good thing came out of it; not understood by most islanders still accustomed to print and unaccustomed to digital, but those who realised its potential invested in it instantly.

The days were rainy and wet, and we took the opportunity to photograph the island in all its wintry shades.

In the long winter months, Lefkada is different and brings out its true character.

As you walk down the streets and paths, you see the island for what it really is and not as tourists see her in August: that is, a tired woman, dressed up and forced to smile at guests.

Lefkada is silent and sleepy, beautiful and wild, neglected and dirty. Yes, unfortunately also dirty.

It is a pain to walk along fantastic paths and suddenly see a dump of old bedsteads, mattresses, obsolete kitchens and fridges and other junk at the side of the road.

"I would pay to be in the moment when they do that.... I'd make them kick all this crap down their throats, pathetic ingrates, living in a paradise and soiling it like this."

"We should report this," Alina replied.

"Yes, but I don't think it would change much. We and the foreign community carry plastic bags when we walk around to pick up bottles and various crap that these people flytip out of the windows and then the genius on duty comes along and unloads a van full of this crap."

Lefkada is also this, absurd nonsense.

"I wonder how the island can tolerate this, it should drive them off a cliff while they are unloading."

Living in a place all year round allows you to get to know it better, to have a broader view than that offered by a skimpy holiday. But even if it is a holiday of a few months, you are still a tourist in the eyes of the islanders; it is quite different when you start living a place as a citizen.

I have learnt this concept having lived in the most diverse places, from Mexico to the Canary Islands: the tourist is one thing, the local inhabitant is another.

And if once you become a local you have privileges, the downside is realising all that is wrong, no matter where you live at the time.

During one of the usual morning walks with the dogs, I arrived at the Australian's peak, which is where the spring trail comes out once the tour is completed.

If you wish, you can do it the other way around from there.

As soon as you pass the peak you find yourself in a paradisiacal vineyard landscape; the surviving saplings from the monastery plantations are still there.

On my way back, for the first time since I have lived there, I saw the gate to the beautiful peak house open and a car parked at the front.

A boxer-looking man was fiddling with something at the entrance, it looked like painting material.

"Kalimera" I greeted him.

The man looked up and returned the greeting.

"Nice house," I continued, the view from up there is something spectacular and that property, with or without the house, is worth millions.

"Thank you, you're the Italian right?"

"Yes," I replied in amazement. "Am I that famous?" I continued, smiling.

"Nobody walks around with all those dogs but you around here."

"Ah that's it... all right have a good day."

"Iasu iasu."

He was the son of the owner. His father was a priest who had moved to Australia years ago where he collected funds for the needy in Greece.

Back home I found Alina splitting pieces of wood with an axe.

Although she used a tenth of my strength, her precision allowed her not to miss a shot.

"I met the Australian," I told her.

"Oh yeah? He doesn't need a baby-sitter, does he?"

"Eh, I'd say he's past the age but if you ask, who knows?"

"Meaning?" she asked laughing

"I think he is the priest's son."

"Was he alone?"

"I only saw him, I don't know if there was anyone else inside."

"Phew," huffed Alina as she straightened up, wiping the sweat from her forehead.

"Bad back?"

"Yes..."

"Why don't you leave the wood to me?"

"Because you take three times as long and mostly produce splinters."

"Oh thank you, very comforting."

"We need to buy a chainsaw."

"We would have to bring it from home. With what things cost here we'd sooner buy wood.... Come on, let me try."

"Good morning" said Dave, in his typical greeting.

"Fabio! Do you let Alina do the hard work?"

"I tell her that too but she insists on calling it precision work and won't let me do it."

"Just splinter the axe and the wood stays whole," Alina taunted, turning to Dave.

"I found someone in Platystoma who sells it cheap, I'm going to have a look tomorrow, do you want to come?"

"Yes of course," I replied, "if it's cheap and it's from last year it would be perfect."

The next day we were on our way to Platystoma.

We arrived in the morning and there was not a soul.

The village is beautiful: perched on the hill opposite Vafkeri, it too overlooks the east coast. The houses are all made of stone with wooden fences, and there are still a few old people raising goats and cows.

The scent of cattle permeated the air, mingling with that of burning wood.

"This is the place Fabio," said Dave.

A pile of timber was abandoned by the roadside, cut too wide and long for our stoves and left to rot under the water of torrential rains.

"Mmm that's not very good Dave..."

"No, come on it's fine, we cut it smaller and it's perfect."

"OK..." I said not too convinced "where does the owner live?"

"Ah I have no idea, I usually see him here chopping wood."

"Ah..."

"Only he's not here today."

"Eh..."

"Let's try asking around."

"Yes... there are chickens over there, wait I'll go ask them."

In addition to the chickens roosting freely in what must have been the tiny village square, there was a plume of smoke swirling out of a low chimney.

"Let's go ask there Dave."

We approached the house and the door was ajar.

"Kalimera," I said.

"Kalimera kalimera" replied a voice, which then continued in Greek and we did not understand what it meant.

After a few moments a woman opened the door: no longer a girl, she looked very beautiful, a flour-stained apron barely held back a buxom bosom and a few unruly locks escaped from the braid forming the hairstyle, hazel eyes looked curiously at the stranger as she wiped her hands on her apron.

She said something more in Greek but we didn't understand a word, the mountain accent is really incomprehensible.

"Xila?" said Dave, pointing to the woodpile.

"Do you want Xila?" the woman asked.

"Ne ne, xila."

"Oh... Here we sell bread. Baked on stone."

We looked at each other stupefied.

She was the miller of Platystoma.

A legend more than anything else, or rather, her mother was the legend.

The daughter, just over forty, had decided to continue the historical business she had inherited from her family despite the fact that it did not guarantee her a steady income, especially in winter.

"Can we buy some bread?"

"Ne!" said the woman, shrugging her shoulders and rocking her breasts.

Dave swallowed, lowering his gaze to the woman's chest.

"Be good, be good Dave."

"Sissi" he replied in Italian."

The woman invited us inside; the place must have been more than two centuries old: it was all stone with wooden beams supporting the vaults, the oven took up an entire side of the wall. Next to it were the tools of the trade – all handmade. I went through them ecstatically.

Years ago, even where i lived, in the Murge region of Apulia, bread was made this way.

Then came progress, with electric ovens and sachet yeasts, and bread, while still delicious, lost its fragrance, its soul, and that unmistakable *mark* with which the baker signed it. By now, stone ovens were almost extinct.

There, however, time had stood still and that beautiful lady with confident movements opened the old hand-forged metal door and baked steaming loaves that filled the room with the fragrant smell of freshly baked bread.

"Choose", she said, "not ready yet".

We chose two forms each and the lady marked them with a knife.

She opened the oven again, the flames dancing in her beautiful hazel eyes, and with a smile she put the loaves back into the oven.

"Twenty minutes, half an hour maximum."

"That means in an hour the loaves are ready Dave."

"OK, we'll wait."

Then he turned to the lady.

"Do you live alone here?"

"Oki" (no)

"Your husband? Children?"

"Oki," he said again.

"Mother?"

"Oki! Den katalaveno!" (I don't understand!)

"Fuck Dave you look like a detective! And leave her alone."

"Oh sorry sorry."

The lady understood the nice Welshman's good intentions, and began to tell her story in uncertain English. We did not understand everything she said, but it was exciting to hear her speak.

In the dimly lit room, she said she was the last unmarried daughter in the family.

Apart from one of the brothers, who was half mad but still managed to cultivate the garden, they were all gone.

The mother was no longer able to bake bread and the oven would have been decommissioned if she had not taken care of it.

She had been engaged to a soldier working at the nearby military base, but when he was transferred she refused to leave the village.

Before, the bakery supplied all the houses in the village, there were no supermarkets and people ordered bread day by day, so as not to throw anything away.

There was also another bakery in Karia, but it had been closed for some time.

Now only a few still came to buy bread from her and her family lived on her parents' pension, cultivating the garden and selling what little bread they could.

She did it more out of passion than anything else; if she had to pay for the wood to light the oven, she certainly wouldn't have been able to afford it.

"Fabio... from today we only buy bread from here."

"Have you fallen in love Dave?"

"Come on don't be an asshole!"

When the bread was ready Dave also paid for me and left a generous tip saying he would be back two days later.

The lady's face lit up and she greeted us, smiling.

"You don't know where Xila? Buy?"

"*Ne*, oil mill."

"Where? Where oil mill?"

"Karia. First Karia right. Straight ahead."

"OK thank you, thank you very much."

"It's a good thing they don't live by giving directions otherwise they would already be extinct," I said.

Dave burst into one of his thunderous laughs and said, "good lady."

"Also beautiful I would say."

"Yes yes also beautiful but I am married and you are engaged, don't be a typical Italian".

"Look, you're the one who couldn't take his eyes off her."

"OK OK... let's go get wood now."

At the junction of Karia and Vafkeri we followed a road that continues into the valley.

At one point we noticed what must have been an oil mill as there were a bunch of old olives abandoned on a trolley.

"I guess this is it," I said.

We entered and a short, chubby man came towards us.

"Kalimera. "

"Kalimera," Dave replied, "Do you have xila to sell?"

"*Ne*" said the man.

"OK we would like some xila."

"One moment, first I finish pressing the olives."

Then he climbed onto a small tractor and approached the cart, hooked it and took the olives to the oil press.

"Don't tell me he presses that stuff."

"It seems so, why?"

"Dave those olives are almost rotten..."

"Oh, you know about oil?"

"I was born on an oil mill, my grandfather was one of the most ingenious oil millers in Apulia, and olives like that wouldn't even make it near the basin."

"Basin?"

"Yes my grandfather cold milled, these on the other hand have that monstrosity on a continuous cycle, you lose flavour and organoleptic properties."

"Oh interesting."

"Jesus Christ, he is really pressing them, I don't believe it.... Mental note: never buy oil from here."

After half an hour, the man came back to us and asked us to follow him to a nearby field where he had some wood covered with a thick sheet of plexiglass.

"Do you like it?" asked Dave.

"Yes, *poly orea* (very nice), how much?"

"One hundred and fifty euro a flush" replied the little man, pointing to his van.

"What?! That the wood is golden?" I replied.

"No, no, Fabio it's fine with me."

"But he's screwing us Dave!"

"Alright alright."

"Brits...that's why prices are skyrocketing on this island.... Look *blatantoil*, we'll take it but I'll load the truck OK?" I told him.

"OK," said the man, shrugging his shoulders, happy to save himself the trouble.

I jammed the wood so well in tetris style that when we arrived at Dave's house and opened the side of the van the load did not move despite the prohibitive slope.

The guy realised that something was wrong as usual but did not explain what.

The second load was crammed in the same way and was unloaded in front of the cottage.

"It's still stealing Dave, good thing the wood is good."

"What alternative do we have?"

"Buy it in Arta, with all the transport we save money."

Alina heard the commotion and came out of the house and began to analyse the wood with expert skill.

"It's a bit big but it's OK," he judged.

"Yes even though we paid too much for it, but at least it is from last year."

"All olive?"

"Yes, it seems so."

"Where did you get it?"

"From an oil press."

"An oil press? You must have felt at home...

... no huh?"

"This week the weather is great for fishing."

"Eh… hopefully you'll catch something, I haven't had fish in a while."

"Yes, buying it is humiliating after spending a summer in a fishing village."

"Don't remind me" Alina replied.

The year before, at the end of the season, I was on a boat in Vliho Bay with a fisherman friend, and while they were choosing which net to use, I asked him if he knew anyone who rented an house in those parts.

I was tired of having to ferry customers from the yacht club dock to the boat anchored in the bay with my small dinghy.

I needed a solution with a pier.

Takis thought about it for a moment as he unwound the net in the water.

The day was beautiful and the sunset set the waters of the bay ablaze.

"There is a flat above my house, but he doesn't want dogs."

"Well I'd say we can discard it."

"You and your dogs – leave them out! And make a baby more than dogs."

"Ah! You fucking islanders will never understand that huh? Can you think of anything else? "

"There is the house of Barba Iannis."

"And who is this Uncle John?"

"He was a fisherman, he died last year. But his grandson rents the house."

"And what is that?"

"The one by the pier with the sloping roof." He told me, pointing to the nearby coast of Geni, his village.

"The one by the water?"

"Yes it is the closest to the water in the whole village."

"Are you kidding?"

"No no, it is available."

"And you tell me just like that?"

"And how should I tell you?"

"When can you talk to the nephew of barbaiannis?"

"We fish now, I'll call him later and let you know tomorrow."

"OK thanks. Takis... I'm leaving next week, let's not make you let me know in a year."

"No malaka, I'll call him today!"

That evening on our way back to the campsite where we had spent the season living in Gypsy, I told Alina that we had found a house facing the sea.

The next day Takis called us to come and see it and it was indeed very close to the sea.

Alina watched me as I counted the steps from the front door to the pier.

"How many?" She asked.

"Fourteen."

Inside it was awful: tiny and poorly furnished, it smelled of stale air and fish.

It had a small fenced-in garden at the front and a huge bbq at the back, where a common porch was covered by a vine.

The owner promised to fix it up during the winter and we specified that we wanted it ready by the end of February.

We agreed on the price, which to be honest was ridiculous, then said goodbye.

Alina was overjoyed, her eyes sparkling.

Then the pandemic disrupted everything.

Already by December I had bookings for day trips on Nitroglicerina, but February arrived and Europe plunged into the darkness of the Chinese virus.

We only managed to arrive in Greece in July, the season was stingy and the neighbourhood turned out to be horrible.

In the end, I was glad to go.

But that was the past, we were now living in a beautiful, cosy mountain cottage, and at that very moment I was driving Gypsy in the direction of the salt flats.

I arrived early in the morning with the sun low on the horizon, and was greeted by a warm, iridescent light reflecting off the thin sheet of water, creating magical plays of light.

The herons were pacing, fishing with their beaks.

I reached my favourite spot, parked behind an abandoned cottage and pulled the already assembled rod out of the car.

I tied an artificial fish to the end and started casting.

It is very relaxing to fish down there.

In front you have dry land with cattle farms, behind you the rolling Lefkadians hills and all around water.

The saltiness of the sea mingles with the acrid smell of the stables.

For the first half hour nothing happened. I threw and retrieved the little fish, making it swim as if it were in difficulty.

Then at some point I felt a tug. Then another.

I loosened the clutch and let go a little bit of the line, then I started to pull back gently but the fish didn't want to know.

It was still sinking and pulling at irregular intervals.

After a couple of minutes the pressure eased and I was able to retrieve the line by working on the reel.

As soon as the fish came to the surface he started to pull again, but by then he had no chance.

It was a Serra, (greenhouse) a killer from the tropics that was infesting the Mediterranean, killing bass and bream.

The day turned out to be very good, I caught two more and of excellent size. For once I would not go home empty-handed.

The sun rose high and the light on the salt marshes lost its mystical aura.

I put the barrel back and walked to the north end of the site accompanied by Bibi, who had been snoozing in the car up to that point.

There, at the end of the path, the gap was clearly visible from where the canal water pours into the salt pans, effectively rendering them unusable.

A tiny fishing boat was hidden under a shrub, moored to a stake driven into the shallow water.

Bibi reached the end of the road and stood there, looking across the narrow arm of water as if waiting for a bridge to emerge from the water to connect the two pieces of land to continue the walk.

"Come on Bibi we are not in Corinth, let's go back."

The little dog turned around, then took one last look at the road that was no longer there and walked with me towards the car.

A thunderstorm was brewing on the horizon; by now I had learnt to forecast by cloud formations.

Every day before going out on the boat, I would talk to fishermen who would explain to me what to expect based on the clouds in the sky at that given time. It was not an infallible method, but when combined with current weather models it had a very good degree of reliability.

"Nothing can replace observing the sky," said a great meteorologist.

This storm came from the south, and it was possible to predict it well in advance.

It was an easy one to recognise, like those from the east.

Babis of Meganissi had explained this to me while observing the clouds over the Psili Korifi mountain nature park, now dotted with wind turbines.

"Come on, let's move or we'll leave Alina waiting for us under the water."

Bibi, almost understanding what I meant, increased his pace by trotting and sniffing here and there.

"I don't believe it..."

"And why?" I replied laughing.

"You really didn't buy them?"

"Are you crazy?"

"But they're huge! These in the oven with potatoes and tomatoes… perfect match!" She said, squinting her eyes and slightly shaking her pretty little blond head.

"Is there any Verdeca left?" I asked.

"Yes we have more crates than we need... I never know where to put them and they take up space."

"I'll make this one easy for you" I replied, and while dinner was in the oven I uncorked a sparkling Verdeca from Tenuta Viglione, an excellent wine that went beautifully with it.

Other fishing trips were not so lucky: on another occasion I happened to catch a couple of nice bass but otherwise they were just frying fish, fun to catch but boring to clean and cook.

It was nevertheless a beautiful winter.

In the evenings, in front of the wood-burning stove, we would lose ourselves in memories of the early seasons when we did not yet live in a house but camped in our motorised T4 van.

The second one in particular was very intense. Nitroglicerina was anchored in Vliho bay and we found accommodation at the Bedrock: a sort of private mini-camping built by a nice, eccentric Englishman.

The land stood by the road from Nydri to Vliho and was surrounded by a centuries-old olive grove with outcropping rocks at its base. Hence the Flintstone-style name.

Rather than olive trees, they should have planted vine saplings on that land, but we are not in the Murge and there is still much to learn in these parts.

Bedrock had not even ten pitches, the shade came depending on the height and position of the sun and it was very nice.

The owner had wanted to replicate Skorpio's grass and in a small portion, the one where the bbq area and hammocks were, he had even succeeded.

There was only one bathroom, small and spartan. Hot water was produced by a solar system.

Privacy was guaranteed.

"If I understand correctly, the owner is a short gentleman with black hair who came through the yard to talk to Makis to try to get his boat into the campsite" Alina told me as we drove to the site.

"For the winter you say? Or he want to put it there in a permanent way?"

" I'm not sure."

"OK let's go and see if they are there, maybe we'll have a chat."

We descended from the Nydri Vliho road down 70 metres of dirt track.

"It is open," I said.

We crossed the threshold and noticed a couple working on an unspecified steel structure.

"Hello!" I said.

"H*aaaa*i" I was answered by a short gentleman with black hair in his marked Devon accent.

"Are you the owner?"

"Of course I am."

"Well, my name is Fabio, this is Alina, we work here and we wanted to know if you rent pitches on a long-term basis."

"Yes of course, we can talk about it."

"Do you accept dogs yes? Because we have two."

"Yes, do they get along with cats?"

"As long as the cats don't disturb them they will..."

"Alright, alright. Come on, I'll show you the campsite. This is Joyce. Oh... I'm Maurice."

"Hi guys," said Joyce. "Would you like a cup of tea?"

"Sure, even better if Assam" I replied.

Maurice and Joy exchanged an astonished look.

"Where do you come from?"

"I am Romanian and Fabio is Italian."

"And do you know Assam tea?"

"We worked on a British boat, I don't know if you have noticed, that big red and white Polynesian catamaran with yellow masts anchored by Konidaris."

"Are you talking about James Wharram's Spirit of Gaia? "

"Yes indeed."

"Do you know James Wharram?"

"Yes... we are great friends also, we have sailed together in his boat between the islands around here."

"So you are telling us that you sailed on Spirit of Gaia?"

"Yes... great boat. At the helm it's very light, then James makes it even easier for you, but hoisting the sails is a lot of work, you know there's only ropes and sails on board, no electronic helpers or anything and it's 20 metres long so the sails aren't really very light."

Maurice and Joy gasped, James Wharram is a legend.

"Sit down guys, you look like two interesting guys."

"Yes, but can we get the dogs out of the car? The windows are open but I can see them anxious to get out for a bit," Alina asked.

"Yeah sure go ahead, in fact we want to meet them!"

"Ah ok... you asked for it huh?"

I went back and released the little pests: Bibi and Pepi began to run all over the place sniffing the new territory, then finally approached Maurice and Joy's camper van, lodged on the best pitch. Even there on the ground was Skorpio grass, thick and soft.

And Bibi baptised her.

"Well guys, this is a squatter camp. Might as well say it now. For the authorities we're all friends, ok? It's still registered as agricultural land, so, it would have been pointless to open a tax number... then I have a few pitches, maybe I'll rent some to people who need to leave a car or boat on a cart like that in the corner."

Near the entrance there was a jeep with British number plates next to a boat trailer.

"Very good, that means there will be no tax to pay and therefore it will be easier to agree on the price" i said seraphically.

Maurice lowered his head with a grunt. "How much would you pay per month to stay in a place like this?"

"Ah I don't know, you're the boss, name a price and if it suits me I accept."

"Yes but how much would you pay..."

"I have no idea..." I didn't want to take the first step. Asking the price was an all-British technique that I didn't want to fall for.

We looked at each other, then I sipped some tea and said,"mmm great, is tea every morning included?"

Maurice leaned his head back, giving that classic laugh of his, made hoarse by cigarette smoke.

"Yes as long as we're here why not, but I think you'll be alone most of the time, we'll be gone all of July and August, you know those are the only months you can live in England without soaking your bones and at the moment apart from that jeep we have no customers."

"No reservation?"

"No reservation, I told you I can't advertise."

"So no tea in the morning for two months."

"No but you will have water, electricity and washing machine included."

"Included in what price?"

"How much would you pay?"

"10 euro?"

"Mmm ok... then let's talk about the price later."

We finished tea in peace, and in the end agreed on a reasonable rent.

I promised to take care of the garden, paying special attention to the areas where Skorpios grass was growing.

It was quite a busy summer. In July Maurice and Joy left and we had a big bbq to say goodbye.

And then we were the only guests in the small squatter camp.

In the mornings I would take clients out on the boat, and return just in time to cross paths with Alina to hand her the bicycle and see her going in the opposite direction, towards Nydri where she worked as a hostess in a glitzy restaurant on the waterfront.

We saw very little of each other that summer, but it was still a fun and very economically productive season.

When Terry arrived it was a real hoot.

Terry is a London taxi driver who had given up his home and his job to travel.

We met him years earlier in Gran Canaria where we experienced an unforgettable winter camping in a Fiat Doblò equipped only with a Maggiolina roof tent.

We still had the tent, and it was my bedroom. Alina, on the other hand, slept in Gypsy, and as a matter of schedule this was a good solution for the whole summer.

Instead, Terry used the large camping tent we were using for storage.

He was an eccentric character, speaking in bursts with that typical Cockney accent of his.

We had remained great friends since that winter in Gran Canaria: him, Pier the Norwegian, Philip... a great group.

We met Terry again before we moved to Lefkada, when I worked as a sailing instructor for the British Academy.

He gave me a hand in the South Italian leg; having a native speaker sailor was great for the young Italian students. Terry taught them some of the dirtiest and most classic English maritime songs... as *Show me the way to go home* for example.

Another whirlwind came in the middle of August when Mirko, a raving lunatic, came to visit us for a week.

Mirko is a very good barman, but completely out of his mind.

He was capable of spending all his savings plus debts on a whim. Like a car.

Once he smashed it into a wall after just two days, he would start again and go on a fixation about something else.

However, it was nice to have him on board, as long as you made him tired you could keep him under control, so I thought well of using him as a human anchor winch.

One of the heaviest jobs on Nitroglicerina.

"Yes the 2019 season was really good," said Alina sipping a Falangaspritz on the sofa, her eyes lost in the flames of the stove.

"Better than the previous one," I said.

"Oh yes much better, I don't want to hear about that yard anymore."

"Come on there were good times there too," I replied.

"Yes of course, in the evening when the cooler weather came down and the sunset coloured the bay, remember?"

"Yes... we used to sit on that abandoned trunk on the shore drinking and smoking, with the dogs running around hunting who knows what."

"Foxes in my opinion," she replied, smiling.

"Yes, it may be, however we didn't earn much that season."

"Well it was the first one, nobody knew you yet."

"Yes it is true."

"What are we doing tomorrow?"

"The weather looks good, shall we take a ride to the west coast?"

"Yes, or we will walk around Lefkada town, it will be deserted with all these restrictions."

"It's better if it's deserted, we get lost in the alleys of the old city, I don't like the mess."

"No come on, let's go to Porto Katsiki, I want to see it in winter, then maybe we'll stretch to the lighthouse and drop by the monastery to pick up some aloe vera creams," she said, smiling enthusiastically.

"All right," I replied, as if I could ever say no to her when she looked at me with that sweet, irresistible smile, those green eyes shining either from the reflection of the flames or from something deeper.

The next day, not quite so early, we got on Gypsy and climbed up to Eglouvi: a picturesque mountain village with a small square shaded by huge, beautiful plane trees.

Just a couple of bars and a tavern, plus the immense notoriety for being the village where the most expensive lentils in Greece are produced and sold.

Actually, lentils are cultivated a few kilometres from the village, in an airy plateau that represents the pass between the west and east coasts.

"Let's stop for a moment," I said as we reached the small church of Agios Donatos.

That place, besides being poignantly beautiful, represents the beginning of the plateau.

A tiny church with a very special square in front of it where no fewer than nine wells sink into the karst rock, from where very pure fresh water flows out.

A few years earlier we had camped there for a week.

I had little work, Alina had none at all, so rather than stay in the sauna at the construction site where we were based, we stocked up on provisions and climbed up there, about 1,000 metres above sea level, enjoying the tranquillity and cool climate.

From Agio Donatos we crossed the lentil plain, a magical place, immersed and protected by a forest in the Apulian Murge style.

"On the way back, shall we go up to Agios Ilias?" I said.

"Let's see if there is time... but let's not go through the abandoned base, I get the creeps from that place."

Climbing a little higher is the highest church on Lefkada: Agios Ilias.

From up there you can enjoy one of the most beautiful views of the island.

To get there you pass the remains of a former American military base, used during the Cold War for radio espionage.

Four huge dishes are still visible and the base is in a complete state of dereliction.

We went there during that week of free camping, but Alina had a horrible memory of it.

"Something bad happened here," he said. "Let's go away... "

"What?"

"Those who have been wronged here still want their revenge."

"Are you OK?"

"Can we please leave?"

I went away against my will.

I also felt something negative in the air, only the view was just too beautiful.

Beyond the plateau, the road begins to descend very steeply towards the west coast, offering views of the sea as far as the horizon.

Looking northwards, one can see the outline of Antipaxos.

We passed through Chortata, a tiny village that is very popular in summer as it is a transit point from the capital to the most beautiful beaches on the west coast.

We passed the junctions for Gialos and Egremni and finally reached the one for Porto Katsiki. We took it and went down to the beach.

The hill was terribly defaced, new houses would soon be built and the lucky owners would rent them out, taking advantage of the view of the more famous Lefkadian beach – at the price of destroying the coastline.

Arriving at the beach car park, the atmosphere changed.

The wind caressed us and brought the smell of saltiness, the view was priceless, the crumbling rock ended up in the sea, colouring it the classic murky blue that has made the island famous: the Lefkada Blue.

Years later, armed with a drone and a lot of patience, I made a video called Blue like Lefkas.

It is still one of my favourites as well as one of the most popular on the Lefkada Official channel.

Descending the stairs to the beach isolates you from the World.

The ugly buildings behind disappear from view: just rock, pebbles and sea.

And that sound, that melody of water stirring the pebbles.

On the right side of the beach there is a cave; when you enter, it's like a huge hug.

You feel protected by the island singing its song to you, the sounds reverberate within and touch chords that have never been made to vibrate before. You enter a state of sensory limbo that sends you into ecstasy.

Time stands still, the colours change but you don't pay attention to it, you absorb it all and then give up until something brings you back to reality.

What brought me back that day was the barking of my dogs.

The tide was rising and within moments access to the cave would have been cut off.

Leaving Porto Katsiki is much nicer than arriving there.

You leave full of positive energy, you know that those awful buildings will not live forever.

But that synergy just experienced – that is immortal.

"Are you OK?" I asked.

Alina turned her head, leaning against the backrest, and nodded, smiling, that beautiful smile of hers with changing eyes, sometimes grey, sometimes green, depending on her mood, the weather and the colours around her.

"Monastery?"

"Are you tired?"

"No we can get there if you want."

"No come on, let's go home, we'll go one of these days and stay there and sleep."

"Yes... good idea."

We held hands and returned to Vafkeri, the forgotten village.

CYCLING IN VASSILIKI

Dave was walking the dog of Kostas, the old shepherd of the village.

"Tomorrow by bike Fab."

"OK Dave, what round?"

"Around Vassiliki... we will see." Dave's 'we will see' was always dangerous when talking about bike rides, and this was no exception.

"OK see you tomorrow, shall we go in my car?"

"As you wish," he replied as he walked away with Mavro wagging his tail happily.

Who knows what would have become of the local dogs if it were not for the foreign community.

There are people here who still regard dogs as work items and feed them with a piece of bread once a week... leaving them on the chain until hunting season starts.

They do not realise that many dogs are far more intelligent than many of their owners.

Mavro was one of them: a beautiful little hound, sensitive and intelligent.

Bella, Alina's hound, had also been Kostas' dog for a few weeks.

Left alone in a hovel she barked for more than fifty consecutive hours before she managed to break the damn wire that kept her tied to a post, after which she lived free for a few weeks before being commandeered by me, who with the help of Dave and his diplomacy managed to get Kostas to give her to me.

She is now happy, microchipped and safe from any second thoughts.

Anyway... the morning heralded itself with splendid sunshine.

I had my usual breakfast of champions, as always before each ride, left the house and found Dave arriving with the two bikes to be set up on Gypsy's rear rack.

"Good morning," he said in his usual accent, trying to speak Italian.

"Hi Dave, I was just coming down to get you."

"No problem."

We started to put the bikes on the rack but could not find the fit despite the fact that it was very easy to use.

"But, they weren't like this last time," said Dave.

"No you're right, let's try to reverse the positions."

Nothing yet...

"Mmm, maybe the black one should be with the gearbox towards the glass, and the white one towards the outside."

"Yes let's try that..."

The whole thing started to become comical...

After several attempts we managed to make the bikes fit *comfortably*.

"Shit Dave last time we got lucky if we got them right the first time."

"OK that's good, now let's remember how we put them for next time," he laughed.

"Good morning!" It was Ann, with her basket full of cat food.

"I'm going to feed the cats at the bottom and I'll be there."

"OK see you by the tavern."

Thank God Anna looked after the feline colony of Vafkeri, or rather, the feline *colonies* of Vafkeri, there was one in the lower part of the village, one near the tavern, and one near our house.

Without Anna's patience and perseverance it would have been a problem.

"Ready?" I said.

"Let's go!"

"Alina everything OK?" asked Anna.

"Yes... I've only had one coffee and I have yet to wake up fully." It was almost ten o'clock.

We gently descended from the hill of Vafkeri admiring the usual splendid landscape of the small islands of the Heptanese, then arrived at Nydri and followed the road to Vliho where I cast a glance at Nitroglicerina, anchored in the shallow water.

"Hi baby," I thought aloud.

"If we don't go cycling tomorrow I'll go out in a boat, I don't know if there will be wind to go sailing, at most I'll go fishing."

"Good show," Dave replied.

We climbed up the road towards the junction for Syvros, and it was there that Dave spilled the beans.

"OK Fab, from here down to Vassiliki will be the first section of today's ride, only we'll do it backwards uphill, then we'll turn for Syvros, another small uphill section and from Syvros onwards it's downhill to the Vassilikiìs growes, from there we'll do the two segments at top speed."

"Oh yeah?"

"Do you like the programme?"

"Do I have a choice?"

"No actually."

"How many kilometres is that?"

"Not even thirty."

"Height difference?"

"A maximum of six or seven hundred metres."

"Ah..."

"You'll be fine, you'll see..."

"I have to adjust the saddle a bit, last time it was too low."

"I have the key with me."

We arrived at Vassiliki, Peter and Little Ann had been there for a few seconds.

"Oh, there they are," said Dave.

"Hey good morning!" greeted Little Ann, sunny as ever.

"Hi guys," said Pete in his rough ex-cop accent.

As we unloaded the bikes, out of Pete and Ann's car came Andrew's beautiful dogs, off to Lefkada for work.

During those months, our friends who lived in the beautiful Villa Dessimi, overlooking the bay of the same name, took care of it.

"Bye guys, have a good ride," the girls said to us as they started their walk.

Dave, Pete and I passed them by going through the new part of the village, that came into being after the tourist boom.

Arriving at the junction with the main street, we began the long climb that would take us over four hundred metres.

At first the road was still damp, the winter sun could not reach that side of the mountain and we proceeded slowly, amidst the scent of mowed grass in the fields and that of wood burning in the fireplaces.

Some chilly locals, despite the spring day, had perhaps decided to light the fireplace.

We climbed up to the picturesque village of Marandohori, beautiful in every season, with its tall plane trees providing shade on the asphalt strip, and their leafy foliage only allowing a few stubborn rays of sunlight to reach the ground in winter.

Past the characteristic and excellent tavern The Old Plane Tree the road climbs further up the slope, the whitewashed walls of the houses standing out in the landscape dominated by the green of the grass and the brown of the tree trunks.

Dave and Pete got a bit of a head start on me as I trudged uphill, and as we moved further away from the town the landscape became increasingly barren and wild.

By the time we arrived at the junction for Syvros I was cooked, but there was only one last small climb to go and then it would be all downhill to Vassiliki grove, the summer training camp of the British gang.

We passed by a small, beautiful and solitary church overlooking the valley. Opposite is an old quarry that, despite having disfigured the mountain, had been colonised by dozens of seagulls.

At sunset the ambience becomes very suggestive, with the birds' cries amplified by that sounding board carved into the rock, and you sit on the bench near the church to admire the surrounding beauty, those sounds, the scents that change according to the season, the yellow church lit up by the setting sun, the valley below, and that feeling of peace that begins to take hold of your soul.

There are many places of this kind in Lefkada, and this is one of them; it almost represents a boundary; in fact, once you pass the little church, you enter the mountains, where the spirit of the island is more alive than ever.

I saw out of the corner of my eye Pete and Dave take a dirt road. Then I heard a loud crash and a booming laugh.

I caught up with them and saw Dave who was doubled over in laughter looking at Pete's legs in the air.

"But why did you come in here? Did you have to go to the bathroom?"

"No no," said Dave, "we wanted to play a joke on you but Pete fell over!"

We took the opportunity to drink some water while Pete recovered.

"So, are the climbs over?" I asked.

"Almost, up to Syvros the slope is minimal, then all downhill," Dave replied.

"Thank goodness..."

"All right Pete?" asked Dave again.

"Yes more or less."

"Sorry not a bright idea of mine."

"As always man, but don't worry I'm used to it."

Those two madmen, after they had performed the great feat *London to Lefkada,* knew each other better than their wives... They were very close.

"OK let's go," Dave called.

The road began to descend well before the village of Syvros, and when we reached it we found it as usual half asleep, with its square surrounded by the canal where a trickle of water from the nearby picturesque waterfalls flows perpetually.

In its farthest corner, overlooking the valley below, is the statue of Alekis Panagulis: the protagonist of the novel *Un uomo* – written by Oriana Fallaci – was originally from Syvros.

The cosy little village bar was decorated with Christmas lights.

It is always beautiful in Syvros, one of those villages that give you a very positive energy.

We often go there both to visit the waterfalls, an out-of-this-world place, and to dine in the excellent tavern.

But it is the waterfalls that are the main reason that drives us up there.

A mystical place, you get there via a narrow, steep climb from the village to this oasis of peace.

The water gushes slow and placid from the rock covered with a soft layer of moss, even in summer. It collects in a long, low pool built of small bricks. You can soak your feet in it if you wish, but the temperature is always prohibitive.

Even in the middle of summer, the water is freezing cold and can cut off your circulation.

The small square in front of the waterfalls is always shaded by tall, leafy trees.

In summer, the leaves allow only a few pinpricks of light to filter through, reflecting in the water and creating an enchanting play of colours.

Even just breathing in that place refreshes you. That cold, moist air saturated with a musky smell enters your lungs and reaches the most hidden corners of your alveoli.

Some of the water is channelled into a fountain and if the air is so special you can imagine what the purity of the water can be. A nutrient icy drink, to be taken in small sips like medicine.

We always leave loaded from there.

Like so many places on the island, it is capable of putting you in direct connection with it. But this is one of the positive ones: as if good and evil were always present in the island's soul and at times managed to reach the surface, this is home to one of the benign points, welcoming to all, especially to those capable of feeling.

We didn't pass by the waterfalls of Syvros that day, we just drove slowly through the village, enjoying its beauty, the small attached houses, the old cars from another era parked and ready for service, the little alleys winding between the buildings, and then all of a sudden the village is overtaken; and a splendid, very fast, adrenaline-filled descent down the opposite side of the hill begins.

"I'd need disc brakes," I thought aloud.

I enjoy braking to the limit by throwing the bike into the crease at maximum grip, but on that descent, on that day, I had to let go of the brakes every now and then because I felt the front wheel lock in the areas that are still damp: those little spots of asphalt where the winter sun rarely shines.

We descended at four times the speed it had taken us to climb, and in no time we found ourselves at the edge of the Vassiliki groves, with the little church marking the boundary.

From there on, a flat segment began, winding through the fields where you had to give your all.

We did not spare ourselves and travelled the last 5 km like hell at over 45km/h.

We arrived at the junction of the main road destroyed and continued downhill without pedalling, then at the entrance to the village Pete shouted: "from the bridge to the bend! Sprint race!"

And we relaunched exhausted in the last extreme effort.

Sitting at the café, enjoying a well-deserved post-ride coffee with the girls, I said "you know, up in the hills a couple of times I've wondered who the fuck makes me do it".

"We all ask Fab, every time!" replied Dave between laughs.

Our big puppies slept blissfully, also tired but satisfied with having chased pieces of wood on the deserted beach.

The sun was shining, it felt like a spring day.

"It looks like the whole week will be like this," said Pete.

"Oh very well, let's plan another round then," Dave replied. "Shall we say Thursday?"

"Fine by me" Pete replied.

"Me too," I said.

"Thursday then," confirmed Dave.

"Tomorrow since it's so nice I'm going boating, she called me today when we passed by her in Vliho."

"Don't make her angry then" Dave said.

SAILING IN THE BAY

The next day the sky was leaden, the kind of colour that between grey and blue goes through ten thousand other shades. Beautiful and fascinating, synonymous with winter.

The bay was silent and there was not a gust of wind.

A light south-easterly was expected in the afternoon, but at the moment there was total calm.

A few solitary migratory birds stuck their heads underwater, fishing with Greek languor.

I caught the mood and started to inflate the dinghy in slow motion, in no hurry.

After about 20 minutes I decided that it was swollen enough, let it slide into the water and started loading it with everything needed for a quiet fishing trip.

On the way down from Vafkeri I had also stopped to buy a snack, woe betide going out on a boat without something to put between your teeth.

I started rowing with peacefulness towards Nitro who was placid floating at anchor.

I got there after a few minutes, she was still beautiful even if a bit neglected.

"Hi Nitro."

She did not reply, looking up at the sky offended that she had been left alone all this time. If it were up to her, she would want me on board at least two or three times a week.

"Yes yes I know.... Don't be a jealous girlfriend now."

I moored the dinghy at the stern and took the new buoy to which I would add an anchor point.

"Did you see what I prepared for you? A new buoy, with a four-foot chain so we don't risk losing the buoys any more."

I stowed the buoy and then opened the lockers to let air into the thin, lightweight hulls.

"OK: let's go for a little ride today, try out the sail modification, go have a look at Leon's boat and if there is wind we'll do two boards."

I started the engine and let it warm up.

I checked for water seepage from the cap's vent, then cast off my moorings and set a course for the bay's exit.

It was a surreal feeling, only a handful of boats were anchored in the beautiful Vliho bay, a totally different sight from the summer view where you needed to zigzag between dozens and dozens of sailboats to reach the berth.

Nitro was advancing quietly, Ruggerino was stretching his piston and connecting rod, which had been inactive for a few months.

We passed the pasture, where the wind usually blows even when there is none, and continued on to Tranquility bay.

Then Ruggerino passed away.

A plastic bag, the huge black kind, had ended up in the propeller.

"Bollocks..."

I lifted the foot of the engine, disengaging the propeller from the plastic, then tried to restart it but it didn't want to know.

There was a knot of current pushing me into Tranquility bay, I used it to approach Leon's boat and then dropped anchor.

I reached my friendly South African friend's boat with the dinghy, and as soon as I boarded it an English gentleman, his eyes very thin and spirited, approached me rowing in a tiny boat.

It was his neighbour. Leon had told me about him, an eclectic guy who lived in a beautiful but terribly run-down two-master: Maramu.

"All right?" he asked in his raspy, heavily British-accented voice.

"Almost well, good morning. I am Leon's friend Fabio, I came to check the humidifiers."

"Oh, ok ok, Leon told me about you, all good then. You made a good anchorage, at a safe distance."

"Actually the idea was to moor my boat alongside Leon's, but the engine thought it was not that good."

"And he did well, it's full of ropes and semi-submerged buoys here."

"Do you live on Maramu?"

"Yes it's my boat, I would love to go out sailing but I have a lot of work to do, I haven't sailed for years now."

"Indeed."

"Eh... at my age things take longer to fall into place."

"Well I'm going on board, I don't want to find myself sailing in the dark."

"Alright alright, have a nice day."

We took our leave and boarded Leon's beautiful boat: El Aquila.

The humidifiers were working great and the boat was dry and cosy wrapped in its scented woods. I closed everything up and rowed towards Nitroglicerina.

I tried to restart the engine, which eventually restarted.

But this would not be the only problem of the day.

I had filled up with watered-down petrol; it had also happened to my bike.

Ruggerino mumbled for a while, moved me forward a few dozen metres and then planted me in the middle of the mud.

I anchored again, hoisted the sails, hoisted the anchor and with a gust of wind I found myself sailing against the current in the narrowest part of Vliho Bay, amidst abandoned buoys and buoyancy aids.

After a good half-hour of edging I managed to gain the exit and a gust of wind began to blow from the south-east.

Sailing in Vliho Bay in winter is wonderful, you have all the water you want, and it is like being in a small lake.

Nitro ran fast, with no waves to slow her down, pulling edges at the side of the bay, gaining the wild east coast, where tree branches lapped the water, and then the more populated west coast, where restaurant piers were secured to the shore for safe wintering, and again from the Makis dockyard where Spirit of Gaia was moored up to Geni, from there to the yacht club and then down to the shallows.

As the wind began to drop and turn slightly to the west, I took the opportunity to pull up one of the daggerboards and prepare for the last board.

After half an hour of pure enjoyment, I started to take the measurements to sail onto the buoy, took the half sail from the hull, made the last tack and calculated the boat's speed according to the distance from the buoy.

At 100 metres from the buoy I tightened the bowline a little so that I could also pull up the other daggerboard and drift.

When I felt the moment had come I tightened the sails and the boat by inertia approached the coloured buoy. I hooked it on the fly and secured its line on the starboard bollard.

"Still... not bad for being stationary for three months, eh Nitro?"

From astern I heard an ironic applause.

"Bravo Fabbiooo!" called Spiros, a friend who has a boat rental on the island.

"Where the fuck did you come from?"

I was so focused that I did not hear him.

"Hella fileee, I saw you sailing in the bay and thought you had some problems."

"Yes indeed, water in the carburettor."

"Ah what malakkia."

"Were you here in the bay?"

"No I was at home, spying on you through the binoculars."

"Holy shit Spiros but what spyglass do you have?"

"Eheh a nice one."

Spiros lives in the hills.

"Thank you file mou, I am sorry to have made you come down."

"Heeella file no problem, in winter there is never anything to do."

"Come on board, we'll have a beer."

Spiros stayed for half an hour and then took his leave.

Sunset fell over the bay and everything turned pink and red.

The shallow water reflected the clouds in the sky in all their hues, the wind dropped completely and just on a whim I made two casts with my spinning rod.

The one-piece carbon flexed and threw the artificial fish over 40 metres.

But I made no catch that evening, put the rod down and stood there in blissful silence, enjoying the last moments of light.

Then I closed the hatches, hailed Nitro with a caress and jumped into the dinghy. I rowed ashore with all the calmness of the World, thinking of the cottage.

Alina had certainly already lit the fire and the little dogs had to be curled up next to the stove, patiently waiting for the time of the evening walk.

Every sailor dreams of a little house in the hills with a piece of land, and while he is there, his gaze flies far out over the sea, dreaming of a boat and the spaces of infinite blue to sail.

I had both, and I was happy for it.

MOUNTAIN BIKE TRAIL

When I got home I saw Alina ready to go out.

"But where did you leave the phone?"

"In my pocket why?"

"Because Dave and Anna came by and asked us to go to the tavern."

The phone was switched off, battery at zero.

"OK I'll take a quick shower."

"There is no time."

"But I am salty."

"Better."

We arrived at the tavern and Dave and Ann were already there.

"Eeee malakka Fabio."

I was greeted with an ovation from all the tavern goers.

It was always the usual ones: Sotiris, Maria, Iorgo, Zaza, the president and the captain.

Plus Lakis in the corner. Always isolated.

After we were seated Dave said, "Not tomorrow but the next day we go mountain-biking."

"Mountain-biking," I replied.

"Yes yes, beautiful," he said in Italian before continuing in English, "let's go around the hill of Poros."

"Where do we start?"

"From Dessimi as always."

"Again?"

"Si sì bellissimo" In Italian.

"You will kill me one of these days with your follies."

"You will see that you will like it."

We dined on Maria's special dish, a stew simmered on a wood stove, a delicacy from another era.

"No too much beer Fab, is not good, now you are a cyclist."

"You are the first Englishman who says he does not drink beer."

"No no, I am Welsh, there is a big difference."

"Are you telling me that the Welsh drink less?"

"No indeed, but still I am not English."

The evening continued amidst the laughter and shouts of the locals, who you never know when they are talking or arguing.

We returned as usual staggering uphill on the road to high Vafkeri.

The day after next we found ourselves in Dessimi: me, Dave and Pete.

The girls took the dogs to the beach while we catapulted down the hill at breakneck speed and then trudged to the Poros junction, a gruelling climb if done on a mountain bike. It would have been a different story on a road bike, and if the weather had held we might have tried it that winter, otherwise it would certainly have been done in the spring.

I arrived at the junction a little behind the two forerunners, then from there we drove through the beautiful, small, picturesque shepherd's village perched on top of the hill.

Tiny roads, designed to fit a donkey at most, prohibitive gradients to the point of having to walk some stretches.

And then the pure adrenaline.

The descent on the southern slope was something unforgettable, both for the view of Kefalonia, Itaka, Atokos and Meganissi, and for the absurd speeds we reached.

I was catapulted back to my childhood days when I rode my first mountain bike through the Mercadante forest, once an exclusive holiday resort on the Bari Murge.

The path was very wet, with completely flooded sections which one passed by floating.

Dave was very cautious on the descent, Pete and I were not of the same opinion, and we dashed off the cliffs like there was no tomorrow.

We walked all around the outer perimeter of the hill, from where Meganissi can be admired from a unique angle, until we reached the isolated and beautiful beach of Kamari.

A tongue of white and grey pebbles with a sea in exquisitely Greek tones, the kind that resembles the colours of the Hellenic flag.

A camper van with two Balkan guys was the only vehicle on the entire beach, and I saw myself and Alina again a couple of years before.

Back then we were also the only inhabitants of the beach, known to be a popular nudist destination, one of the few on the island.

There is something libertine, ancestral and amniotic about swimming naked, it sends you back in time to the moments before your birth.

We spent unforgettable days on that beach listening only to the crashing of the waves on the pebbles, the cries of the birds, the wind in the branches of the olive trees, nothingness: just us and the island.

And that feeling of being embraced, cherished by she who is able to recognise who loves her and who does not.

The only thing that made us leave that beach was the wonderful news of the birth of Alexander, my beloved nephew. We packed everything to go and meet him.

"Goo Fabiooo!"

Dave roused me from that dreamy state, the beach had already passed and we were trudging uphill. Below us was the cliff bordering the end of the foreshore, the water bubbling and tinged with blue, green and azure in a play of iridescent power.

As we approached Dessimi, the landscape lost its wild side.

Man had colonised that side of the beautiful bay, one of the most beautiful on the island, and several houses were springing up among the trees. Earth-moving machinery was tearing up the hillside to make way for concrete blocks with millionaire's views.

As we reached the entrance to the bay we heard a rather familiar barking; it was Cody, who from the dry stone wall of the beautiful Villa Dessimi had recognised us despite his blindness.

Abandoned in Saudi Arabia by his former owners, he had been adopted by Andy and Kristen who found him wandering blind on a freeway.

We climbed the steep slope leading to the terrace of the villa.

From there you get one of those breathtaking views of the bay.

"Ehy you look exhausted."

"Those two are crazy Ann," I replied breathlessly.

"Yes I know... come on sit down, there's cake and coffee."

Little Ann's coffee is always great, you down three cups like nothing else.

We relaxed, sprawled out in the armchairs with the two big Australian dogs asking for a rope toss. A game that once you started you couldn't escape for hours on end.

"It was fun yes?" Pete asked.

"Too fast for me." Dave replied, "going down the hill at that speed is dangerous, I don't have the reflexes I used to have."

"I stopped because I couldn't pedal after lowering the saddle, my knee was giving me too much discomfort," said Pete, whose kneecap had been had operated on a few weeks earlier.

I preferred to devote myself to the excellent cake, then after the third cup of coffee that accompanied the second piece of cake I said "you are crazy... anyway I recorded everything on the gopro, give me a few days, maybe a few weeks and I'll make a nice video out of it..."

THE DOLCE FAR NIENTE

In February, the island's climate changed for the worse.

The days grew colder, cold northern winds whitened the mountain peaks to the east, the Mount Psifi wind farm was a splendour: barren at the base and hooded in white – like a wise old man with a Franciscan haircut.

There was not much to do in the village, although at least there we were more isolated and protected from the collective madness that was taking over the World.

In the capital, the lockdown was tougher, the police stopped incoming cars and controls were stricter.

In Karya, however, they didn't give a damn: the bars were open and no one dared protest against the inhabitants of that ancient Lefkadian village. They were mostly all hunters who were already pissed off enough about not being able to practice their favourite winter activity, so the police preferred not to give them another reason to use their rifles. The village elders sat comfortably in the cafés sipping coffee in the morning and tsipuro in the evening.

In Vafkeri they had it no worse. The Platanos had become a clandestine tavern: although someone had sung and it was now public knowledge that at Christmas the entire village had gathered there, it was still possible to spend pleasant hours there, but only if you were *admitted*.

And the new and younger inhabitants of Vafkeri were.

The walk from the cottage to the tavern was always evocative, despite its brevity.

At times the fog enveloped the hillside, making the landscape ghostly, the yellow lights of the street lamps struggled to pierce the nimbus-like mantle, and at their tips mystical halos reminiscent of church candles shrouded in incense smoke.

The paved road was always damp and on the coldest days the crunch of ice could be heard with every step.

The smell of frost mingled with that of burnt wood and wet grass.

Cats were sheltering under old abandoned cars, there was an old blue Austin Morris van; it wouldn't have looked out of place in some British museum:, certainly if some enthusiast had scouted it out he wouldn't have waited a moment in making an offer to the owner and restoring it in a maniacal fashion.

But who would have scouted it up there? Half-hidden by the doors of a barn.

The whole island was a small museum of old cars left in a sad state of disrepair.

I happened to notice a number of vintage Alfa and Lancia, Toyota vans from the 1960s with the company crest in metal that would have made an elderly Japanese nostalgic turn his eyes, not to mention the Vw T-Series. Those were a dime a dozen.

But in Vafkeri there was only the old blue Morris, just before the shortcut from the alley to the tavern, a passage so narrow that it reminded me of the narrow streets of old Giovinazzo village or some alley of my Palese, in Apulia.

If you ever find this narrow passageway, remember to turn your torso to pass through it or you risk touching the walls with your back before you reach the square of the Platanos, the ancient and centuries-old guardian of the village, whose leafy branches shade the church and the tavern patio.

I knocked on the closed door, screened by the purple curtain, and as always the thin, inquiring face of Sotiris Santas appeared with the usual cigarette between his lips.

"Hela Fabio pame"'come Fabio pass.

"Thanks Sot... that's cold! Holy sour tzatziki!"

"Eheh... *crio crio...*"

I entered the warm atmosphere of the tavern mingling with it, took my place at the usual table and glanced at the living flames dancing in the wood stove.

A pot with stifado smoked, flavouring the air with spicy scents.

"Fabio, ena tsipuro?"

"You also make two Sot."

"Eheh... water?"

"No no smooth."

"OK smooth."

Sotiris disappeared into the half-light of the kitchen, filled a glass with a good dose of tsipuro and left it on the table where I was sitting.

Almost without stopping, he walked over to the wood-burning stove and lifted its lid.

"Mmm perfect," he said, sniffing its contents.

Then he took a wooden ladle resting on a nail in the wall and used it to fill a centuries-old-looking bowl.

He put the ladle back, closed the lid of the huge pot and brought me the handmade bowl.

"Oh... the spoon."

He disappeared again almost running and returned with a spoon in the same style as the bowl.

"Hela Fabio, bon apetit."

"Thanks, but don't speak French to me or my hunger goes away."

"Oh, bon apetit is not Italian?"

"No in Italian is buon appetito."

"Ah! True true, well: buon appetito."

"Thanks Sot, gosh it's spectacular!"

'Eheh... that's how my mother did it, and her mother before her: cazarola, slow fire, free-range chicken, some beef and pulses. But not supermarket pulses.... Never!"

"Where do these come from?"

"Oh these Maria grew down in the valley, you don't need to water them you know, the spring water comes through the gutters."

"What a sight, never had such a good stew."

"And you will never eat it."

"Listen Sot but do you like wine?"

"Wine? No no. No wine for me."

"And what do you drink? Besides water I mean."

"Whisky and coke, I really like whisky and coke, or a little campari with orange juice, but in summer."

"Mmm ok, too bad... I have some Primitivo pugliese at home that would go perfectly with this stew..."

"Bring it next time, at most I'll taste it."

"Yes, but don't put water in it because it is illegal here."

Sot laughed heartily and said, "Yes, but here we are in Lefkada."

"Yes, but the wine is Apulian, and I am a sommelier so I have a licence to kill the innkeeper who waters down the wine!"

"I have heard this story."

"Yes it is a true story, but it goes back to the Egyptians who apparently, God forgive us, are still believed to be the inventors of beer."

"Oh yeah?"

"Yes... in Roman times Pliny the Elder in his Naturalis Historia called it Egyptian filthy water worthy only of infecting the plebs.

"However, even before that, in Hamurrabi's time, there was a law that the watering innkeeper was drowned in his own beer."

"Really?"

"If they have deciphered the hieroglyphics of the code well, yes."

"Fair enough."

"Me too."

"Iamas."

"Iamas" and we lifted the goblets, clinking them, and then poured out the liquid they contained.

"Another one?"

"Yes thank you Sot, stifado is good but thirsty."

"Eheh it's the spices, family recipe."

"Which of course you will not reveal to me."

"Well... it's a secret but I can tell you something."

"Oh, thank you..."

And he walked away again, taking the glasses with him.

This is how life went in Vafkeri in winter, in the morning a walk with the doggies, then a light lunch, a nap, a good read and then to the tavern.

"Didn't Alina come today?" said Sot, returning the two glasses filled to the brim.

"No it is Lent."

"Yes it is true, I should make it too since I am Orthodox like her but I had this free-range chicken that... did you taste it?"

"Yes it is really good."

"And so because it is Lent, Alina is staying at home?"

"No, it's just that she was sure we would eat meat and didn't want to be tempted."

"Ah! Good girl."

"Yes, sometimes."

"Hela Fabio... you are lucky to have a woman like that who loves you."

"Ah yes I know, I'd probably be dead by now if it wasn't for her, or in jail at best."

"Why, did you kill someone?"

"Not yet that I know of but you know how it is..."

"Yeah... you know Fabio... when I was young, I can tell you now, in the days of the colonels... I was a spy."

"A spy?"

"Yes, a secret agent."

"Oh yeah?"

"Yes, a lot of action, a lot of adrenaline... we would go after dissidents, I would mingle among them and then zac! I'd get them arrested."

"Interesting."

"Yeah... then the regime fell, my file was destroyed and I was out of a job."

"And it's a good thing or you could have ended up in a fucking Soviet gulag."

"Yes it is very likely."

I used up my stifado.

"You want more?"

" I'd better not."

"Hela Fabio pame." he said, and taking the bowl he headed back to the stove to fill it.

"Yes but then it will take me another tsipuro and we'll never get out..."

"You don't have to drive anyway."

"Eh... that's true too."

Sot returned to the table with the bowl full and steaming.

"Thank you Sot."

"My pleasure Fabio." He took a long drag on the cigarette and contemplating the smoke as he exhaled it resumed his narration.

"You know in those days...I always had a gun with me. A Tokarev, those Soviet ones you know? They knew me as a revolutionary infiltrator.

I had long hair, dressed like them and frequented those places in Athens you know... A bit strange."

I nodded even though I wasn't sure I understood what he was talking about, let alone where those strange places in Athens were, I only realised he had a Tokarev and that was as far as I got, being a weapons enthusiast.

"Dangerous people, bad people, I've had a lot of them arrested you know..." then smiling he lost himself in the memories of his fantasies.

"Did you ever meet Alekis Panagulis? He was from Syvros."

Sotiris' face became grim.

"A lot happened here during the civil war, but the locals don't like to talk about it, they prefer to forget. The island was the nerve centre of the civil war... but I hardly ever operated here."

"And where did you usually stay?"

"In Capital."

"Wasn't it worse than around here?"

"It depends...

"Once... ah no I can't tell you that..."

"But come on it's been so long now..."

"Yeah but you know there's a girl involved..."

"Ah! You old rascal with a moustache," I said in Italian.

"What?"

"Nothing, i said the leopard doesn't change..."

"Its spots… eheheh, is there also this proverb with you?"

"I think it is international Sot."

"Yeah... Anyway there was this girl... only I was married you know... a very awkward situation."

"What happened to her?"

"Ah I don't know... they arrested her with her boyfriend."

"Which was not you I suppose."

"No no no... I did what had to be done: I provoked when I had to provoke and a scuffle ensued, the police came and arrested us all, but they already knew who they had to arrest and where they had to come..."

"I guess I guess."

"But I felt that girl had something towards me, some attraction you know?"

"Yes," I said as I ate.

"If not, the guy, that idiot, stinking big-haired guy, if not, he wouldn't have taken it so badly, I mean, that one ate me with his eyes, you know, an infiltrator, armed, who knew sensitive information..."

"A mouthful in short."

"Eh..." and he tilted his head to the side, winking.

"Who is that hottie on TV?" I asked looking at a beautiful girl spinning letters in a game show.

"Oh this is Valia... Valia Hagitheodorou."

"That's a real mouthful."

"Eheh."

The TV went without volume, and was on just to give the tavern a homely air in case of checks that never came.

"Sot I need some wood, the one I had in the back I cut it all down and almost finished it."

"But didn't you go with Dave last week to get it?"

"But that you have the C.I.A. here in Lefkada?"

"I told you, I was a secret agent."

"Yes. It costs too much wood at that one, I don't have a British pension like Dave and last year it's not like I worked that much."

"Try asking Zaza."

"To Zaza?"

"Yes, he sells it."

"I guess it's worse than in Karya."

"Well... ask, see."

Sot stood up and without asking, filled my glass again.

"Is it the third or the fourth?" I asked.

"I have no idea, I'm not counting."

"Fine, and how many shall I pay you?"

"None, we are officially closed so..."

"Come on Sot, stop this."

"Hela Fabio... I make food for myself, two or three more dishes that is, I use the wood anyway and if I don't finish the stifado then it goes bad..."

"Yes, but tsipuro?"

"And that you want to eat without drinking?"

"You remind me of an Italian saying, which goes something like this: how sad it is to eat without wine, so much so that you almost don't feel like eating...".

"Right, I agree... you know my father was a philosopher, in Athens, and he often told me anecdotes like that."

"A philosopher huh? Yes you told me about it."

"Great person, you know my greatest legacy is not the house he left me, but his books."

"All in Greek?"

"Yes, of course."

"What a mess this is; I was in the bookstore, looking for some books on the history of Lefkada but those translated into English are very few."

"Yes, I don't know why they never translate enough of them, as if they were jealous of them.

"The history of Lefkada is very fascinating you know... it was not an island, the canal was artificially created."

"Yes I read it."

"Besides, you know this is not written everywhere but: this is the real Ithaca."

"What do you mean?"

"Eh you know..." said Sot lighting a cigarette and preparing to tell one of his interminable and at times interesting stories.

"The translation of the Homeric texts from ancient Greek lends itself to numerous interpretations, a bit like the Bible and the Gospels. The true translation has been lost over the centuries and has been shaped as it has been modified."

He took a puff from his cigarette and blew it to the side, letting his gaze wander over the wooden walls.

The flame of the stove illuminated him, giving his face a surreal aura.

"My father once told me that there are three main passages Homer wrote on this subject, among others.

Two in the Iliad and one in the Odyssey, as Ulysses remembered his beautiful homeland of seventy waterfalls."

"Seventy waterfalls?"

"Exactly."

"But in Ithaca there are no waterfalls, I have been there, they using desalinators."

Sot tilted his head to the side nodding in agreement, then dropped some ash from his cigarette and before taking another puff said, "And that's one."

I remained silent, he now had my attention.

"In another passage," he resumed, "the mother of Odysseus asked Patroclus: *did you come walking? Or by rowing fast?*"

"What do you mean by walking or rowing fast?"

"Lefkada at low tide could be reached on foot, walking. At Ligia semi-submerged there are still the remains of an ancient road used to transport flocks and built on the shallows, another passes by the small church of St Nicholas, you know the little church on the island."

"Yes yes I know her."

"Here, and it goes all the way to Preveza."

"Unbelievable..."

"No, just history... and by the way you can't even get to Ithaca by rowing fast."

"And the third?"

"The third is the one that lends itself most to interpretation, but Homer in one passage said that from the south of Ithaca it was possible to admire two islands, well we in the south have Atokos and Arcudi, with in the distance Ithaca and Kefalonia looking like one island seen from here, in fact one interpretation of the translation said that it was possible to admire the outline of three islands."

"Crazy..."

"No, just history, now tell me from south Ithaca what do you see?"

"Well... Zante, and the Dragoneras if there is Mistral."

"Yes, and not as clear as the three you see from south Lefkada."

"That's for sure."

"Yeah..."

"What's all the fuss about then?"

"My father believed there had been a simple mistake in the translation. A similar name in short... they were talking about an island, and Lefkada was once connected to the mainland. So they made a mistake in the translations somewhere in the story."

"And how did the inhabitants of Ithaca take it?"

"Ah... they disprove everything, as always."

"But I read that Ulysses' palace was recently discovered over there."

"The palace of Ulysses was discovered by Dorpfeld and was where Nydri now stands.

In Ithaca they discovered *a* palace of *a* Mycenaean king, but in those days every island had its own king, they cannot know whether it was Odysseus' palace or not, they just used the story for publicity."

"A translation error..."

"Yeah." he said, and put out yet another cigarette in the ashtray.

"Like with Primitivo and Zinfandel at the end."

"Like what?"

"Ah, nothing... Primitivo... wine, and Zinfandel.... are genetically the same thing. But a mistake in the tag of a plant that was shipped to America to the New York municipal nursery created a misunderstanding that was only resolved after it was noticed in the 1960s how similar the Zinfandel and Primitivo plants were and how much the organoleptic character of the two wines resembled each other."

"Oh, interesting... but I don't like wine."

"Yeah well everyone has their flaws Sot but the story of Ithaca is crazy..."

"It is, it is true."

"Where can I find out more? Where can I go further?"

"You have to learn Greek first."

And at that point I made a face that, if translated into words, would have meant blasphemy.

I staggered home, trying not to slip as I trudged across the slippery pavement.

I thought of Ithaca and the incredible story I had just heard.

I wasn't entirely convinced that Sot had been a secret agent, to be honest I didn't believe a word of it.

But if it was true that the translations of Homeric texts lent themselves to interpretation, well: I believed that other story. Or at least I was tempted to.

The road climbed gradually revealing the wine press monument in the wine square, the small old church and then the larger one near the cottage, dedicated to St Marina.

How beautiful the cottage was, a ghost of solid stone shrouded in mist hiding the smoke blown out of the chimney of the wood stove.

"Honey? I'm home!"

"You fucking look like Jack Nicholson in The Shining."

"Do you know that this is the real Ithaca?"

"You've been drinking huh?"

"Just a few tsipuros..."

"Yes some..."

"Anyway really, Sot said that his father was practically a philosopher, so he said that by translating the Iliad he discovered that Ithaca was in Lefkada."

"And Ithaca is what?"

"I don't know he didn't tell me."

"Eh... next time ask him."

"OK."

"You asked for wood?"

"Yes we have to ask Zaza."

"Ah good, we're in a tight spot then, if it snows we'll freeze."

"Well it's very likely... because it was about to start – a few flakes I saw."

"Yes yes..."

"Really!"

At that statement even the dogs raised their heads and looked at me suspiciously.

"You don't believe it?"

Pepi sighed and went back to sleep muttering.

Alina burst out laughing.

"You ungrateful *bbastasi* I had to leave you on the side of the road. Or worse, in a kennel."

I turned around, opened the door and soft, white snowflakes were beginning to settle on the ground.

"See? It's snowing."

Alina jumped off the sofa and looked out.

"It's really snowing!"

"I've been telling you for half an hour."

"And what do I know, you talk about Ithaca, philosophy, bullshit."

"And instead it snows."

"Madu how nice! I'll get my jacket!"

"Where are you going?"

Alina had already dashed off and from the other room replied: "To take a walk in the snow!"

"Cold-blooded Transylvanian..."

The dogs anticipated Alina and came out running, jumping and trying to bite the flakes.

Pepi returned after seven seconds and went to stand almost under the wood-burning stove.

Instead, Bibi took the opportunity for one last extra evening piss.

Alina grabbed her SLR camera and tripod and walked out with a smile accompanied by a funny noise of happiness.

"But really go to—"

"Come on!"

We walked about fifty metres down the driveway towards Dave's house.

We took two shots using the light of the street lamps, then went back and took more shots in the wine square.

"Tomorrow we'll go around, if we can go up to the little church."

"OK..."

"Brrrr fredoooo, it's OK we can go back in."

"OK..."

She was like a child at times, a little something was enough to send her back to the memories of her childhood, a difficult childhood, lived during a dictatorship.

In those days they had fun with nothing, learning to appreciate what little they had.

And that little today was of immense value – and Alina was transformed in an instant from that beautiful, sensual woman to whom it is impossible to say no into a sweet, tender little girl.

Good match... I was simply fucked.

To witness that rare event of Ali waking up early in the morning is something so rare that it can be told to the grandchildren.

That morning was not one of them... but we came close.

As always, as a good sailor, I was quite an early riser.

I got out of bed, made a fire and started fiddling with the cooker in the kitchen, making a hell of a mess.

After a few minutes, Alina came out of the room with her usual stunned face and approached the window.

"Mm and nor eve?"

"Hi cicci... said something?"

"Phew..."

"OK drink your coffee eh? Take care."

After about ten to fifteen minutes, the minimum time it takes for Alina to become humanly tractable, I saw her make her first smile of the day as she lit a cigarette sitting on the fireplace mantelpiece, near the wood stove.

"Are you among us?" I asked her.

"Yes...now yes."

"Oooh good."

"Don't mock me," she said, frowning.

"No no not at all... we'll take all the doggies yes?"

"I don't know. Pepi might want to stay here in the warmth."

"Boh ask him."

Pepi, as if sensing that we were talking about him, curled up on the sofa near the wood-burning stove, enjoying the warmth radiating from it.

"But yes let's bring them all, they will have fun in the snow."

"Yes for ten minutes maybe... do you remember what happened in Romania?"

"But what does it matter, there it was minus eleven degrees and on the ground everything was frozen."

During a couple of sub-zero winters in Alina's hometown, the doggies got used to leaving the house for a few seconds, just long enough to do what they had to do, and you would see them return at the speed of light, jumping on the sofas covered in warm woollen blankets.

It was very curious to see them pawing around trying to limit the contact between the icy ground and their paws as much as possible.

I left the house to turn on Gypsy's extra heater, the legendary Vw T4 camper van.

After not even five minutes, the cockpit reached a temperature that allowed you to stay in a short-sleeved T-shirt, despite the -4°C atmosphere.

Alina took a little longer to get ready, so I took the opportunity to let the doggies stretch their paws and to let them finish their little walk by jumping in the car instead of going home.

Pepi was not happy about this.

"Come on don't make that face... couchide."

"Don't insult my love!" said Alina peremptorily.

I started the engine, let it warm up for a few minutes and then manoeuvred down the hill to Vafkeri.

"It's a good thing the road has these two so rougher parts otherwise you know what a slip..." On the stone slope two concrete lanes had been dug in horizontal lines to help the tyres grip.

"Do you think we can get up to the little church?"

"I don't know, until Eglouvi it should be easy, then we see."

In fact, as far as Eglouvi it was easy, the landscape whitening as we climbed in altitude.

An increasingly thick layer of snow greeted us at every hairpin bend.

"Let's go by Karya and see what the situation is like there."

The main square was whitewashed. A couple of children were playing snowballs and throwing them at each other under the eager eyes of their mothers.

The road was completely passable, we were still too low in altitude.

We turned around and took the steep path to the *pass.*

Once in Eglouvi the situation changed.

There was a lot more snow on the ground and on the streets only a couple of old people were enjoying the unusual landscape.

We continued uphill and after a couple of hairpin bends Alina said "Stop stop! Look at the view from here!"

We were at a height where we could photograph the village so famous for its lentils from above, with its white roofs and plumes of smoke spiralling out of the chimneys.

"Summer tourists do not even imagine that Lefkada can wear white."

Alina did not listen to me, engrossed as she was in adjusting the white balance of her SLR camera.

"Come on, let's go up or it will all start to melt, look at that sunshine," he told me a few moments later.

We continued to climb until we reached the pass, the church of Agios Donatos with its nine wells.

We love that place, we feel an inner peace take over every time we go there and to see it like that was really surreal.

After a few more shots, we continued uphill, passed the abandoned military base and took the narrow, shabby road that leads up to Agios Ilias, the highest church on Lefkada.

"What?" asked Alina.

I had stopped, something didn't feel right about the road.

I got out of the car and took two steps forward, then approached the side of the road and there I realised that under the asphalt there was nothing but emptiness for at least half the carriageway.

"From here on we walk," I said on my way back.

"Why?"

"There's a sinkhole under the asphalt, it's dangerous to go through it with Gypsy: we're too heavy."

I parked in a recess in the road, I doubted that anyone else would go up there because theoretically we were in lockdown and it was forbidden even to leave the house without a justification.

The little dogs flew out looking around bewildered, too white.

Ali took the Nikon and we started the long uphill walk to the hilltop, dominated by the blue and white church.

On the way we stopped several times to admire the scenery and take some shots, the air was pure. Very few cars circulated on the island in winter and the north winds had cleaned what little smog there was to clean.

Ice, earth and brackish were the scents that dominated the atmosphere up there, at an altitude of over a thousand metres.

There was no wind that day, and thank goodness.

The air was still, as if it too was frozen.

In the distance, the buildings of the capital and its lagoon stood out against a white backdrop that included the mountains of the mainland.

The snow had not reached sea level and that contrast was rather curious.

Alina seemed perfectly in her element: her sparkling green eyes, her off-white skin dotted with freckles, and that curious woollen hat with two dancing balls framing a childlike smile.

As we advanced up the hillside, the first thing the little church showed us was its blue dome, caressed by a dusting of white.

At the top, the landscape was unique.

The absolute and respectful silence towards that sacred place, the village just below asleep in its stillness, the lentil fields covered in snow and that feeling of bliss that always pervades you in some places on the island.

I inhaled deeply.

"Do you hear that?" asked Alina.

I nodded my head.

"The island loves us," Alina said, smiling.

"Where else do you feel this feeling so strongly?" I asked her.

Alina pointed to the abandoned military base with her head.

"The base?"

"Yes, but in reverse."

"And the positive instead?"

Ali looked up as if searching for an answer.

"I don't know... so many places but every time it's different, the feeling I say."

"Yeah, I wonder why."

"They are the ancient spirits of the island. Each one of them transmits something different to you, even if it is a benign feeling, each one is unique."

"Do you remember that lady we met at the tea bar?"

"Yes... the one with the different coloured eyes."

"Yes. She said something about."

"What was that?" asked Alina, interrupting me.

"Thunder... at least I think so."

"But there are no clouds."

"Then an earthquake tremor."

"But not a leaf moved."

"And then I don't know."

"Maybe we are just talking too much."

"It may be..."

After spending an hour or so in that magical place and saying a few prayers inside the little church, we started walking towards Gypsy.

"Is that a police car on the path?" asked Alina.

"I see nothing."

"It is now covered by the hill."

"Ah yes here she is..."

"*Kai tora?* What do we tell them?"

"That we have come to bring the dogs around."

"Yes... from Vafkeri to here?"

"And why not?"

Ali shook his head in disapproval.

"Wait... It's a military machine. It will come from the Army base."

In fact, after a short while the jeep reversed course and went back the way it came.

"What do you say we also go to the west coast?" proposed Alina.

"It's already melting, but if you want to..."

104

"Let's go all the way to the other side of the pass, maybe some more nice shots will come out."

We walked across the lentil-growing plateau and came out on the opposite side of the island.

Although the view was splendid, the most beautiful and characteristic place of the day remained the plateau.

The little wind that had been there during the night had cleared the western side of the hills of snow. While there was still some on the plateau and it was still falling on the eastern side as well, below Vafkeri there was nothing left: it was too warm for it to remain on the ground.

"Come on let's go download the photos and light the fire, if it's out it will freeze at home."

"OK. I'll stop at Platanos though," I said.

"Whatever, bring me something good?"

"If Maria has prepared a little something fancy yes, preferences?"

"No no, Maria's special is fine."

We returned to Vafkeri through the idyllic landscape of the Lefkada mountains – dressed for the occasion in the most typical winter attire.

"We should do a photo exhibition at the end of this year.... Lefkada in the four seasons."

"Eh, not a bad idea," Ali replied.

"Sure... I'm not blonde like you."

Ali glowered at me with that gorgeous look of hers, then gave me a half-lipped smile and a cocky grin.

I drove home, parked and walked to the tavern.

There was little movement, chestnuts were opening in a pot resting on the wood stove.

I took a tsipuro, had a chat with Maria and then with a bag of hot chestnuts went home.

I found Alina in front of the computer with shining eyes: the photos had turned out to be much more beautiful than expected.

"Really?" I asked.

"Look at this!"

"But it's from this morning, during the lap with the doggies. I took it up at the Australian's peak."

The photo showed snow-covered karst rocks in the foreground and the islands of Scorpio, Meganissi, Kastos and Kalamos in the background.

"Yes indeed, the ones in Vafkeri are more beautiful than the ones around."

"I told you it was pointless to stray..."

Ali elbowed me in the belly.

"I really love this one."

"Yes, I wanted to capture the plume of smoke."

A beautiful picture depicted a whitewashed roof with a smoking chimney against a backdrop of islands and snow-capped mountains.

"Yes, you can get something out of it... if not an exhibition at least a calendar."

"Yes next year we do it!" said Alina super excited.

"What do we eat?" I asked.

"At Platanos there was nothing?"

"Yes I had a small plate of cold meats and cheeses and some chestnuts."

Ali turned, tilting her head to the side, and with eyes that had become two slits said, "tell me you brought two chestnuts..."

"They were very few... I would have liked a few more too."

Alina then made a sad little face, sticking out her lower lip.

Then I pulled out the steaming bag. "But you're such an asshole you know that? Just professionally!"

And as I snickered she continued laughing, "You are such a despicable person... bad on the inside."

"Wait till I uncork a *Sellato*," I said." There is nothing better than a vintage Primitivo to accompany them."

And so we spent the evening discussing the photos we had just taken, with a glass of an excellent, award-winning wine in hand, and munching on Vafkerian-style chestnuts.

"Ehy buonasseraa."

"Ohoh that must be Dave," I said, heading for the door.

"Hi Dave! Hi Anna!"

"Hi guys, have you been out and about? I saw that the car wasn't there before."

"Yes, we've been up there doing some shooting."

"Ah, OK. We wanted to know how the road to Nydri was."

"Under Vafkeri there is nothing, go quietly."

"OK thanks."

"And what, but come inside. A glass of wine?"

"Oh no thanks Fabio we have to go do some shopping."

"Look I uncorked a 2016 Sellato."

"OK then."

"Come on in," I said with a smile.

I took two more glasses as Alina greeted Dave and Ann.

"I am sorry but we have run out of chestnuts, Maria made them down at Platanos."

"Ah, castange? What are they called in Italy I remember in Rome they used to call them...'

"Caldarroste," I finished.

"Ah yes cadarosta"

"No Dave, caldarroste, two r and e final."

"Cazzarrosta OK."

"Yeah whatever, here you go have some Primitivo which is good for your pronunciation."

"Pronuzzia."

"Here... wait till I let you taste a pecorino that Sotiris recommended, I finally found a cheese smoked like Christ commands here too," I said as I put on the table a delicious goat's cheese, which he insisted on calling pecorino, smoked and not very mature.

"Who took those pictures?" asked Ann.

"Most of them Alina... but the most beautiful ones are mine." I said already knowing the face the little blonde on my right would make... who indeed looked at me smiling and shaking her head.

"Yes, today is Fabio asshole day."

"Oh isn't it every day?" said Dave, backing up Alina.

Who knows why the neighbourhood in these playful matters always sided with her and never with me.

"But they are beautiful!" said Ann.

"The chimney one there... who made that?"

"Fabio..." Ali replied.

"Oh... and that one there the number..."

"Fabio..."

A snigger was heard between sips.

"More wine?" I asked. "It is rude to leave a bottle unfinished, especially when it is such a wine."

"I do thank you," said Dave.

"We should organise a wine tour in Puglia Dave, at the first opportunity we will embark, go raid and return."

"I'm in! But if you have to go before you organise it, bring me a couple of crates of this please."

"Will do. This is my favourite winery, they even have a b&b on the premises you know, after a good tasting... you never know."

"Yes, good idea."

"Then we eat fancy so we fall on our feet."

"Speaking of eating, are you guys coming over for dinner the day after tomorrow? Pete and Little Ann are also there."

"Sure thanks, when are Andy and Chris coming back?"

"Next month."

"They will bring the spring then."

"Eh let's hope so, so we can cycle more often."

"By the way, that white bike... you're not selling it, are you?"

"Andy wants to buy it too," she laughed.

"And you don't listen to that kind of kangaroo, then what do you say?"

"Fab it's a bit too big for you, in my opinion you need to get a *54* considering your height and instep, at the first opportunity try Pete's, in my opinion it's the right size for you."

"Come on let's see, I guess it's too expensive for one like Pete's."

"Yes, but you see if you are comfortable with the size and then decide on the model you prefer."

"Well guys, we really must be going, thank you very much for the wine and cheese," Ann said.

"But mostly for the wine," Dave added.

"I'll bring a couple of bottles to the dinner the day after tomorrow, OK?"

"Oh perfect thank you!"

"OK bye beautiful see you."

"Bye!"

"Nice..." I said, closing the door. "Finally, the neighbours I always wanted."

Ali looked at me with that infra-green ray gaze of hers that meant so many things....

like today meant something like...

and no, it cannot be written.

THE MONASTERY OF SAINT NICHOLAS

Night fell cold and serene, the icy air entered the nostrils filling the lungs and purifying the thoughts.

"What are you doing?" asked Alina, seeing me on the little wall tinkering with the weather station.

"I'm calibrating the compass."

"In the dark?"

"Oh yes; the sky is perfect today and I can align it with the North Star, see? It's that one there."

In fact, the starry blanket was splendid up there in Vafkeri, where there are very few artificial lights and those of the neighbouring villages are far away.

The winter sky offered a firmament to make the remotest places on earth envious.

Certainly looking north-north-west one could perceive the disturbance of the Santa Maura lights, but the main constellations were there, as drawn: Ursa Minor & Ursa Major, Cassiopeia, Orion, the Pleiades.

I love the winter sky, I contemplate it often, from anywhere.

During our winter in the Canaries we bought a small amateur telescope in a shop that sold second-hand items. We went there often, partly for the budget, partly because the friendly foreign owners donated a large part of their income to the island's shelters for stray and abandoned dogs.

During that long, warm winter, we enjoyed getting to know the stars, camping with the legendary Doblò, equipped only with the roof tent, in the most remote places on the seven islands.

"Now it is pointed perfectly, the first adjustment with the hand compass had not been optimal, too much junk around here."

"Meaning?"

"That is, metals create magnetic fields that deflect the north compass."

"Ah... OK... are you coming in now?"

"Don't you like it out here?"

"Yes, but we're not in the Canary Islands, it's not even three degrees."

"Yes... I was thinking about the Canary Islands too."

"Every time you look at the stars you think about it."

"Yeah... we should go back sometime."

Ali had left the door barely ajar and the dogs had taken the opportunity to sneak in.

Outside they too seemed drawn to the starry sky, or perhaps they were just trying to understand what their humans had to look up there for.

"I guess they don't agree with going back in..."

"OK let's take a walk."

Vafkeri in the evening was a nativity scene: silent, fragrant, cold and cosy.

We walked up the slope leading first to the president's house, then to Klaus'.

There you come to a fork in the road, to the left you go down to Dave and Ann's and further down you come to Olga's, to the right you continue uphill and pass Villa Mistico and the water cistern before climbing up to the Australian's peak.

From up there the view is even more spectacular.

The lights of Meganissi and Scorpio were tiny dots that blended in with the stars, looking up vertically it felt like being inside one of those round souvenirs that, when shaken, simulate a snowfall inside them, as if they were micro-worlds in their own right.

"But do you realise how peaceful it is here?" said Ali.

I inhaled, turned towards her and nodded my head.

A gentle breeze came from the forest, passing through the trees like a sigh: the breath of the island.

"If the wind continues to blow from the north-west tomorrow it will be another beautiful day," I said.

"Do you want to do anything in particular?"

"We could go to the lighthouse."

"Yes why not, let's also drop by the monastery to pick up some aloe creams?"

"Of course," I replied.

We walked home enjoying the silence, the scent of the grass and the peace that the island can give you.

The next day the wind continued to blow from the northwest, calm and without too much force, just enough to keep the atmosphere clean.

The morning air was fresh and crisp and after a rejuvenating breakfast we got the dogs into the car.

I drove over the mountains to the other side.

The snow had now melted, only a few piles strenuously resisted at the roadsides in places where the sun could not reach them.

The sea on the west coast was milky.

That colour, which has made the island so famous, stood out in contrast to the blue sky on the horizon.

The road was deserted and every now and then we had to avoid boulders that had broken loose from the rock and rolled onto the asphalt strip.

They would have to wait until the start of the season to be removed, the islanders are like that: siga siga...

Once past the Porto Katsiki junction, the landscape becomes ghostly, beautiful and wild. Goat herds alternate with shrubs and olive groves.

The road narrows to the point that two cars would struggle to pass.

We arrived at the monastery and found the gate closed.

"What does it say on that sign?" I asked.

Alina got off Gypsy to read more.

"I think we'll have to wait half an hour. There's mass at this time."

"Ah ok... let's go back to that clearing we passed, the dogs will like it."

I drove to a piece of land with a single tree in the middle and a lot of grass all around.

There was only a watering trough for the goats, then nothing but mown grass.

The dogs, as expected, loved it: they launched into wild runs and chases, pretending to fight and then rolling on the grass.

After half an hour of playing they were exhausted.

"Of course the nuns chose the place well to make a monastery," I said.

"Yes... it's very peaceful up here and the view from them is incredible."

"Did you know it was dedicated to St Nicholas because the 80 sailors from Bari who removed his bones from the Ottomans stopped here?"

"Yes, I read that somewhere, that must be why this place is so magical."

"Yes... there should be a small road or path from the monastery down to the sea. It is the same path used by sailors at that time."

The wind increased in intensity, moving the branches and causing the last leaves to fall, which, in a final embrace with life, had tightened their grip, dying where they had been born.

The dogs stopped and all three looked towards a fixed point in the bush.

The wind in the bushes sang, it was a young girl's voice.

Bibi started barking and I called him back.

Then in the distance a shape hovered in the air.

Like a cloak, it rose into the sky to fall back a little further, hidden from view.

Before we realised it was the remains of a shearing, we were a little surprised.

"Sometimes this island is strange," I said.

"Yes... I don't know if strange is the word but still, yes, something is."

Then, as if from nowhere, the silhouette of a shepherd appeared.

All wrapped up in his coat, with his long white beard, he approached, clutching his gnarled staff in his hands.

His eyes were the same colour as the Gaidaros sea in a storm: that milky white tending to light blue.

His face was furrowed with deep wrinkles and his tousled hair waved in the wind.

Without stopping, he lifted his stick and pointed to the spot where we had seen the lint fly off, then nodded his head and smiled, displaying a row of almost transparent teeth.

And as he came, he left.

The air seemed lighter and the sounds became more distinct, as if they could be separated from each other.

A deep, guttural background hum began to vibrate at an independent frequency.

"Why didn't those three bark! It could have been anyone!" cried Alina.

"These are the moments when I miss Tarallo... "

"Yes, Tarallo would have started barking two hours ago!"

We got back into the car and drove back to the monastery.

This time the gate was open and I drove to the car park.

It was and still is a beautiful place, there is a tiny church with unique icons and frescoes, a small shop that looks like something out of a bazaar from another era and a wooden bench that contemplates a breathtaking view, as if it were an ordinary sight.

Further on are the nuns' cells, the vegetable garden and a small farm.

We entered the shop and a very nice nun greeted us with a beaming smile.

"Ciao! Italians?"

"But how ca—"

"Fa! We are in a monastery!

No, sister I am Romanian, he is Italian".

"Ah Romanian, so Orthodox!"

"Yes, I am Orthodox."

"Brava brava! And where are you from?"

"From Pitesti."

"Ah yes, I know some monks from that area came here on pilgrimage years ago."

"Yes? My uncle is a monk."

"Ah yes?"

"Yes we are very religious in the family, my aunt is also a nun, then my brother is a priest."

"Brava brava."

The shop inside resembled an old-fashioned shop.

There was honey, medicinal herbs, handmade creams and candles, lots of icons and several crucifixes.

Alina spared no expense and chose several products that proved to be very useful.

She gave me a crucifix and as Sister Gerasima placed it around my neck, blessing it, she said: "You must become Orthodox!"

"In the sense that..."

"In the sense that if you do not become Orthodox, you cannot marry this beautiful maiden!"

"Ah in that sense there..."

"Has he already proposed to you?" the nun asked Alina.

"Yes, look sister let's change the subject."

"So he asked you. But he hasn't been baptised yet."

"No not yet... as soon as we go to Romania again though, he said he will get baptised by my brother."

'Hmm, that's OK then,' said Gerasima squaring me sternly.

"Sister, don't you remember us? We have already been here several times."

"Yes of course I remember!"

"Does that shepherd with the flock nearby ever come around here?" I asked.

"Pastors?"

"Eh yes shepherds... you know the ones with goats."

"Yes I know what shepherds are, but there are no shepherds here in winter."

"But we saw one just this morning before we came here."

"It's not possible, in winter the shepherds bring the flocks down to the valley, only in summer do we see them up here."

"Yes but today there was one, his face was all wrinkled, old and his eyes almost white."

The nun became serious.

"You have not seen a shepherd. Those are not shepherds. And you should be baptised!"

Then she disappeared behind a curtain and returned with a small bottle containing black liquid.

"This is very strong," she said, turning to Alina who is the galleymaid.

"You can put a few drops in water and drink it a little at a time. Or you can put a few drops in your mouth but it is very bitter. It is a root extract and the plants we get it from grow on this hill, where the wind beats all year round and the saltiness strengthens them. This helps you."

"Help with what?"

"To think."

Then she turned to me again.

"If you ever see any of them again, don't look them in the eyes and don't try to talk to them, they speak an ancient language."

"Please, I don't even speak Greek..."

"Neither do they. Take it once a week, and whenever you need it."

Alina tried to reach for her wallet again but the nun quickly stopped her.

"This is not something you can sell. It is a gift from me."

"Thank you but you shouldn't have..."

"Yes I should, don't worry."

Then she sat down in a funny way, her hands framing her cheeks, and looked at me, tilting her head to the side.

She turned to Alina and said, "but are you sure you want to marry this one?"

Ali burst out laughing and said, "Yes... yes of course I wouldn't marry anyone else."

"Hmm," said the nun, turning back to face me.

"All right then... but get him baptised!"

We left the monastery with Alina almost unable to contain her laughter any longer, I looked at her amused, shaking my head.

"Are we sure that thing she gave us works? No, because if she uses it too, I wouldn't want to be like that after a month or so."

"Come on she's so nice!"

"Yes of course she is nice, maybe a bit strange but nice... she almost seemed to want to baptise me."

"No only priests can baptise someone in the Orthodox Religion."

'This is nice here...' I said with a sigh.

"Yeah... what do you say we stay over?"

"Yes why not, is there something in the galley?"

"Mmm I think a few tins and some seasoning, but there is no bread."

"Eh no if there is no bread no..." I said jokingly.

"Come on there are crackers."

"There are no beers, not even wine... good thing we have the thing there that the nun gave us."

"Yes but I don't think it's alcohol."

"It may be... but it is certainly hallucinogenic."

"Shall we stay then?" asked Alina doing that tender childlike look mixed with her irresistible smile.

"OK..." I said, opening the small bottle to sniff its contents, then started coughing.

"What is it?" asked Alina.

"It's not alcohol, more!"

Alina sniffed it in turn, then said, "I realised what it is, Visarion, my monk uncle, made me taste it. Just a few drops he said, it's serious."

"Yes yes..."

Ali looked at me in that way of someone who admits no reply when certain topics are touched upon, then prepared a delicious dinner using Gypsy's alcohol stove, which was always ready for the occasion.

We drank some of that bitter mixed with water and the starry mantle opened up before us.

The peace that reigned in that place was surreal.

We stood gazing at the stars, listening to the waves in the distance crashing on the cliffs and the wind in the branches of the trees.

Winter scents permeated the air.

The dogs were sleeping, growling in their sleep and trying to bark.

"I wonder what they dream about," I asked.

Ali looked at them lovingly.

"Maybe they dream about that pastor," I continued.

"He was not a pastor..."

I looked at her, raising my eyebrows.

"You too now? What was he if not a pastor?"

"I don't know, maybe one of those island spirits you hear about from time to time around."

"Sssi... no more amaretto for you eh? I'll take this one I would gladly take another sip."

"Yes you finish it I'm fine... and rest assured: they can't come in here," Alina said, rolling up in her sleeping bag.

I looked at her in much the same way as I had looked at Sister Gerasima, then I also drained my glass and looked away.

Two bright dots shone in the bushes just beyond the fence. Then they disappeared.

A fox. Or a cat. I thought.

Then I curled up in my turn and fell asleep.

The night went quiet and still.

Gypsy was a white dot on the jagged coastline of Cape Lefkada.

The monastery turned off all external lights at night and only the lighthouse with its monotonous flashing revealed the tip of the island, marked on every nautical chart and famous since ancient times.

Before dawn I was awoken by the sound of light footsteps.

A black, hooded figure was walking down the driveway and had arrived at Gypsy's height.

The view was not good as the windows were fogged up, the stove had worked well during the night and we did not feel cold.

The figure was getting closer and closer, massive and decisive.

Until I saw her tying a bag to a rear-view mirror.

Bibi was sleeping on the seat closest to the mirror but gave no signs of life.

Then the figure left.

"Congratulations Bibi," I said to myself.

"If Tarallo was still there at this time, he would have woken up even the deaf nun who sleeps with earplugs two floors below."

Then driven by curiosity I opened the sliding window and stuck my head out to get a better look at the bag.

Nothing much, an anonymous white bag hanging from the mirror.

Only it had a peculiarity: it smoked.

I climbed out of the warmth of the sleeping bag against my will. I opened the hatch and no one, neither Alina nor the dogs moved. Bibi even snored.

"What guard dogs... fantastic."

I slipped on my shoes without tying them and stepped out into the cold night.

I stepped on a puddle and heard the dry sound of breaking ice.

We had gone below zero.

I went around the car and approached the steaming bag.

Inside was a paper wrapper with eggs and a piece of cheese.

I got back into the car and the sound of the sliding door closing finally woke up the merry company.

"What are you doing... it's still dark" protested Alina.

"Technically it is dawning; and since we are in the middle of winter, dawn means 8:30 in the morning."

"Emmè?" said Alina using a Bari intercalary meaning: *What about this?*

"And I don't know about you, but I'm hungry."

"You are always hungry..."

"We had visitors."

"Oh yeah? Who?"

"I don't know, she was big, fat, and hooded in black."

"Mmm did you see it or dream it?"

"See, she even left us a souvenir."

"Meaning?"

"Hard-boiled eggs and cheese."

Alina then raised her dishevelled head doing that typical funny look of hers that characterises every morning when her brain is at 3%: that is, every morning in the pre-coffee phase.

"Really?" she asked.

She was beautiful: her platinum blond hair all tousled, her eyes bright green and her cheeks with a sprinkling of freckles.

"Yes apparently there is someone who cares about our breakfast."

Ali approached the bag, moved the edges with her hand and looked inside.

"It must have been the nuns."

"You think so?" I sang to her.

"Mmm ciiii!" She mumbled streching "you make the coffee?"

"Oook."

That morning we had breakfast of boiled eggs, cheese, dry bread and coffee; a real Greek breakfast.

The day turned out to be cold and bright.

There wasn't a cloud in the sky, the dogs were stretching their paws in the car park sniffing who knows what among the blades of grass, the scents of that part of the island are unique: in spring they reach their peak with the blossoming of heather and white thyme; in winter the smell of wet earth, the perennial saltiness and the ever-present smell of stables prevails.

These aromas swirled in the air, carried by the wind, and invaded the nostrils, awakening dormant sensory scents.

We spent the whole day walking among those deserted places.

During the season the monastery is much visited, especially by Balkans, but in the winter months it feels like being on another planet.

It was very cold.

"What wind is this? Mistral?"

"Yes, full house," I replied.

"Well at least if there is Mistral it means it won't rain."

What a sailor she was becoming...

We went to the lighthouse to admire the sunset, which comes very early in winter.

There was no one there either, just the immensity of nowhere where the gods play.

Apollo ran swiftly, pulling the sun in his chariot: a yellow trail to the west that ended its race plunging into the dark blue of Neptune.

The clash of the Titans was a silent explosion of colour that tinted the sky in shades of pink and pastel – as if the palette of those who painted Eden had been overturned.

SAILING FISHING

During some days of that long winter, the sun seemed almost unwilling to come out from behind the hill.

Low on the horizon and almost listless.

The positive side of this natural phenomenon is that the colours are fantastic, the landscape takes on the appearance of a just painted picture with hues fresh from the palette.

A winter dawn always has something magical about it: the dry, icy air, the total silence, the island sleeping like a hibernating wild animal.

That February morning I woke up early, well before dawn.

I prepared myself a frugal breakfast trying not to make too much noise, took my fishing gear and slowly loaded it into the car.

"I should have thought of that yesterday..." I said in a whisper, observing Bibi wagging her tail looking at me with that sweet little face of him.

"Ok come on let's go for a little walk." At these words Bibi catapulted towards the door, Pepi on the other hand turned around on the other side curling up on the couch grunting something that in canine would have meant *"you two are crazy, I'm not moving from here."*

We stepped out into the darkness of the Lefkadian night, walking along the paved path of the village.

Every 40 metres or so a streetlamp emitted its pale yellowish light, there was no fog or clouds, the air was clean and crisp that morning.

We walked to the top of the hill and turned back; someone had put up a net barring access, perhaps to avoid some wild boar or other wild animals from entering the village.

Beyond the fence, however, I saw movement, it was dark and I could not make out what it was but it was there. After a few seconds whatever it was disappeared up the path to the top of the hill.

"Come on back, it's cold!"

It was four degrees below zero that day, good thing there was no precipitation forecast otherwise the snowpack would have thickened, and not just a little.

Only Bibi did not want to go back and walked along the path leading to a beautiful pink house.

When we reached almost the halfway point, he began to growl, raising his fur on his back.

Like a shadow, the old shepherd of the village walked past us.

He looked at Bibi pointing his stick at him and continued with that cadenced, almost floating step of his. He greeted me with a nod without looking at me and disappeared, as if he were invisible.

What is Kostas doing here in winter? I thought. His flock was down in the valley.

We went back inside and I let Bibi in the house, took my boat backpack and got into the car.

It was cold and the engine started reluctant, it would have had time to warm up all the way down to the valley as the road was all downhill, thinking about it, it would have been possible to travel it even with the engine off.

As usual, I did not meet anyone until Nydri where the only shutter open was that of the fish market.

"Kalimera."

"Kalimera Fabio," the friendly fishmonger told me with a smile. "Some sardines?"

"Yes, thank you."

The lady turned around and emptied a bag, then wrapped it in two plastic bags.

"Where do you go fishing?"

"I don't know yet, I'll get in the boat and then decide."

"And when are you going to take me for a ride on your boat?"

I pretended not to understand and greeted her.

Arriving in Vliho I continued to the bakery to buy something to eat as a snack.

There was no *focaccia barese* in Lefkada, so every time I had to make an exception to the family tradition that *you don't go out on a boat without focaccia.*

That morning I settled for a couple of cheese pastries and a sad slice of something that would emulate a pizza.

What I miss most here in Lefkada are the typical Apulian dishes, but I am a traveller and I am used to that.

I parked Gypsy on the waterfront and in twenty minutes inflated the dinghy.

I no longer had that nice electric outboard I had bought the summer before for cheap because some starving man had stolen it from me.

On the other hand, I had two new, well-balanced oars.

The gurgling of the water on the blades was the only sound in the bay.

I rowed towards Nitro who was there, at anchor. Beautiful in the liquid gold colours of dawn.

An imperceptible mist began to rise from the surface of the water, increasing that mystical aura that always hovers there.

I could not resist. I stopped, opened my backpack and grabbed my SLR, which as a good photographer is always at hand.

I took a few shots of Nitroglicerina reflected in the water with perfect symmetry.

The following year that shot would end up in my first island calendar.

I looked around, enjoying that stillness.

The silence was as palpable as the mist that thickened by the second.

Then the cry of a bird ripped through that veil of magic and its wings waving in the air made curls in the nimbus mantle in front of me.

This is not real. I'm at home and I'm still sleeping.

I looked at Nitro about ten metres away and started rowing again.

When I reached it I found it covered in a thin layer of frost.

In some places it was icy.

"Hi Nitro, did you sleep well? I see we got below freezing here in the bay too eh? Let's hope Ruggerino feels like leaving today."

I climbed aboard holding the dinghy mooring line in my hand and turned it to the stern bollard.

I opened the lockers and stowed the fishing gear.

It was even colder in the bay.

After a few attempts, the engine started muttering and spitting out a plume of smoke.

"Bravo Ruggerino, come on we're not going far. At most we will arrive in front of Sparti."

I went to the bow, released the moorings and engaged the forward gear.

Nitro moved delicately on the water: very light and with minimal draft, it needed minimal buoyancy to move forward.

I took the helm and set a course towards the mouth of the bay.

It was deserted.

In summer you had to pay attention to how many boats were at anchor zigzagging between them, that day I counted six.

I had the whole bay to myself, the light now illuminated even the contours of the mountains well.

A dense, deep, saturated blue coloured the cloudless sky.

When I arrived at the narrowest point I gave a few revolutions by increasing the speed.

"Hopefully some wind will come in in the afternoon, it would be nice to sail back in eh Nitro?"

I passed Tranquility bay, the beautiful cove where several foreigners moored their sailboats.

The name, however, is not so apt, since every time the Mistral or Libeccio comes in, the quiet bay turns into a trap.

There are many wrecks that witness these rare but tragic events. Nowadays, even anchoring in Tranquility bay is a risk given the number of boats that inhabit its depths.

Just beyond the bay is the beautiful little church dedicated to Agia Ciriaca, the patron saint of fishermen.

Legend has it that during an unexpected and violent storm, several fishermen who were outside the bay were taken by surprise. The rain was so thick that they lost all visual reference, and the electromagnetic storm unleashed by the lightning drove the compasses of those few who had them crazy.

At one point, the families of the fishermen, who had gathered on the headland where the church now stands, saw their loved ones' boats return one by one.

The next day everyone claimed to have seen a light coming from the cave closing the bay.

So from then on its interior was painted white and candles burn there perpetual.

A beautiful little church was built under the cave, which all the sailors greet on their way out and in, praying for a safe day.

As soon as you step outside, you have the feeling of being in a lake.

The islets of Sparti, Scorpio and Madouri are there, like submerged hilltops.

Further east is the beautiful Meganissi, and further still are Kastos and Kalamos.

All this splendour is closed to the north by the mainland and to the west by Lefkada.

To the south is the channel to Ithaca and Kefalonia.

The pearls of the Ionian Sea – one of the most beautiful places in the world.

A mythical place, where legend and truth are intertwined, lost in the Homeric poems.

I went as far as the shoal at Sparti, a very good fishing area.

I anchored at the edge of the shallow water and with Greek calm prepared the rods.

All this morning work had given me an appetite, so I immediately took out the first of the cheese pastries.

I had learned to appreciate the calm that accompanies fishing days, and it had taken me a long time to learn to do so.

I, who have always been a lover of any adrenalin-pumping activity, from go-karts to racing catamarans, had realised that going fishing transports you to another dimension in time and that it doesn't matter if at the end of the day you come home with dinner or not, the most important thing is that very slowing down that makes the day go longer, there in the middle of the sea, enjoying one of the most exclusive views on the planet.

Sparti is an uninhabited island, there is only the skeleton of what should have become Alexandros Onassis' villa, started by his father Aristotle and never completed following his son's untimely death.

It is now owned by a rich Russian tycoon who will sooner or later turn it into a super-luxury resort, as is happening in Scorpio.

Lost in my thoughts I did not realise that several hours had passed, I was awakened by the sound of an outboard.

A small cabin boat was approaching my position.

I took out my binoculars and saw at the helm the unmistakable face of Babis, the friendly manager of the Porto Spilia Tavern in Meganissi.

Behind him was his brother, Vassili *spiderman,* famous for his boardings of huge yachts from the tavern's pier on his small dinghy piloted strictly in surf style.

His technique is rather peculiar: he arrives at the side of the yacht on duty and with the mooring line clamped between his teeth climbs up the side. He then secures the line to the yacht's hawsers or wherever it can be secured and goes to talk to the captain, offering him the services of the family tavern.

In defiance of any rules concerning permits to board or boarding, this technique has made their fortune.

The wives in the kitchen churn out traditionally cooked delicacies, the children help serve at tables and berths, Babis is at the cash desk and Vassili is at the boarding house.

Two guys as nice as they are traditional.

"Hela Babis cala iste?"

"Oooooh captain. In winter here too?"

"Yes of course, this year I tried."

"Bravo bravo. Who told you about this fishing spot."

"Nobody, I studied the nautical chart."

"The nautical chart huh? And tell me what other places do you know?"

"The shoal of Paleiros and the shoal between Scorpio and Meganissi."

"Malaka... yes but don't tell anyone eh?"

"No, don't worry, even because of the foreigners who go fishing on this slope in winter, there is only me."

"And good, got anything?"

"No not yet, my tops are too stiff, they're eating my bait and I don't notice, maybe I should try the lures and the spinning rod but it's too nice to be here relaxed."

"Yes yes, sleep; he who sleeps doesn't catches a fish."

"True," I said with a smile. "How are things in Meganissi?"

"Well well, but we in winter live in Lefkada."

"Oh yeah?"

"Eh yes you know the guys want the big city, Meganissi too small."

"Big city eh? They study in Ioannina?"

"No no in Lefkada town."

"Understood, well say hello, I will see them this summer at your place."

"You came a little last summer."

"But if I came two or three times a week."

"And why not every day?"

"Because some customers prefer to go to Paleiros and the mainland beaches."

"Fuck mainland, Paradise is in Meganissi."

I lied at the time: I believed that if I told him the truth, that many customers I had taken to Varka Family in Kalamos, one of the best restaurants in the Ionian Sea, Babis would sink my boat on the spot.

There were interesting rumours about him, legends more than anything else.

My old sailing instructor, Mimì, had always been a skipper and used to hang around Croatia and Greece in summer.

He told me that at the time of the Kosovo war you could find everything from bombs to Kalashnikovs at Babis.

I had never given too much credence to those rumours, maybe it was about some hunting rifles that everyone has over there, but you know... at sea one can never be too careful.

"Alright captain, we're going towards Meganissi, we'll leave this place for you."

"Look you can stay if you want, I'll hoist the sails as soon as a bit of wind comes in and do two boards."

"Eh little wind today, and from the south you see?"

Babis pointed to a spot in the sky where there was nothing.

"No I don't see anything."

"Eheh in Summer I taught you how to see, but in winter you still have to learn."

"Babis there is not a cloud how do you understand that—"

"No cloud! Colour! Look!"

The sky to the south was a different shade, but I attributed this to the sun's natural rotation.

"Little wind today, south."

"How soon?"

"One hour, maximum one and a half hours."

"Well I still have some relaxation then."

"Eheh see you captain and visit me more often."

We said goodbye, Vassili smiled and nodded his head, he never spoke, he was one of those silent but very efficient ones.

After about an hour or so I decided that I had had enough. I stowed the equipment, fired up the Ruggerino and hauled anchor.

"Let us go into the wind..."

I got a little closer to the island, and as soon as the view to the south was clear I saw the water rippling in the distance.

"You old sailor wizard, you have got it right again."

Babis' forecasts are famous, every time I visited him in summer he always taught me something about observing clouds in that particular microclimate.

I loaded the dinghy on board to have as little resistance as possible. There was an upwind current of at least a couple of knots, so going upwind in that situation would have been a bit tricky without a nice little help from the wind.

The wind arrived, puffing light and weak but enough to get Nitroglicerina moving, very light and equipped with an airfoil mainsail immense for its length.

Gradually, as I tacked into the bay, I gained the entrance to the bay and experienced the great pleasure of sailing into it, which is absolutely impossible in summer.

The return was like the rest of the day, quiet and relaxed.

FEBRUARY - THE STORM

"Have you seen the forecast for tomorrow?" asked Alina.

"No, I have not yet written the weather for today."

"Give it a look OK? The gusts are bad."

"Which direction?"

"North west."

I sighed in concern. I don't like it when he comes in from the north-west.

In the bay, the Mistral is self-powered.

By a strange phenomenon it is diverted southwards and following the conformation of the bay it rotates back to the north, giving strength to the incoming north-west.

"Yes tomorrow won't be pretty, I should go and have a look but there's not much I can do."

"Yes, also because it will come at night so..."

I finished my breakfast and got ready to go fishing.

I am not an experienced fisherman, I do not respect timetables, nor do I respect the tides or the phases of the moon. When I feel like spending time at sea I simply grab my rods and go.

That day went like many other days, little fish and a lot of peace.

On the way back, I stopped in Vliho, passing my friends' boats: Dave, Mike, my Nitro at anchor, a catamaran anchored on the other side of the bay and, further north in Tranquility bay, Leon's boat.

The Libeccio was beginning to strengthen, temperatures were still high for the season, and a jump to the north-west was expected during the night with gusts of over forty knots.

As soon as I got home I glanced at the weather station and saw that the jump was on.

It was coming in from the west, it was only a matter of minutes before the Mistral arrived announcing itself with icy gusts.

I compared my data with the weather stations of Lefkada town and Platystoma on the net, which confirmed this.

"Hey, how did it go?" asked Alina.

"As usual..."

"Good thing I cooked," she said, smiling.

"I guess we'd better take the dogs for their walk now, it'll be here soon."

"OK, how is Nitro?"

"She sleeps peacefully."

The little dogs went crazy as always when it was cold, chasing each other and rolling around on the grass.

Then the Mistral arrived.

I did not sleep well that night; despite the perfect anchorage I was always afraid that some other ploughing boat might hit Nitro.

The gusts were respectable and I knew the direction was such that in the bay a force five could generate a force nine.

In the morning after a quick breakfast I went down to Vliho to check the situation.

I did not look at anything until I could see the Nitroglicerina mast.

There it was, with the chain nice and tight and the trampoline on the bow fluttering.

"I knew it... I should have taken it apart last time."

I had left it because it was convenient to use when I went fishing. Anchoring without a trampoline was more risky.

Now, however, it was flapping in the wind, the hooks had certainly broken and a couple of lines had blown off.

Then I looked around and realised I was lucky.

One sailing ship had the Genoa in tatters, further ahead Dave and Mike's boats were at an odd angle.

I ran up to their berth and realised that something was wrong.

I remember after an expletive I just said, "I have to call Dave."

My friend's boat crashed against the pier, a hole had opened in the stern and as if that wasn't enough, it was resting on Mike's, the beautiful wooden ketch from 1963.

Both boats were on a catamaran that had been moored there for years.

I managed to board Dave's boat and realised that the damage was extensive.

The starboard gunwale was bent and part of the side damaged, but this was nothing compared to the damage on Mike's: the port side was completely smashed in, fortunately above the waterline.

I went to the bow and saw that the anchors had ploughed in, they had no more grip.

I called Dave who immediately answered.

"Hey Fabio! How are you mate?" he said in his unmistakable Scottish accent.

"I'm fine Dave, but maybe you should fly here my friend. There was a big mess yesterday and your boat suffered some damage."

"Fuck!"

It was the worst thing a sailor could hear. Or almost... the worst is best not written.

"OK Fabio, can you try to tug on the anchors?"

"OK I'll try."

He had three of them. One at the end of a large rope and two others in a line on the chain.

I easily dug my way to the other sheared end.

"OK Dave, you're missing one."

"Which one?"

"The one on top."

"Shit! OK, can you try operating the other one? Try the electric winch."

I opened the locker and pressed the button marked up.

"Nothing Dave."

"OK, I disconnected the battery."

In the meantime, the wind blew icy from the north-west, less than at night but still strong, and made the boat bend, which kept crashing into Mike's boat.

"There is a handle Fabio, try operating it by hand."

I grabbed the handle and started to tug, but a shackle with a line was attached to one link of the chain that I had to remove.

"There's a rusty shackle Dave, I need to find a clamp, I'll call you back."

"OK, is there much damage?"

I went around the boat on video call and was not happy to let Dave see what had happened, then went ashore with the intention of going to look for a clamp in the van which was parked at the other end of the pier.

I stopped near a boat where the owners were reinforcing the moorings and asked them for one.

I went back on board Dave's boat, released the rusty shackle and operated the hand winch again. I barely managed to get the anchor under tension, but not enough to detach the boat from Mike's wooden one.

I observed the situation and realised that I could do no more until the wind had decided to have enough. I only managed to put two fenders between the hull and the pier and between the two boats, then I went ashore and set a fender on Mike's boat as well.

I called Dave back and informed him of the progress.

Then Terry arrived, not the taxi driver but a friend of Dave's who had the keys to the boat.

"Hi, you are Fabio?"

"Yes, you are Bill?"

"No Bill is in Tranquility bay, he cannot go ashore at the moment there is too much wind."

Bill is a gentleman who used to look after the boats of the British between Vliho and Nydri.

I immediately thought of Leon's boat and hoped that it was OK.

"OK, let's go get a coffee and in the meantime I'll call Dave to calm him down a bit."

Terry was nice, he had lived on the boat for fifteen years, then he got bored and decided to sell it.

"Boats boats boats!" he said, "if you don't want to sleep at night, buy a boat."

"You're telling me..."

"Ah! A continuous job, from when you buy it to when you sell it, just a continuous job, a money pit... fifteen years I lived on the boat, and I still remember how well I slept the night after I sold it."

We stopped at the bakery at the end of Vliho and had two coffees, then Terry called Dave.

"Ehy Dave, don't panic my friend, you got it worse last time"(!)

"You have a hole in the stern above the waterline but I don't think it's deep enough to let water in.

"Mike's boat has its side smashed in, so I hope you're insured, anyway don't rush, Fabio has put additional fenders on it and it's all right now, as soon as the wind drops a bit we'll go on board and try to tug on the anchor to bring it back on line ok? Don't panic, it still floats".

British... If it had happened to me I think I would have died.

"Good," he said after ending the call. "There's not much we can do now. That madman... let's hope he secures the boat."

"What did you mean by last time was worse?"

"Oh it's not the first time he crashed the boat on the dock you know, last time it had a leak all along the stern line, but Dave has hands that can do everything: he repaired it without taking it out of the water."

"Are you kidding?"

"Not at all. Dave at the age of thirteen started working on his father's fishing boat, in the Hebrides north of Scotland, a bad place to go to sea you know, then became a ship's engineer and there's nothing he can't fix."

"I remember that in the regatta he tuned Nitroglicerina like crazy, it was so fast. He made a splice on the mainsail tackle that held more than a shackle."

"And I believe it, let's go back to the dock, maybe Bill has arrived."

When we got back to the boats, the Englishman's bicycle was leaning against a bench and he was on Mike's boat doing the damage count.

"Hey there!"

He had a hoarse voice, altered by saltiness and cigarettes. He had lived on a boat for years. *Three Boats Bill* they called him. He had, to all intents and purposes, three boats, all three gifts from their owners as a token of thanks for looking after them for years.

Others called him *Bicycle Bill* since he had no other means of land transport.

Terry took an envelope with keys; he had a bunch of them, St Peter's style. He fished one out and gave it to me.

"This is the one from Dave's boat," he said.

I took it and climbed aboard.

I opened the hatch and savoured that typical smell of a boat that had been closed for a long time: a mixture of wood, oils and varnish. A familiar smell I had known since childhood, first smelt on Alnilan, my uncle Vito's small, fast speedboat.

I always felt a reverential pleasure in boarding a boat, that respect for her and her owner, that aura of intimacy that envelops small objects.

I first checked the bilge... and immediately called Dave.

"Ehy everything is OK, there is no water" and we both breathed a sigh of relief.

"OK Fabio, does the battery have voltage?"

I glanced at the led indicator on the chart table, which read 14.5.

"Yes it does, the photovoltaic panel works well."

"Perfect. Go to the bow, next to the dinghy engine there is a switch, a battery disconnect; put it *on* and then you should be able to operate the electric anchor winch from the bow."

"OK."

I found the switch, operated it and went to the bow. The winch pulled a few metres of chain aboard.

The boat finally started to straighten up by breaking away from Mike's.

I immediately called Dave back, who was delighted.

"Perfect! Leave the battery attached, maybe you need to give it another pull. I'll be there in two months."

Bill was waiting for me ashore, helped me disembark since I had to jump onto Mike's boat first, and thanked me.

"Very well, I will come again tomorrow to have a look," he said.

"Yes, me too," I replied. I have to go aboard my boat, I left the trampoline on the bow and it jumped off."

"Oh well I'll be here working, maybe we'll meet again."

"Yeah why not, I want to have another look at Dave's boat in the absence of wind."

"Well, let's make it roughly one to two?"

"Yes of course from one to two is fine."

Terry shook his head, smiling.

"We're all getting Greek here eh? From one to two..." he said wryly.

We all three smiled, Terry was right after all.

We were glad we had sorted it out, we weren't finished but at least we had secured the boats. Not bad in that wind.

"How was Tranquility?" I asked Bill.

"Not quiet at all, but no boats were damaged."

"Good thing, there is one of my friend's, the outermost one towards the west."

"El Aquila?"

"Yes indeed."

"It should be OK, no problem."

"Just as well, I was there a few days ago to check the dehumidifiers, I should go back but some bastard stole my electric outboard and it's a long row there."

"It is becoming impossible... a few years ago you would leave the boat open and no one would touch anything, but today it is becoming bedlam."

"Yeah... alright come on, then I'll see you tomorrow."

"OK, one to two o'clock."

We said goodbye with a smile and I drove to Nydri.

I stopped to do some shopping and saw that Alina had called me.

"Now if I tell her about the trampoline it will be a laughing matter" I said, thinking aloud.

Alina had asked me to take it apart at least seven times since the season ended.

I sent her a message telling her everything was OK.

As soon as I got back I told her, "we did well, Dave's boat got damaged, Mike's boat even worse, but Nitro held up great.... Only the trampoline fluttered."

Ali looked at me with that irresistible look somewhere between reproachful and amused, then shook her head and continued cooking.

FRIENDSHIP & SOLIDARITY

The next day I returned to the bay to meet the two Englishmen.

The wind had calmed down, not completely, but the situation compared to the day before was paradisiacal.

I passed by Dave's boat and was pleased to note that it was in much better shape than the day before, then continued on to the end of the pier.

I parked, untied the dinghy from the car and inflated it.

After half an hour I rowed towards my Nitroglicerina.

"Hi baby, everything OK?"

Everything was OK... a salt coating covered the boat but everything was OK, zero damage.

Only an old rope holding the trampoline to the cockpit had come off, but the rings were in place and so were most of the sacrificial hooks.

We were lucky.

It was worth it to break your back to re-anchor.

By the end of the season, I had tripled the haul to 30 metres of eight-millimetre chain attached to a pair and had moved the huge anchor that I was using as a dead body to a much shallower seabed, almost close to the shallows.

I had spotted a muddy spot in the middle of the Posidonia and had dropped the anchor there, which had taken hold immediately.

"Very well..." I said to myself.

I opened the two mini-cabins to let some air circulate and then set to work.

It took me about ten minutes to dismantle the trampoline, and I had to cut the end of a few ropes where the knots were too tight.

No water had got inside the cabins, just a bit of oozing so I took one of the mattresses and put it in the dinghy, I would wash it at home.

I closed it all up, kissed Nitro goodbye and returned to the floor.

Once the small dinghy was moored, I loaded the trampoline and mat onto the van and went to check if Bill had arrived.

I found him in the company of Terry near Dave and Mike's boats.

"Ehy good morning!"

"Buoon gioornooo," Terry replied in Italian.

"Are you OK?"

"Oh much better than yesterday!"

"Yeah..."

"I heard from Dave, he will call the yacht club to have the hole closed."

"The yacht club?"

"Mmm yes..."

"But does he know that the same guys are not working on it this season as last year?"

"No I don't think so..."

"Mmm come on let's call him, if I'll do the job, at least he won't pay anything."

"OK let's give him a call."

We called him on video and Dave answered after almost a minute.

It was clear from his face that he was asleep. It was almost twelve o'clock!

"Oh sorry Dave... did we interrupt something?" asked Terry.

Dave laughed into the phone.

"You looked just a bit busy, I'd hate to think a sailor like you was still in bed at this hour."

"What's up guys?" he asked, laughing as always.

"Fine with us, we're here trying to float your boat while you're... but are you alone?"

Dave laughed louder as he looked around in an evasive way.

"Oh God this was fucking" said Terry, shaking his head.

"You know my friend I am of a certain age, it is not nice to remind an old man like me of the pleasures of life," he continued.

"But no I was just in bed."

"Yeah yeah right... show us your boyfriend."

When two sailors start mocking each other there is nothing more to be done, in person it would end with a smile or a fistfight, but video telephones made things much more complicated.

After about fifteen minutes in which Dave was called the most absurd epithets that ranged from homosexual pervert to gutless Casanova, just to name a few that could be politely spelled, we finally got back to talking about the boat.

"So," Terry continued.

"Fabio had an idea, and he said you could get paid work done by whoever you want or he could try to patch it up himself but at least for free."

Dave as a good Scot smiled and immediately opted for the second solution.

"Very well, we'll go and buy the equipment and I'll advance the money, OK?"

"Great, thanks a lot guys."

"Wait until you see the work before you thank me, say hello to your boyfriend."

Terry ended the communication and handed me the phone, shaking his head and smiling at the same time. "Crazy bastard, what do you think he was doing?"

"He was asleep," said Bill.

"For me it was with that great American hottie girlfriend of his," I said.

"Eh that was one hell of a hottie," added one of the two whose name I won't mention out of respect for Dave.

"Good! Come on Italian, let's go shopping. Let's take my car."

I got into the car with Terry and we drove to a nautical equipment shop.

"OK, buy everything you need, I'll pay."

"Whatever."

I took a sheet of fibreglass about a metre square, some two-component epoxy resin, gloves and a couple of brushes.

"Is that all?" asked Terry.

"Yes the rest I have in the van."

"Ah! good boy."

Terry paid and we returned to the pier.

"Well, do you need help?"

"No, I'm good, maybe just pass me the materials in the dinghy. I'll prepare the resin ashore so I don't risk spilling anything."

Prepare the bi-component in a graduated container, when using epoxy it is essential not to get the proportions wrong otherwise it will not catalyse and you will waste time and money.

Then I climbed into the dinghy, gave it a quick scrape while Terry continued to mix the resin, cut out a piece of fibreglass and applied it to the damaged hull.

In about fifteen minutes of work applying progressively smaller sheets I managed to close the breach and sent a photo to Dave.

The hole was repaired, it had gone really well.

If water had entered the aft locker, it would have seriously damaged the heating system and the hydraulic piston of the autopilot.

"Bravo Fabio," said Terry, "I have an idea."

"Let's hear it."

"How about if we put one more in the north direction?"

"Which is a great idea, do you have a good anchor? I have a couple at home."

"We borrow one from the catamaran here."

"You say the owner won't get pissed off?"

"The owner is in some mental hospital in England, otherwise it would not explain why he abandoned such a boat."

"Yeah... it's a nice cat."

"Yes it is, good for living in it. Bill's keeping an eye on it."

"She has two unused anchors in the portside locker," said Bill. "We can use one until Dave gets back, then we'll put it back in the spring."

"Well then, is there also chain?" asked Terry.

"No, no chain," replied Bill.

"I'll take care of the chain, I should have twenty metres or more," I said.

144

"Then we're good," Terry concluded.

"OK, so tomorrow I'll recheck the repair and before we dry the dinghy we'll do this work."

"Perfect, Dave will be pleased."

Maritime solidarity is beautiful, people who may barely know each other or who had never met before become inseparable work colleagues, and just because a single incident has confronted them with the will to help a distant friend.

Who knows, maybe it's the hope that if it were to happen to them they would want someone there to take care of their unattended boat, or maybe it's just sheer camaraderie. The fact is that in the end Terry was right: the best night's sleep is the one following the day you sold your boat.

The next day we met again to finish the job.

I took over 30 metres of chain with me, which was secured to a 26-kilo anchor.

A rope was attached to the other end, which was placed on the boat's bollards.

While I rowed, Bill laid the line first and the chain afterwards.

Terry from the ground was signalling me the direction to take.

It was an easy enough job, yes of course with an outboard rather than the oars it would have come out even better, but you had to make do.

At least with this second anchor the boat would not be unprepared in the event of a second storm from the north.

"Very good." Said Terry. "I'd say we've earned a good beer."

"Well said my friend!" replied Bill, who never skimped on beer.

"But I don't want that piss they sell in the tavern, let's get three beers from the supermarket and drink them here on the pier."

"Come on Bill, let's go to the yacht club.... My treat."

"Ah well then..."

"Go for the yacht club, they have Guinness there," I concluded.

We walked as if we were old friends to the nearby lovely yacht club.

It was run, and probably still is, by an Anglo-Irish couple.

We took our seats at the large square counter just across the threshold.

It was the summer area, but they had insulated it with plastic panels and a wood stove heated the atmosphere.

I had my Guinness, while Terry and Bill opted for a blonde.

At the counter were the usual patrons, people who lived by boat in the bay and used the yacht club as a reference point for receiving mail, doing laundry, printing documents or any other need.

Years ago there was a real hurricane in the bay, some boats capsized and a Frenchman drowned.

Ruairi, the owner of the yacht club, together with his strictly British boys, were in the water giving aid to those in need. On that occasion Ruairi dived and pulled a girl from her capsized catamaran saving her life and deservedly becoming a local hero.

In recent times there were other guys working on the boats, but inside the yacht club there was that typical British style atmosphere, which you could also find in the dishes.

I don't know about you but a breakfast of scrambled eggs, sausages and bacon is about as rejuvenating as you can get before starting a day. And there you have it.

"You don't want to have breakfast now... do you Bill?"

"Why not?"

"Because it is almost noon."

"Well take it as brunch... you always pay for it yes?"

"Beer is..."

"Come on don't be a Scot."

"Oh God... OK go for your breakfast. Fabio you take anything to eat?"

"No thanks, I'm going on Guinness."

"The similarities between the Italians and the Irish will never cease to amaze me..."

"You are not the first to say that. There are several, excluding red hair."

"Yes I noticed..."

146

At that moment Ruairi entered.

"Ehy Rory good morning."

"Hi Terry how's it going."

"Well thank you, congratulations on the boat."

"Ah thank you."

And he left on his way to the office.

Ruairi was like that. Few words and many deeds.

"Did you put your boat back in the water?" I asked.

"Not yet, but he finished it."

"The ferro-cement one?"

"Yes indeed her... his little girl."

"What a sight. I know it well, my first season I practically camped under it with my van."

"In the construction site?"

"Yes, I moored mine there too."

"You are crazy do you know that?"

"Yes I know, but what was I supposed to do? It was the first season, I didn't know how it was going to go and I didn't have the money for a house... so I asked the owner of the boatyard if I could stay there and he was fine with it. The boat that was casting the most shade was Ruairi's so I parked down there. In the water I only saw her in pictures."

"Ah yes, the picture on the wall inside the yacht club."

"Yes exactly, man what a photo gallery they have in there."

"Yes she is pretty."

The interior of the yacht club was very cosy, all wood, pictures of old sailing ships on the walls and a corner with sofas and a nautical bookcase.

"Did you really do a whole season in one yard?"

"Yes I told you, some people do it in winter, at least I did it in summer."

"That also has its reason... now you have a real house instead yes?"

"Yes," I replied, smiling, "in the mountains it would be hard to go camping in winter."

"And I believe it, but camping is a way of life you know... a bit like boating."

"True, the following year in fact I spent it at Maurice's in Bedrock."

"Ah! That other fool... Maurice and Joy, what a pair."

"Yes very nice. Nice place too."

Meanwhile, breakfast for Bill had arrived.

Two mega eggs with sausages, mushrooms, bacon and bbq sauce.

"Then they wonder how it is that the British die so often of heart attacks," Terry said.

"For football" Bill replied with his mouth full, "every time we play against Italy, a few get dried up..."

We all three laughed out of heart, then Bill dived onto the plate.

WANDERING AROUND THE ISLAND

Winter lasted longer than usual that year.

It was a cold March, with the Mistral blowing frosty from the north-west, bringing with it northern European storms.

The mountains on the mainland remained covered until April, while on Lefkada's highest peak, Mount Elati, snow appeared whenever the temperature dropped below zero at night. And this happened very often.

"We won't be able to grow Canary Island aloe here either," I said sad, looking at the dead plants after the last night frost.

"Yes, too cold" Alina replied.

"Who knows maybe we can ask Andrew and Kristen to keep them at Villa Dessimi, over there I don't think the temperatures are so cold."

"Yes, although I see them more interested in vines than aloe."

Andrew wanted to become the first person to make good wine in Lefkada.

He was convinced that with the right plot of land and the right winemaker he could achieve great results.

We talked about it several times and I agreed. The Lefkada Mountains remind me in some ways of the Murge Baresi, with their karst rocks and red earth.

With an altitude between 400 and 700 metres, the right slope and a southern exposure, one could obtain sensational grapes.

We still ran out of wood, the cold did not let up and Spring was stalling.

"I guess I'll ask for another load today," I told Alina.

Then the phone rang.

It was Elio, with his unmistakable Romagna accent.

"Hello Fabio!"

"Hey Elio good morning!"

"Eh good morning... not so much you know. I can't go more than ten steps without having to sit down."

"Yikes... Back problems again?"

"Eh my back... I have problems with my identity card other than my back."

"Eheh, those come sooner or later for everyone."

"What are you doing bothering you?"

"Not at all, I was just considering I was almost out of firewood and thought I'd go for a bike ride up the hills around here."

"Eh, you go if you can. Listen: but there in the tavern at your place, when do we make a piglet or a lamb again?"

"I'll just go tonight, I'll ask and tell you. Do you have a particular day you'd rather come?"

"Look, for me Sunday lunchtime would be perfect, so I don't have the workers in the house and I come back down with the light."

"Alright let's see what we can come up with."

"Very well, thank you then see you soon."

"Bye Elio I will call you tonight."

I closed the communication and took a knowing look at the bike.

"Was that Elio from Sivota?" asked Alina.

"Yes, he wants to come and have another go."

"When?"

"He would prefer Sunday lunch."

"Mmm ook."

"I'm going for a bike ride, it looks like it won't rain today."

"In this cold?"

"Yes I will try the new jacket, it should be perfect for these temperatures."

"You are sick..."

"Yes I know, that's also why you love me."

I dressed in my winter cycling clothes and left the house.

It is wonderful to ride a bike in winter, when it is not raining, of course.

The island is deserted, there is none of that sticky humid heat that characterises summer, the air is cold and crisp and you have the streets to yourself.

Coming down from Vafkeri it is almost all downhill towards Karia, you pass the spring that overflows in winter and the pure water invades the roadway, then you begin to follow the road that winds westwards, bend after bend.

When you arrive at a T-junction you have two choices: left for Karia and the possibility of descending to the west coast, or right and follow the hilly Platystoma-Alexandros road.

That day I chose the second option, and the easiest.

I didn't feel like slaughtering myself, I wanted to take a quiet stroll admiring the scenery.

The tiny village of Platystoma was as deserted as ever, a surreal silence hovered among the alleys.

I took the road that climbs up to the church and then dips down to Alexandros; another pearl of a village before which one passes through bucolic landscapes and cattle farms where the animals live free in the grounds.

As soon as you enter the village, a delightful little church welcomes you on the left.

A small stray dog that has lived there since time immemorial was lying quiet in the middle of the road. He just raised his ears and then turned his head. He seemed happy to finally see a new face as he began to wag his tail, but he did not move, not considering me a danger he remained motionless.

I continued pedalling in the religious silence that enveloped the beautiful little village and passed it after not even a minute.

The road continued to wind its way through the landscape.

It was a perfect day for cycling. There was little wind, a shy sun was shining up there in the blue Lefkadian sky and the birds were chirping happy, no longer in danger since the hunting season had ended the month before.

I passed a fountain and decided to stop there to refill my water bottle. The water was cold and had a mineral taste, thick and nutritious.

I resumed pedalling with calm and met a family of wild goats.

You recognise the wild ones because they have longer horns, no cowbell and are much faster and more agile.

They had a couple of kids with them.

I passed very close to them, but a sort of sixth sense, as well as a memory of a close encounter years earlier in Fuerteventura, induced me not to stop and to continue pedalling.

I arrived up in Lazarata and turned left towards Pinachori, another small, semi-deserted village.

In the central square of this remote mountain village, sitting under the veranda of an old building, there is always an elderly gentleman who sings every morning.

And that day was no exception.

Now: as a scene it was quite picturesque, but let's say I would not have liked to be his neighbour, or even have a little house there, on the main square of that beautiful village.

The road continues to wind its way to the entrance of Pigadisani and from there we can consider ourselves on our way back.

You start climbing again, the roadway narrows to a point where a bus would struggle through.

There was, as always, a lady cooking with the windows open, and the usual feeling of hunger flared up in the pit of my stomach like a vice as soon as I smelled the scent of food cooking.

On the Pigadisani square there is a tiny tavern bar run by a nice big guy who, besides being a restaurateur, is also a dancer of typical dances.

I remember years earlier seeing him lift a table with his teeth during one of those absurd performances that have little to do with dance.

After leaving the village and travelling down a couple of quick hairpin bends, we finally arrive in Karia: the village of carpets and olive wood artefacts.

It is the second most populous village on the island. Second only to the capital.

Nestled in the centre of a fertile valley, it is alive even in winter, by Greek island standards of course.

There is a supermarket, a pharmacy and a couple of bars. This is enough for the islanders to live peacefully and hibernate at the slow and pleasant pace of the town's gushing fountain.

Once past Karia, you start to descend and the cycling becomes more demanding.

In no time at all we find ourselves at the junction with Platystoma and from there to Vafkeri there is a kind of competition between us island cyclists: three kilometres of bends and ups and downs where you have to give it your all.

That day I had saved myself by enjoying the scenery so I had energy to spend and I remember that I made a very good time.

I arrived home exhausted, with Alina seeing me red and flushed and shaking her head as if to say: *but who is making you do this?*

Yeah... good question.

After an hour of couch immobility and a restorative shower, I threw myself headlong onto the plate that Ali had so lovingly prepared for me.

"Good?" he asked.

"Yes, very good."

"Are you going to the tavern today?"

"Yes, I have to order Zaza some more wood and I have to ask Maria if she will prepare something good for us on Sunday."

Then we heard the sound of an engine coming up the hill and once we reached our house a couple of honks let us know that Ann and Dave were finally back.

We opened the door and greeted them.

"Hey welcome back."

"Hello neighbours, Thank you."

"Did you miss Vafkeri?"

"Ah! You can't imagine how much."

"Going cycling one of these days?"

"Sure!" said Dave, pointing to the beautiful carbon bike disassembled and lying on the back seat.

"Did we go shopping?" I asked.

"I can't wait to try it!"

"And I believe it. We may be going to the tavern with friends on Sunday, would you like to come?"

"Yeah sure, why not."

"OK, I'll ask Maria what's good."

"Everything, as always after all."

"Come on, let's not take up any more of your time, you'll be wiped out after the trip."

"Yes, thank you see you later, bye."

"Hello, Mavro will be happy to see you again."

Mavro is a beautiful big dog that the village shepherd always left on the chain in a fetid hovel.

I had managed to free Bella and take her away, now Mavro was there and Dave was in charge.

We didn't understand what the hell the owner was doing with a dog when he only ever kept it tied up by feeding it one slice of bread a week. Denounceable!

In the late afternoon I went down to the tavern and found Maria and Constantinos there.

"Ehy kalispera."

"Yassu Fabio, Ola kala?"

"All's well, all's well, except that I'm wrecked because I slaughtered myself on the bike, there's not a time I can just go for a quiet ride."

Costantinos laughed heartily with his ever-present cigar at the corner of his mouth.

"Hey Maria," I asked, "can we organise a little lunch on Sunday?"

Maria took the translator and it took us a few minutes to realise that I wanted to know what was fresh to eat, for how many people and if it was possible to have Sunday lunch.

In the end we realised, an excellent roast lamb would brighten up our Sunday lunch.

I still didn't know if we would be two or seven.

I sent a message to Elio who was delighted.

After a few minutes, Zaza, the Georgian, arrived.

I asked him if he still had any wood available and he first said no by putting his hands crosswise, then said he still had some but it was dry.

I wasn't sure I really understood what he meant but I ordered a van anyway because we were running low and the cold didn't seem to be abating.

He told me that in four days he would bring it to me. Let's *hope so...* I thought, here when they tell you two days it is not unusual that they mean two weeks.

But Zaza is Georgian, and occasionally he was more punctual than a Greek.

Gradually the tavern filled with the usual patrons, so Kostas and Andreas started playing cards, Lakis as always sat in his little corner doing nothing, Maria was knitting and I was trying to understand some of those cut and mispronounced words that were the Lefkadian dialect of the mountains.

There was no way, I would never learn Greek from them and maybe not even their dialect.

I remember that I learnt Spanish in four months of Mexican life and I learnt it so well that whenever I speak it with native Spanish speakers, they always ask me if I am not South American.

This happened to me again and again during a winter spent in the Canary Islands where most of the inhabitants emigrated to Venezuela before returning home.

Who knows... Maybe I still had hope, but it was the will that was lacking.

My other neighbours were all British and English is the second language on the island being a popular tourist destination.

And between you and me... what was the point of learning Greek if by speaking in a narrow dialect and at the speed of light they could still not be understood?

I drank my second beer, stood up, asked again to pay and Maria, as always, signalled for me to go.

"Maria on Sunday though I want to pay OK?"

"Ne ne ne... avrio," she said without looking up and continuing to knit at an absurd speed.

I walked out of the tavern and headed for home, tackling one step at a time that stone-paved ascent amid the scents of winter slowly giving way to those of spring.

AGIA KIRIACA

Spring exploded with a riot of scents and colours.

The hills surrounding Vafkeri turned into colourful fields of flowers, inebriating with their scents the lucky few like us who had chosen the Lefkada mountains as their residence.

It had been a couple of days now that temperatures had returned to double digits.

"Finally," sighed Alina, "my favourite season has arrived."

I looked at her smiling with love.

I like winter, the cold one with the snow and the wind howling through the window openings, the fireplace burning, the fresh citrus fruits, the frosty air.

"Yes I would say that this winter has lasted long enough."

We had even had sub-zero nights in late March.

"Today is 25 March," said Alina, "Greek Independence Day, how about going for a ride? There will be celebration everywhere."

"It's also my cousin Francesco's birthday, I must remember to wish him a happy birthday even if he won't be too happy... he's turning 50!"

Ali took the cup of hot coffee in her hands and brought it to her mouth, taking a long sip.

She was beautiful... sitting there by the fireplace, her legs crossed and her eyes still sleepy. Her hair was tied up in a ponytail and her blonde fringes came down over her green eyes.

"Let's have a little walk with the dogs first, OK? Then we'll get ready and go down to the valley."

Alina nodded, smiling.

I took the leashes and went out into the garden where Atina and Ella were waiting for me.

They barked, bellowed and howled in joy.

They understood that they were going for a walk and this was their way of showing it.

Even the dogs sensed the change of season and greeted it with a newfound happiness.

No more long, cold nights spent shivering in the kennel. At least for Atina.

Bella had now taken possession of the cushion next to the wood-burning stove.

We climbed the Australian's peak as usual and then stretched a little down into the flower-filled Vafkeri valley.

Alina seemed to be at a funfair. She took her SLR camera with her and took hundreds of photos of the colourful flowers in the fields.

"Look how beautiful this piece of land is!" She said, violating a private vineyard planted with low trees.

"It even has a bit of a sea view!"

"Yes alright sea view... we would need the telescope."

"Yes, but you can see it." And she smiled again.

There is nothing to stop her innate enthusiasm.

I cast my gaze upwards in a bird's eye view.

The entire valley was planted with vines and in the middle was a peasant bent over a hoe working the land. His movements were slow, light and rhythmic. It almost seemed as if he made no effort at all.

We continued the long walk being guided by the dogs until they took a steep uphill path.

The narrow road became narrower and narrower between the rows of trees that were closing in on each other making shade.

Then we came to a small clearing with a shabby old abandoned building in the middle.

"I wonder what it was..." Alina said almost to herself.

"It looks like a madhouse," I replied.

The building was ugly, white and boxy. It ruined the clearing, which on the other hand was beautiful.

The majestic pines over the years had covered the ground with their needles.

The shade and coolness were more than pleasant and even from that point, there was a semblance of a sea view.

"Look!" said Alina who had her head stuck to a window.

"What?"

"There's a blackboard on the floor and those look like wooden desks! Maybe it was the school..."

"Ah that's why I feel this awful feeling of discomfort."

I had never had a good relationship with school, too many rules, too much bullshit and too much time wasted studying things that did not interest me explained by bored state officials.

With a few rare exceptions that I could count on the fingers of one hand, I have always hated my professors.

"Come on, I always had fun at school," Alina replied, smiling.

"Yes, me too, every time I didn't go, how much focaccia I ate on the Bari seafront instead of going to school you can't even imagine, especially when beautiful spring days like this arrived."

Ali broke away from the wall with a smile and said, "we could ask the president if he will let us use this land, if it is true that the bills have skyrocketed we can buy a caravan and park it here."

I smiled at her with affection. I love that wild and spartan side of her.

We resumed our climb and came out at the entrance to the village.

From there we went up the Platanos shortcut to the cottage, but we preferred to lengthen it by going round the north side of the village.

When we arrived home we saw Tanassis' van parked nearby and just then the old man's deep, friendly voice echoed through the air.

"Good morning Mr Fabio! Good morning Senora Alina!" He often confused Italian and Spanish.

"Hello, good morning."

"See what a beautiful day?" He said smiling.

"Yes, great indeed," I replied, looking at the envelope Tanassis was holding.

He waved it in the air and said, "Good news, very good news!"

"Oh yeah? The electricity bill is never good news."

"This one is, remember when you told me you thought you were paying too much?"

"Yes I remember, I tell you every time you bring me one."

"There indeed you were right! Look at this."

I opened the envelope with curiosity and it was... negative."

"What do you mean?"

"It means you are in credit with the energy company, for the next four months you owe nothing."

I was stunned, "Oh yes... that's really good news."

Alina took the bill from my hands and she too was incredulous.

Over the past month, all islanders had been complaining about the incredible increase in energy costs.

We stayed for a few minutes talking about this and that with the elderly gentleman who then asked, "So what are you going to do? Are you going to stay?"

"Yes, for sure the whole summer and who knows maybe even next winter."

"Well good, because I wanted to have you install one of those things that heats water with solar panels."

"That would be great, thank you."

We continued talking and then Tanassis said goodbye.

"See?" said Alina. The island doesn't want us to leave.

"And yeah... do you want to go down to the hill?"

"Yes yes, today is a good day."

We got into the car and drove slow to Nydri where the celebrations were about to begin.

Lots of kids, babies and older children were dressed in traditional Greek costumes. Flags were scattered.

The anthem started and a more or less sorted column began to parade waving the colours of Greece.

The parade was closed by some boys on horseback.

People were beaming, everyone had poured into the streets to exchange greetings.

They felt that date very much, after all they had freed themselves from the Ottomans so how could they be blamed?

After an hour or so of rejoicing we looked at each other and without saying a word we knew we wanted to leave.

"Gyros?" I proposed.

"Yeah, how about we get it takeaway and go for a picnic in Agia Ciriaca?"

"Sure."

We passed by Stathis and ordered a couple of gyros, which were ready in a few minutes.

While we waited, Iannis, the massive owner, arrived and greeted us warmly.

"Hela file ti canis? Ola kala?"

"Hey Iannis you OK, you?"

"Ne ne ola kala ola kala."

Between smiles and pats on the back we gained the car and slipped out of the bedlam.

"Man it looks like an August day for how many people there are," I said.

Ali was rolling a cigarette.

We arrived in front of the junction for Dessimi.

"Hey look," said Alina

"The new supermarket is open, let's stop on the way back, we have no more water."

We entered the junction keeping to the left for Geni.

"It still bothers me to pass through here," I said.

"Again! Come on think of good things..."

Good things materialised before our eyes in Vassilis and Alexis, the two fishermen brothers.

Especially with Alexis I had been through a lot while living in Geni.

"Look at those two," I said, slowing down.

They were setting up a barbacue.

"Hey mobsters all right?"

"Eeee Italian mafioso how are you?"

"All good all good, what are you doing roasting?"

"Eh eh today is a celebration. What are you doing?"

"A ride to Agio Ciriaka with the dogs."

"Good friends."

Alexis laughed all the time. With what he smoked, it couldn't be otherwise.

We arrived in front of the junction for the church. From there we could only continue on foot.

We parked, dropped off Bibi, who was the only one of the three we had brought with us, as Pepi preferred the sofa to the car and Ella on sunny days would squat in the garden, rolling in the dust.

We took the path to the church and that typical, eternal feeling of peace that we feel every time we start walking down that path took hold of us.

We passed by Tranquility bay, with its boats moored for years.

Some now sunk, some forgotten, others still waiting for an owner who on some occasions will never come.

At the end of the bay was the boat of Leon, our South African friend.

"There it is, I said."

"Look there is the neighbour."

"Yeah maybe on the way back I'll ask him if he'll give me a ride in the dinghy so I can go check the dehumidifiers."

"When was the last time you checked them?"

"A couple of months ago."

I had agreed to check Leon's boat from time to time, the idea was to check it once a month but then I had problems with Nitro's engine and rowing was a long haul from Nydri. Not impossible but long, Bycicle Bill did it every time his outboard let him down.

We passed the ancient tomb of Dorpfeld, the German archaeologist who first raised the hypothesis that the real Ithaca was Lefkada.

"Great place to rest huh?" said Alina.

The tomb stood on a low, shady, lush promontory. The air became purer all of a sudden, and the feeling of bliss became more intense.

After a few steps, there is the small church of Agia Ciriaca, at the end of the arm that closes the two bays, that of Vliho and that of Nydri.

The little church is beautiful, tiny and carved into the rock.

At its slightly higher end is the cave, reached by a ladder.

Inside the whitewashed cave are icons as well as candles that are always lit.

It was the time of low tides, at least half a metre lower than average.

We sat in the sun and consumed our meal alone and in total bliss, gazing at one of the most beautiful sights in existence: the yellow house on the island of Madouri, still owned by the heirs of one of the most famous Greek poets, further north Sparti and hidden to the east Scorpio and Scorpidi.

It is a place where few words are exchanged because it is always emotions that win, the kind of emotions that silence is able to amplify.

A fisherman passed close to the mouth of the bay with his small, mumbling wooden fishing boat, and in keeping with tradition made the sign of the cross in the Orthodox manner addressed to the small church.

The sun rotated in the west, illuminating more and more that small piece of Paradise.

"You think the owners of Madouri would let us stay on the small island?" Ali asked.

"I don't know, why should they?"

"Maybe they need a couple of guardians."

"I've seen that a fisherman often goes there, he opens the house from time to time."

"Man I would live there more than go there sometimes."

"Eh... it wouldn't be bad, especially in winter or now in spring."

"I would live there all year round."

"Who knows, maybe when they come back we will ask them."

"You long for it."

"You think it could work?"

"Yes, anything you really want always comes true."

I looked towards the beautiful and lonely yellow house, built since time immemorial, when fishermen's boats had nothing but sails as their main propulsion.

We stayed a while longer, I saw a shoal of sea bass go by and the urge to go fishing returned.

Then almost in unison, as if driven by an external force, we got up and with calm walked down the path.

Leon's boat neighbour was no longer on deck, maybe he had gone down to his cabin to take a nap, the day was ideal for that.

It must have been about fifteen degrees and more.

As we drove up to Vafkeri the wind began to howl and when we parked in front of the cottage the tree branches were dancing.

She greeted us by barking, her huge bloodhound ears flapping in the wind.

It was at least five degrees lower than on the coast.

"Eh... my beautiful Vafkeri," I said.

"Gorgeous and wild."

But as I was saying this, I was thinking of the peace and blissful feeling I experienced that afternoon at Agia Ciriaca, the little church dedicated to the saint to whom I too, every time I go out on a boat, address a prayer asking her to get me safely back into the bay.

INAUGURAL TASTING

Among the various advantages or disadvantages of spring, depending on how one sees the world, is the reawakening not only of the flora, but also of the small mountain villages.

While on the coast, businesses were beginning their clean-up preparations for the season, the small mountain villages saw their houses reopen.

Relatives who returned for a few weekends, those who went on holiday to their second home, the foreign community who came to enjoy the spring warmth.

Between them I saw John and Ann appear, as all of a sudden as usual.

The first British people we met in Vafkeri, those who had welcomed us the year before.

"Hey Fabio!"

"Oh oh welcome back."

"Yeeeee how nice, finally in Vafkeri!"

"Did the trip go well?"

After the usual goodbyes and a rendezvous at Platanos for the usual *evening beer,* which always ended in something roasted between litres of Mamoz, I returned home to give Alina the good news.

"Hey they just got back John and...—"

"Yes I know," said Alina as she was gripped by the sewing machine.

"Ah, did you hear us from outside?"

"No Ann texted me about Dave and said we're all in the tavern tonight for the *welcome back.*"

"Ah..."

"Eh..."

"OK I'm going for a bike ride to prepare for the event."

The *welcome back* consisted of a heroic meal with an English-style drink, which, as per tradition, did not betray expectations.

After the merry dinner Ann had a great idea.

"We should have a wine tasting."

"Yes, very good idea," nodded Dave right away, glass in hand.

"Yes, with your Pugliese wine I mean," continued Ann Mystico.

"We did one at Dave's house this winter."

"Yes I know, and that's where I got the idea, we could do it at Villa Mystico or here at Platanos."

"Yes, I can ask Maria only I don't think I can reconcile the idea of the portion of food used in a tasting with that of Vafkeri..."

"Yeah, that might be a problem but... let's try it, worst case scenario we do it at my place."

I looked sly at Maria, who was lounging with incredible skill at her usual table, her cigarette burning in the ashtray, a smile on her lips.

"Yes tomorrow I'll talk to her, doing it today with an army of beer bottles on the table seems unprofessional."

The next evening I spoke to her for real and as expected Maria had no idea what a wine tasting was.

She and Costantinos, the managers of the taverna, were always very kind and understanding with me.

They never objected if I often asked to bring wine from home when there was a particular dish on the table to be paired with something more structured and important than the tavern wine.

They did not like the taste, being used to the local wine, but they let it be, watching curiously as the Italian sommelier sipped his wine in the goblet, tasting it with every mouthful.

When I explained how the tasting was to be conducted, I knew immediately from their bewildered faces that it would not be an easy task. We got stuck on the subject of glasses right from the start.

"No Maria I can't do a tasting with just one glass, but I'll bring those, don't worry."

"But I have many glasses, look."

Yes, she had many, I decided to involve her as much as possible.

"OK these can go for whites, perfect. But the reds need special glasses, I'll take care of those."

"Aren't these good?" asked Maria with affection.

"No Maria, those are beer glasses."

"Ah. Beer."

"Don't worry Maria, I'll take care of the glasses, we use a few: one for the sparkling wines, these of yours for the two whites, and mine for the reds."

"OK, I'll take the racomelo though in small glasses."

"Do you want to bring the racomelo to finish?" I asked worried.

"Eh yes eh!" she said peremptory, "we are in Vafkeri."

"OK, let's close with the racomelo and dessert."

"Bravo," she said, smiling.

The most difficult thing was to make them understand that they had to wait between courses.

Usually in the Taverna you get almost everything together and fill your plate with a bit of everything.

We devised an easy menu and timed it.

"OK we start with the sparkling wines, now let's see if we can pair them with some cold cuts and cheese; if not we'll take the sparkling wine outside, at seven o'clock it will still be daylight."

"OK," Maria replied.

"Then as soon as we start with the whites you bring—"

"The Maria special I made you taste yesterday!"

"Yes very good, that will be a perfect match."

Perfect would have been to have fish crudités, but we will slowly get there. I thought.

"Then wait for the barbecue, I'll give you the nod."

"OK," said Maria, all happy.

I couldn't ask for more, as having a different type of meat for each red would have been too much, so with the meat on the table I could direct the tasting of the scheduled reds.

I called Anna Mystico to give her the good news.

"OK Ann the tasting is taking shape, Maria only has glasses for the whites; for sparkling wine and structured red I'll see to it but I'm missing a set for the young red.

"I'm on it."

"Great."

"Ann... it will be a test this eh, don't expect an Italian style tasting, there was no way to fit the cold cuts in and it will be a miracle if the courses don't all arrive at once."

"But yes Fabio don't worry, we do it just for fun."

"Maria asked me how many we are."

"Mah... we'll be seven or eight at most, I've told a few friends."

...

The night before the tasting Dave dropped by the house to invite me for a beer at Platanos.

As soon as we entered we found the table already set for the next day.

"Hello beautiful ones!" exclaimed Sotiris.

"Ehy Sot," I said, "do you have guests or is this our table for tomorrow?"

"Tomorrow? But isn't the tasting today?"

"What? Sot the tasting is Wednesday, and Wednesday is tomorrow."

"Oh fuck!"

They were off to a good start, they were a day early....

Maria arrived stunned and said, "That was for today, I even marked it in the diary."

"Maria we texted a few friends and got together for tomorrow. Today we happened to drop by for a beer."

And thank goodness. They were already preparing everything: the half-cooked dishes, the lit grill....

"OK don't panic," I said.

"It will mean a test tonight..."

In the end it was a blessing, because we realised that the food was just too much, and we eliminated a couple of dishes.

The next day, however, when I arrived at the tavern very early to fix the glasses, it was still closed.

When Maria came downstairs, she could not understand why each guest had to have four different glasses in front of them just for wine.

"Well Maria we can remove the one for water, I don't think it will be needed."

The canonical eight were soon joined by Lukaz and Magdalena, a nice Polish couple they had met the year before.

The previous summer, thanks to the speed of social media, we managed to put them in touch with a vet and their wonderful dog who had been bitten by a snake was more than happy.

"Well come on, ten of us are equal," I said.

Then Dave C. joined in. a distinguished Englishman who set up a charity to help the island's stray dogs.

"OK, give eleven no problem." It was seven thirty and the sun was still shining outside.

It was great, so we uncorked the first sparkling wine to be tasted: an excellent Verdeca brut.

We were on the terrace in front of the small church and the huge plane tree after which the tavern is named, and right from behind the tree three more people emerged.

"Hey guys I hope they are not your friends because then we would be too many," I said.

"Oh yeah..." said Dave C. in quiet British phlegm style "I've invited three of my friends from the association... I hope that's not a problem."

"OK... fourteen then."

"It seems so."

"Well... wine and glasses."

Dave and Alina immediately understood that I would need help.

"Is there anything I can do Fabio?" asked Dave Edwards.

"Yes Dave what glasses do you have at home?"

"What do you need?"

"One set for sparkling wine and one set for structured red."

"No white?"

"No, Maria has them. And I can use my white ones for the young red."

"OK I'll go."

"Ah Dave... could I use your decanter too, I uncorked the reds at half past four to make them perfectly oxygenated by nine but... I'll have to uncork some more."

"OK no problem."

"Alina..."

"Yes?"

"A *Sellato*, a *Passione* and a *Negroamaro*."

"OK."

"Ah... and the decanter."

"Ooook."

The newcomers realised that they had created a bit of a stir but as good Englishmen they did not mind too much.

The tasting continued as planned, Maria was perfect in bringing the dishes at the right time, and our guests were enchanted by the story about the indigenous Apulian grape varieties used in the wines being tasted, as well as by the notions about the tastevin, an ancient instrument that is now in disuse but still very impressive.

The wines did the rest: award-winning Apulian pearls of Doc Gioia del Colle, my land: the beautiful Murge Baresi.

In particular, they were impressed by Primitivo, both in its sparkling and still versions.

The *Sellato, a* thoroughbred Primitivo, was the star of the evening.

At one point from the self-named *'vip'* table – that of Dave, Ann Edward, Alina and the Polish couple – there was a shout followed by a roaring laugh that startled even the kittens at the door.

I was in the midst of explaining the difference between maturing wine in casks and large barrels when I was interrupted by Dave.

"Fabio you have to hear this one! Do you see this picture? Show him the picture Luk."

On a smartphone screen were Luk and Magdalena sitting on the bench outside Dave's house.

"OK... So?"

"Do you know when it was taken?"

"Of course before I poured the wine..."

"Yes, a year earlier!"

"That is, is it from last year?"

"Yes! They were in front of my house wondering whose it was, and now they showed me the photo and asked if I knew the owner of my house!"

And yet another endless laugh.

"I mean, if we had been sitting at the *boring table* we would never have found out! Do you understand?"

I love Dave, especially when he is in that state of excitement.

There had been a very sad moment at the beginning of the year when he had decided to do that ridiculous *dry* January, or alcohol-free January.

He had become so boring that his British friends had nicknamed him *boring Dave.*

Then at the end of January, when I was preparing him a welcome back to the world of the living, he came up with that *dry 2022* idea... no it was just too much.

With Ann, we concocted a trap of the finest kind: a light dinner that turned into a barbecue, and as a finishing touch I brought a decanter with the latest 2016 vintage Sellato in it.

Dave's favourite.

"You know... it's the last one I have" I began sad and disconsolate "Probably the last one in the whole of Greece, and as far as I know in the whole world... for sure the producer finished it."

The year before, we tried to buy it again but only the 2018 vintage was available, which was still a spectacle.

But Dave had a soft spot for 2016, a kind of veneration. There he fell...

It was good to have him back.

He was overjoyed and bursting with joy.

The tasting ended with Passione, a fantastic *Primitivo-Nero di Troia* blend in which the grapes of the former are left to dry on the vine while those of the Troia are picked at the right ripeness, i.e. three months later.

An incredible, reflection wine.

Everything went well until Maria arrived with racomelo, or hot tsipuro with honey.

To tell the truth, after the first two or three drinks things were still going well, after the fifth a little less so, then memories are vague and get lost in the singing and dancing.

The next day, strange but true, the glasses were all intact. Even the decanters.

Various items of clothing, a set of keys and a telephone were found on the tables. All returned to their rightful owners.

The pair of glasses in their elegant red leather case, on the other hand, we never discovered to whom they belonged.

During the day only a few reassuring messages were exchanged in the internal village chat, Dave C. had stayed over at Villa Mystico, where the evening continued with a bottle of excellent Scottish single malt and an innocent stumble in the pool.

Her friends had returned to Nydri and were delighted with the evening.

It was only after two days that I decided to return a couple of sets of white glasses to Ann.

"Hey from home, anybody home?"

John's athletic figure peeped out.

"Hey Fab," he replied in a hushed voice.

"Everything OK? John?"

"Eh more or less, we couldn't get out of the house yesterday."

"Well if I had a house like this I wouldn't go out that often either, my friend."

"Thanks, but I think it was the whiskey," he said, laughing.

"Yes I think so too... the view of Scorpio and Meganissi with Kalamos and Kastos in the background eventually tires, you are right."

John laughed again, shaking his head. Then Ann came out wearing sunglasses.

"I would say that went well, yes?" she said.

"Oh splendid, beyond expectation, the idea of the certificates then..."

At the end of the tasting Ann Mystico had taken out certificates of participation in the inaugural tasting of the Vafkeri clan from her briefcase.

It was a surprise even for me, who had signed them one by one as a sommelier, and Maria was also happy to sign them as a chef.

"Oh I forgot, Costantinos was hurt that he didn't sign anything."

"Oh God, I don't believe it."

"Yes indeed..."

"OK next time we will sign him as..."

"We in Bari call them *mest fueg*."

"Mest what?"

"Those on the grill."

"Oh okay... whatever then, you will dictate it to myself and write it down.

"I have good news," Ann continued full of anticipation.

"Have you heard yet that we haven't broken any single glass?" I said.

"Oh no I didn't, really?"

"Yes not even one, I thought that was the good news."

"No no, more beautiful."

"Oh... this is getting serious."

"Yes, very serious."

"Go I'm listening."

"You know my friends from Syvota?"

"Yes of course."

"They were thrilled."

"Good, I'm glad."

"Yes, but enthusiastic to the point that they would like to make one at home."

"Even?"

"Yes, and they have a very nice house in the hills of Syvota, something great will come out of it."

"Wow, I'm glad."

"She really liked your way of talking about wine in such an evocative way and your knowledge of Apulian vineyards; I took the liberty of giving Marina your number."

"You did well, in fact thank you, it was your idea after all."

"Are you kidding? In fact... we should do it again."

At the time, I still had no idea how many more times we would do it.

EASTER IN THE FAMILY

Orthodox Easter was approaching, with some taking the opportunity to reopen restaurants and others closing them to spend this important holiday with family.

The rumours from the tavern were that it would be closed, no one had told us anything yet, but then again no one should have told us. It would have been nice to spend it with friends like we do in Italy and I was sure that with the British gang we would have organised something.

Then one day Maria took us aside to talk to us.

"Hello Fabio, hello Alina, ola kala?"

"All is well Maria thank you, you too?"

"Well well, thank you... ehm... I wanted to warn you that for Easter the tavern will be closed and....

We wanted to ask you if... well, would you like to spend Easter with us here at Platanos?

The whole family will come from Athens."

Alina and I looked into each other's eyes in amazement and a little embarrassment.

"Maria but it's between you in the family, thank you but we wouldn't want to disturb you."

"No no, you are like my family: Please come."

On Easter morning, the sun was shining on Vafkeri.

Spring was taking hold and temperatures were rising day by day.

The scent of flowers saturated the air and the gentle spring breeze carried the pollen in little swirls of colourful clouds.

The valley was a concert of chirps with a constant low hum in the background.

If God ever thought of drawing inspiration from something to depict the valley of Eden that something had to be very close to the valley of Vafkeri on that Easter day.

It was the first real day of spring.

We walked out the driveway door and stood on the white pavement of the street.

Taking a breath of fresh air early in the morning is a panacea that gets your day off to a better start.

I removed the waterproof cover from the bike to see the splendid electric blue of the fairing shining in the sun's rays, turned it on for a moment to rev the engine and let it and its one hundred and fifty horses breathe some good air.

"Finally..." I said. It started at once, no more coughing fits from the cold, damp winter air.

The motorbike was also feeling the change of season and was raring to go for a ride in the hills of the island.

"Another time," I told her, switching her off. "Today we are invited for lunch."

"What a nice motorbike!" said Dave as always when he saw it uncovered.

The British gang led by my friend was walking down the driveway: in shirtsleeves, Bermuda shorts and sandals on their feet they were perfectly at ease in the spring warmth.

"Hi Dave, everything OK?"

"It's OK Fabio, I just didn't expect this invitation that's all."

"Yes neither do we, it is amazing to be considered not only islanders but part of one of the oldest families of Lefkada."

"Yes, that doesn't take away from the fact that I wasn't expecting it. Are you ready?"

"Yes, I cover the bike and we go."

"Leave it uncovered!"

"No too much pollen around, say she's allergic?"

"Oh Fab! You and your Italian romanticism."

"And what can we do..."

I finished covering the bike at the same time as Alina closed the front door.

We walked down the paved driveway following the steep slope, leaving the wine square with its huge old press on the left.

Once we reached the shortcut alley, we arranged ourselves as always in single file as it was too narrow to pass side by side.

At a certain point, you have to advance sideways to get through the narrowest part.

We passed the alleyway and entered the small square of the bar, arriving after a few steps on the terrace of the Platanos.

A huge table awaited us, shaded by flowering trees.

Many people, most of them strangers, greeted us with smiles and incomprehensible greetings.

Alina and I along with Dave, Ann and the rest of the troop looked at each other bewildered.

They beckoned us to take a seat and immediately our glasses were emptied.

A toast of happy Easter.

A poor but delicious lamb was browning on the grill and the smell of meat made the mouth water.

There were noisy and happy children, parents, uncles and various relatives in that complicated web of kinship that holds a Greek family together.

Between one glass and the next came courses of delicious dishes, those made in the family using recipes handed down by word of mouth, and some of those dishes were not new to me having already tasted them there, thanks to Maria and her grandmotherly cooking.

The husbands of Maria's daughters, on the other hand, were responsible for the perfect cooking of the lamb, which, alas, we discovered tasted unequalled.

There was a time when I tried to eat less meat, when I saw a little lamb playing with my dogs and realised that there is not too much difference between the two.

Only in Greece, especially on the islands, it doesn't work that way.

Traditions are something deeply rooted in these kind and hospitable people, and only now are some of them beginning to realise what great joy a dog can give you if only you see it differently from a working tool perpetually tied to a chain.

Maria is one of these people.

She has her terrible, little *Pocket*. A tiny dog who in another life, I think, must have been a kangaroo.

The lunch was something momentous, the atmosphere reminded me of the Easter holidays of my childhood when with friends and relatives we would gather in the countryside at the *Casa Rossa* for memorable days.

Throughout the meal, Maria's family members would ask us if everything was OK, if we wanted this or that, if everything was good.

I cannot remember a single one among them who did not ask these questions at least twice.

'It's amazing this generosity,' Dave said at one point.

I nodded my head, every word being superfluous.

When the time came for the racomelo, one began to distinguish those who had hair on their stomachs from those who began to drink water.

And then the dancing started.

Endless sirtakis with four generations dancing all at once. Something never seen before.

In between dances Dave said to me, "Fabio I think this is the right time to hear from an authoritative voice the true story of the tavern." That being a subject that had always intrigued us.

I never understood who picked up on Dave's unasked question, the fact is that a fairy tale started from there.

Greek style of course, as the history of one clashed with that of the other.

Tempers flared and tones rose until the oldest person at the table, the son of another Maria or as they say the *original Maria*, took the floor, silencing the most agitated spirits.

"I am pleased that you are interested in the history of the Tavern, because the history of the Tavern is the history of my family."

At those words a surreal silence fell over the small square. Even the children grew quiet, like good old-fashioned grandchildren waiting to hear a story from their grandfather.

"My grandmother was widowed very young. You know in those days there was little living and there was only a small hospital in Santa Maura but getting there was not easy.

"The good road ended in Karia and to get to Vafkeri you had to dismount from the donkey, the path was only good for goats."

Maria smiled, nodding her head as she poured another round of Racomelo.

"Wasn't there even a road to Nydri?" asked Dave.

"No, in those days Nydri did not exist," the man continued, smiling.

Ann elbowed Dave, signalling him not to interrupt.

"Here in Vafkeri there were only shepherds and my grandmother with a small daughter could not look after the goats, so she had an intuition.

"She sold the flock and turned what was house and stable into a small warehouse."

He said, pointing to the door of the Platanos.

He noticed that all of us foreigners looked at the sign above the door dated 1807, he turned and said smiling 'oh no... that's the year the house was built.

"At first they only sold grains and seeds, only later did it become a refreshment point, hot coffee more than anything else."

In fact, the sign said cafeteria.

"Shepherds used to come here and refresh themselves during the long summer days.

"Little by little they began to ask for something to eat and so a small wood-fired kitchen was set up, which still does its job.

"The shepherds and the few people passing by ordered the meal for the next day, and those who had not ordered anything made do with what was left over, if there was any left."

The narrator took a long puff from his cigarette.

"Little Maria grew up, came of marrying age and then my sister and I arrived.

"My mother did everything she could to make us study, she wanted something different for us, something more.

"So he sent us to the city, where my sister met her future husband and together they had a child," she said, pointing to a boy who was now an adult and father of two.

"Unfortunately, she also left us very early," he continued, lowering the tone of his voice.

At this point one of them pulled up his nose, turning his gaze to hide his shiny eyes.

"I became a doctor and moved to Athens, while my mother continued to run the cafeteria until the first tourists arrived.

"And with tourism, what was once a refreshment point has become the Taverna O' Platanos that you know today. I hope you will be able to appreciate the authenticity of the flavours of the past, the flavours of when this giant was nothing more than a small tree," he said, pointing to the immense centuries-old Platanos tree that on one side has its roots deep into the island's karst springs and on the other shadows the church and the Taverna that stands next to it, the guardian of the ancient art of mountain cuisine.

We were all a bit speechless, then the narrator smiled, pointing at the Platanus.

"You know my great-great-grandfather planted it," he said, sipping wine.

"He planted it at the birth of his first child: my great-grandfather.

And after a short pause he went on to say:

"He also left us young but who knows... maybe he never really left us," he concluded, looking lovingly at the tree.

At that point the glazed eyes were no longer just a pair.

THE MAY RAIN

It seemed that summer wanted to start early, the heat was rising relentlessly day by day.

Then May arrived and fortunately a low pressure brought some coolness.

The rain brought a touch of life to the plants and the earth, and while the clouds shielded the island from the sun's strong rays, temperatures returned to the seasonal average.

Lefkada began to repopulate.

Dave and Mike arrived, not overjoyed at the damage to their boats but nevertheless pleased to see them still afloat, and the rain came – just to make the British feel more at home.

In the mountains, it was always a spectacle to watch the clouds enter the valleys and climb the hills, clambering over the treetops.

The smell of dampness permeated the air and Vafkeri disappeared from sight.

"How about going to Egremni?" proposed Alina.

"Why today of all days?"

"Well it's not hot and we can go down and up again without killing ourselves."

"Look I'd rather go by boat than on that ladder, but if you want to..."

She convinced me (as always) and so we went for a walk on the west coast.

Arriving at the junction for Egremni, we took the narrow, winding road that ends abruptly at a gate.

On the way down there is a house with hundreds of shoes tied to the fence, shortly afterwards you come to the end of the line.

Here, roads collapse quite easily, the earth is crumbly and earth tremors are very frequent.

We parked and approached the edge of a small clearing.

You had to hold on to the trees on the slope, it was almost sunset and the light was the kind that makes you dream.

We looked down and our breath stopped.

Her majesty Egremni... wild, immense, mystical.

The view from the top is one you don't forget, something that enters your soul as every hair on your body stands on end.

The scent of Mediterranean scrub permeated the air: thyme, eucalyptus, salt and maritime pines with their resinous barks.

We went through the gate and after a few hairpin bends we arrived at a square and the new staircase: scary, anchored in the crumbling wall.

Starting to descend, it is still possible to observe the remains of the old staircase carved into the rock.

"I don't believe it, they anchored the new ladder in the old one," I said, touching a tie rod that ended its run in a rock step.

"I wouldn't want to be here in summer, climbing one of the 300-plus steps with the sun bringing temperatures to cremation levels in the hope that a tremor won't come just then."

"Yeah, that's why I wanted to come here today," Ali replied, smiling.

"Maybe... but I prefer to get there by sea."

Further down, a tongue of pebbles under a talcum powder-white ridge matched the Lefkada blue sea.

We arrived at the beach and birdsong welcomed us to paradise.

We started walking along the shoreline barefoot: there was no one there, we had Egremni to ourselves.

We didn't talk, there was no need.

What we felt was the sensation of being connected to the wild spirits of the island, with the senses amplifying their receptivity: the view swept westwards towards infinity, and long waves broke on the pebbles singing the sound of the sea and releasing the scent of the Ionian Sea.

We had the unique taste of saltiness on our lips, and the contact with the bare earth gave us the feeling that we were not alone walking on that eternal beach, accompanied by an invisible but tangible presence that our sixth sense, even more awake, perceived.

We sat hugging each other admiring the sun dipping into the sea.

"I think we will remember this season," I thought aloud.

Alina nodded, not even imagining how much that summer would change our lives.

The sound of thunder woke us from our idyll, we looked at each other and smiled.

Alina's eyes sparkled.

She took me by the hand and we walked towards the stairs.

In the middle of it, clouds came in from the east, darkening the sky even more, a fiery red tongue still held out to the west.

Then it came, fresh and purifying.

The May rain poured down on us, we welcomed it with a smile, spreading our arms wide. Then we kissed, and after an indefinite period of time we looked into each other's eyes and the rain faded away. I don't know how long that kiss lasted, but I know I can still feel the effects now.

In the car we turned on the heater to dry off a bit.

As soon as we arrived in Vafkeri we inhaled a breath of the purest air that only the Lefkada mountains can provide.

The cottage was there with its windows lit, the dogs had recognised the sound of the engine and were barking happily.

Every time we came home, we felt like we were living in a fairy tale.

Vafkeri is magical and always welcomes us with love into its spiritual arms.

It almost feels like being on another island.

So many small bright eyes were spying on us from every angle.

It was the village's small feline colony.

I looked at my bandaged hand, a few days earlier in picking up a kitten to take to the vet for sterilisation I had hurt myself.

The cat, usually always very quiet and sociable, had realised that something was wrong and turned on me, biting my hand.

One canine was sunk into the palm until it touched bone.

I did not let go because there would be no way to get her back; according to the vet, that pregnant kitten was too small to survive a birth and she was pregnant.

So I had gritted my teeth and managed to get her into the carrier.

One day maybe she would have thanked me, but at the moment she was not to be seen, although I was sure she was spying on me from some corner, with those tender yellow eyes of hers.

There were also two other eyes in the darkness. I didn't notice them at the time, they were a bit bigger and a different colour.

They shone less than the others but were deeper and more penetrating.

A background sound dispersed through the valley dark and silent. Perhaps more thunder, but it did not matter.

The feeling of peace I felt at being back home prevailed over everything.

THE ISLAND OF SAN NICHOLAS

Summer came in the form of a two-week interlude in mid-May.

We noticed this as the walls of the cottage began to heat up and the temperature outside began to exceed the temperature inside.

Writing the daily weather for the island gave me certain advantages and made me more aware of certain changes.

"The heat is on," I announced.

"That's nice," Ali replied, doing her classic childish grin.

Alina loves the heat; I, after a five-year interlude in which I had lived chasing the summer, could no longer stand it.

"I have to postpone my departure to Romania by a few days."

"Why?"

"On 15 May is the feast of St Nicholas and they open the little church opposite Diavassidia."

"See! Who told you that?"

"Sotiria, he said that on the first Sunday after 8 May they open the little church on the island."

"And how do you get there?"

"Fishermen ferry people as a vow to the saint."

"And how do I tell Dave that you are still here during the Triathlon?"

"Well just tell him you don't want to go."

"He will be hurt."

Dave tried hard to convince me but the truth was that I did not want to participate in that competition.

Andrew, the owner of the beautiful bicycle on which I used to train, also helped me out. He called me and told me he wanted to take it to Saudi Arabia, which is where he worked, only in the end he couldn't and left it in Lefkada, he warned me but we never told Dave anything before the Triathlon date.

To be honest, I wasn't trained at all and I was just showing off.

15 May arrived and the mercury rose above twenty-five degrees.

That morning we took our usual little ride with the dogs, then we got on the motorbike and drove off the island.

"You say they embark from the tip near Diavassidia?" Ali asked.

"I have no idea, that's certainly the nearest point but to get there by car there's a bit of dirt road, I say we continue to the fishermen's landing stage, if there are cars parked there it'll be there for sure. At the very least we'll go back, I don't want to go on the dirt road with the Ninja."

The Ninja is my first bike. A Kawasaki for strong hearts, the last model of that series that still had carburettors. Four Klehins that over 7500 rmp make it spurt away with a brutality capable of breaking frames. In fact I broke two of them, a factory defect, but who cares. Adrenalin pumped to seven bars.

I went slow that day, as always happens when Alina occupies the back seat.

We arrived at the landing stage and a long queue of cars made us realise that this was the embarkation point.

We went down to the piles and I stopped.

I switched off the engine, put on the kickstand and we set off together on the rickety wooden footbridge.

The view was mind-boggling.

A wooden stilt house with a sheet metal roof stood in a precarious balance on crooked planks that sank into the crystalline sea.

Like a wader, it had a chimney protruding from one of its 'walls'.

Night and winter shelter for intrepid fishermen who dressed up as Charon for the occasion.

The difference was that they transported living people and not souls, but the destination was, yes – something that had little to do with earthly life.

We boarded the small boat, as always we did not understand a word, but with gestures the fisherman managed to make himself understood. He was trying to balance the boat.

They were very unstable mini-barges, the only nautical means capable of advancing in those few centimetres of very clear water.

Once detached from solid ground, the mind goes into hibernation and sensations that only the soul can feel come to life.

The church of St Nicholas gets bigger and bigger, and after a wide turn to avoid the shallows, our ferryman points to a small stone pier.

We touch land and realise that we are in one of the few remaining almost untouched paradises on earth.

The only building is the small church made of wood and stone.

A small room with a cot and a fireplace is part of the small building, a veranda and inside the liturgy room.

A melodious litany came from the sacristy, the scent of incense mingled with that of saltiness and seaweed.

The colony of seagulls flew in frightened by this sudden human incursion.

A mother with a threatening manner was guarding two little ones not yet able to fly.

We attended mass in religious silence, the only foreigners among the locals.

Once the liturgy was over, we walked away from the small church to explore those tongues of sand that change shape with the tide and swells.

A few dozen metres further on, silence enveloped us in its most total form.

It was us in connection with nature, nothing else.

It was on these shores that Sikelianos wrote his verses, a hermit a stone's throw from the mainland.

Vegetation on the island is almost absent, except for a few bold shrubs that try to survive by feeding on the little rain they need.

Clinging to the sand, twisted and low to offer as little wind resistance as possible, it created an image that blended in perfect way with its surroundings.

Pilgrims kept coming and going from the little island and we had the distinct feeling that we were experiencing something out of the ordinary.

It is one thing to visit the island on any summer day, quite another to visit it during this day so sacred to the locals.

St Nicholas has left his mark around here.

You can see him from the monastery on the opposite side of the island dedicated to him and from this tiny church on a small island of sand and shells.

As if he wanted to embrace the whole of Lefkada from one end to the other.

The liturgy is an ancient Orthodox rite, the icon of the saint is carried out of the church to the spot where it is believed his remains were landed during the journey that took him from Mira to Bari.

The place is full of energy, the waves break far out over the reef, the lagoon, on the other hand, is surreal calm.

Alina, as always in these situations, is very quiet.

Me too, on the other hand.

It often happens when one is in a place of haunting beauty. There is no need to speak.

We wait for most people to leave, there are few of us left.

The silence becomes even more intense.

We already know that we will get on the last boat, and in fact it is us, the priest and his children.

Yes, Orthodox Christianity allows priests to be married. Good thing I would add.

The boat glides on the silent water, the priest asks us where we are from and we discover that he speaks Italian. He has also been to Romania several times.

I ask him why the feast of St Nicholas is so strongly felt in Lefkada, although I already know the answer.

He smilingly explains to me that truth and legend many times coincide.

There are many islands that claim a stop during the famous translation of the Saint's bones.

But something happened here in Lefkada during those ancient years that remains written between the yellowed pages of the books kept in the basement of the monasteries.

Lefkada has never sought publicity. Even if it is the true homeland of Homer, or his protagonist Odysseus, even if those intrepid sailors stopped here for real, even if a tombstone was found in the ruins of the ancient capital with the name of Jerusalem engraved on it.

There are many secrets this island holds that it does not need to reveal.

Also because what would be the point? Who would be interested in changing history?

Certainly not to most people, who today are much more interested in other things instead of culture.

And so the island keeps these secrets to itself.

Whispering a few stories only to those able to read between the lines.

Without realising it we touch land, we disembark and feel different. Lighter, better and more full of love.

It is not the first time I have had such a feeling, but it is always wonderful to experience it.

Alina is radiant and beautiful, when the sun begins to colour her skin copper, she becomes, if possible, even more beautiful.

We say goodbye to the priest and our elderly ferryman, his boat full of nets and the balancing piling.

We get on the bike and the roar of the four-cylinder brings us back to reality.

I drive slowly, we enjoy the scenery.

We returned to the island by following the coastline to Perigiali.

At the entrance to the driveway leading down to the harbour I noticed the unmistakable curly, golden hair of Francesco. The owner of the splendid Ionian Spirit.

He was intent on drilling a pole.

"Kalimera."

"Hela Fabio how are you?"

"Very well... What are you doing?"

"I am attaching the boat signs."

"Ah... on a signpost?"

"Yes, there must have been a stop sign or I don't know what before, anyway it's free now, I'll put my boat sign on it."

Greece...

Hearing Francesco speak is a hoot.

Half Sicilian and half Athenian, he never lost his Sicilian accent.

Ionian Spirit is moored at the fishermen's pier, beautiful and happy.

Next to Francis is Minas, the intrepid commander.

"Come on board, we'll have a drink together."

Getting on the Ionian Spirit is always nice.

The fragrant woods, that unique character of an old boat with thousands of miles on its back.

Francis restored it to its former glory and now wants to make something unique out of it.

Private wine tastings and luxury outings.

"What have you been up to today?"

"We went to St Nicholas Island, it was open and today there was the liturgy."

"Nice, we on the other hand have been working like every day even though it's Sunday... would you like a Mojito?"

Alina and I looked at each other, "OK why not."

Lefkada is an island that gives you a mystical experience like the one we had in the morning and then throws you aboard a historic boat to drink cocktails.

"So Fabio, when are we doing the inaugural outing?"

"Ah anytime, the wines arrive the day after tomorrow."

I had loaded Spinazz's car with twenty two cases of Tenuta Viglione wine.

Alina was going to Romania, Marco Spinazzola was coming to Lefkada. He would be at my place of course... Crazy times were ahead of us.

We continued talking about prices and how to publicise it.

"I have to introduce you to a friend of mine who has an agency, I worked there my first year with Nitroglicerina. They have several Dutch customers and anyway they are good, attentive to the type of clientele you ask for."

The day continued like this between drinks, then we went back up to the cool of Vafkeri.

The dogs were, as always, delighted to see us again.

It is incredible the variety of sensations one can experience in the same day.

The goats' bells echoed in the valley as they climbed up to their summer barn.

The village shepherds had just finished their transhumance.

Down on the plains it had become too hot and now the forest on the hills was in bloom.

Figures that looked like something out of a history book, wrinkled and curved like a stick of rough olive wood.

The days were getting longer, the sun was radiating its light late into the night.

Everyone in the tavern was now outside, spring was like a season in between.

It ferried us from cold winter to hot summer.

"Let's just hope it's not as hot as last year's," I said, thinking aloud.

"Yeah... I'd like it if it was always spring," Ali replied.

"I don't know, in my opinion it would be boring, in the end every season is beautiful because it has to be waited for.

I love the cold after the summer oven, as well as the bloom after the cold and snow."

"Yes, but I don't like the cold."

"Sometimes I wonder if you are really Romanian."

"That's exactly why I don't like it, I have lived in the cold too long."

How can I blame her? Alina felt the same way about the cold as I did about the heat.

Anything experienced in an excessive manner in the end gets tired.

I know it well, after several winters spent in the Caribbean, Mexico and California, consecutive to summers in sunny southern Italy, I still remember that feeling of purity and bliss I felt when I saw snow again after five long hot years.

WALKING AMONG THE ISLANDS

"But when was there ever a queue to go into town? I almost miss the days of that pantomime pandemic, where everyone was holed up at home and no one went out, peace in the streets."

"How bearish you are!"

"Yes I know and so what? What can I do about it? I can't stand chaos. If I liked it I would have stayed in Los Angeles and not moved to a Greek island."

This was a classic early-season dialogue between Alina and me. It was something habitual, cyclical.

As a good Aries, I love tranquillity, calm and solitude.

Alina, who had lived the first part of her life in Romania during the communist era, had developed a free and rebellious personality, in total contrast to the totalitarian style imposed by the dictatorship.

"My life will be far from here," she used to repeat to her parents who could not imagine any other life beyond the border than the one dictated by party rules.

She envied the stamps on my passports, the countries I had visited, my experiences; in the early days of our story, when we were still just getting to know each other and our wonderful relationship had yet to blossom, she would fill me with questions: what is this place like, what is that other place like...?

In the end it depends on how you experience them.

It is like wine.

Some Germans love the wine they served at Platanos before I arrived.

Now: everything can be said about Platanos except that they served good wine. But then again, it is also true that everything can be said about Germans except that they understand wine....

Things have changed since I started doing wine tastings there.

Except for the tastes of the Germans, they still don't understand much.

The cellar was shrinking, the wine was flowing in an oenological cascade and there were few reinforcements beyond the Adriatic.

I was waiting for friends like a godsend. At the time, the law provided for something like twenty four cases of wine per person for personal use.

The problem was not the law, the problem was finding someone who would come and have enough space.

On the first round I overtook myself by carrying some five hundred and more bottles ambushed in Gypsy.

But the tastings took off and the wine went like hot cakes.

After tasting it, customers started asking me for crates upon crates, even friends asked me for it and I sold it to them without any mark-up.

An importer was needed. So that the tasters could buy their own wine and I could use my bottles for tastings.

There was just no way to convince the local importers to import anything other than what they already imported. They did not want to vary their boring routine.

The days passed quietly, spring was advancing, flowers were blooming and birds were singing.

"We didn't go out even once with Nitro," I said.

"True, we should go do some nautical camping."

It was a good idea; to go to Frixia, the next day perhaps to Arcoudi, then on to Atokos and why not, perhaps as far as Ithaca.

It was something we had always promised ourselves we would do but for one reason or another had never done. At least not with our boat.

The memory of that wonderful 2019 holiday in Kefalonia and Ithaca, where we had a fantastic couple of months as soon as the season was over, was still fresh in our minds.

Two beautiful islands, even more beautiful when experienced in a van.

At those thoughts, the island grew gloomy, jealous.

Almost envious.

Lefkada is like that. It cannot bear to hear good spoken of its hated neighbours.

We could appreciate Meganissi, the little sister, but Ithaca! Never.

Yet it is beautiful.

Get there by boat, appreciate the beaches, the tranquillity.

It is something I love to do, and countless trips take me to those shores during the summer season.

Not only Ithaca, but also Atokos, Kalamos and Kastos with their idyllic bays and secluded taverns.

One day like so many others I got a phone call, it was an American gentleman who had read an article of mine published on the blog lefkadaofficial.com in which I described a boat trip among the islands.

Here are excerpts:

One of my favourite places from which to start a boat trip is the bay of Dessimi: the crystal-clear water, the cave of San Nicola, a safe harbour when you return in the afternoon with the Mistral tearing at your clothes and you there, at the helm protected by the bay.

There is a jetty, a wooden hut that serves as an office, and dry palm fronds for shade.

And then there is Malù... the Dessimi mascot is there in the shade, watching over everything. The cutest little dog in the bay is now an attraction, cuddled with love by all.

...

The day always starts with a caress to Malù, a goodbye to friends and a crazy run at 20 knots in a southerly direction.

I always arrive early, often on my motorbike.

Parking in the shade is provided by Fanì, an intrepid sailor from Geni who fishes with her small fishing boat in winter and runs this shady car park in summer.

And I enjoy Dessimi early in the morning.

Then when Spiros and Malu arrive, a good coffee never fails, yet another despite the fact that the day has just begun.

"Where are you going today Fabio?"

"Atokos and Ithaca I think."

"Ah man, not to Meganissi?"

"Hmm, if we don't stop to eat in Gidaki maybe we'll pass."

The customers arrive, Malù sniffs them out, signals to me that they can go, and I seat them on board.

I let go of the moorings, engage the reverse gear for a few seconds, then move forward with the starboard engine and the boat turns on itself.

I set a course, give it a few turns and the bow rises, the guests lay out their towels and slather on sunscreen, I let them.

Cody barks loudly from the hillside of the beautiful Villa Dessimi, he recognised me... that sweet little blind dog adopted by a couple of dear Australian friends.

To the southeast, the cave of St Nicholas is still asleep, the bay is a mirror and the brackish smell permeates the thick, pure air.

I increase the revs again, the bow rises and the customers smile, I say "shall we go?"

They answer yes and I sink the throttle, the engines scream and the boat glides, sputtering at over 20 knots. I adjust the trim, partialise the throttle and Dessimi pulls away fast, to starboard runs the beautiful Arcoudi with its natural pools, in front of us Atokos.

After half an hour of furious running we reach the south-western end of one of the most beautiful islands in the world.

The kaleidoscopic water that awaits us as we turn east is something to be seen once in a lifetime.

A vertical wall that shimmers and reflects the morning sunlight shot at it from the sea with the shadow of the boat flowing under twenty metres of crystal-clear water.

And a tiny beach all to ourselves.

You have to come there early in the morning and hope it goes well, especially in the busier months. In June there is no such problem, in June it is a dream in any case.

The swallows flying around you and those scents that only places where man has not yet destroyed anything can give you... An enchantment broken after an hour of blissful solitude by the first boat of the day, the first after yours.

We haul anchor and sail past Atokos to its most famous bay: the Bay of Pigs.

Here are the only buildings in Atokos: an open church dedicated to St John and a shabby little house.

Beautiful place, lovely out of season, a little too crowded in summer, but an almost obligatory stop; if only for a dutiful prayer in the little church and a swim in the clear green water.

Continuing on our route I always take a diversion.

Few people know this place and those few with good reason do not tell you where it is, not even me.

Have you ever seen a tree grow upside down?

A seed that fell among the rocks, who knows how it managed to cling to life and grow upside down.

It has not yet touched the water but it is a matter of a few years, for now it is there, swaying blissfully in the wind like a circus performer.

We fly away to Ithaca and its Dionysian bays.

They are endless, once we arrive we idle and the song of the cicadas covers that of the engines, olive trees clinging to the rocks that have inspired acrobatic goats over the years, red earth, white rock and blue, sky-blue, now green sea.

No wonder the gods chose this place to live, where else?

The customers don't speak, some take photos, others don't even manage it anymore dazzled by the incredulity of so much beauty.

Incredible is the right word.

We sail along the beautiful and mythical island to the bay of Filiatro.

Now: there are two bays here, one is the beach most frequented by locals, the other you only reach by boat. That's where I point my bow, and that's where I drop anchor.

I challenge customers to bring me some sand.

You dive in and go down, down, down and down and most come back up empty-handed.

Filiatro is one of those places you never want to leave, which is why I always choose it before lunch, it is your stomach that pushes you to the next stop: the beautiful and famous Gidaki.

Reaching it only by boat, a small kiosk that prepares some of the tastiest souvlaki on the island welcomes you amidst wood and dry palm fronds.

Ice-cold beer and a well-deserved rest lying on the soft white sand.

The boat anchored and secured to the ground by a rope to that log there, always him.

Then comes the little boat with tourists from Vathi with the beautiful Miriam, the half-Greek, half-Venezuelan hostess.

"Hola Fabio, como estas?"

"Todo bien Miriam, is work going well?"

"Yes we have just started again"

"Eh we too..."

"What, are you tired of Lefkada?"

The parochialism...

From here, it is the weather that decides: if the weather is good, you go to Vathi, with its splendid statue of Ulysses and the cosy old town, a walk that restores the soul; if, on the other hand, the weather promises bad winds, better to start heading back towards Arcoudi and its magnificent pools.

We skirt the mythical island at 15 knots, quiet, the guests don't notice anything, I, on the other hand, notice the inevitable change of colour in the sea there to the north, when the protection of the island ends and that angry midnight blue streaked with white lines begins.

There will be dancing, I know... there is always dancing. That's the price you pay for going this far.

But I don't say anything to the customers, it wouldn't help, I let them enjoy this beautiful view.

Then it comes.

The first wave sends you flying and you reduce your revs, eleven knots still too much.

Another flight, down to seven, then six, then five.

Then the ever-present message from Spiros spying on you from the GPS:

"Hey captain... everything OK?"

"Yes, don't worry, we'll make it, don't worry," and here I am always reminded of my grandfather Tonino, who used to tell me: "don't ever worry.

Taking the piss obviously out of my innate and boundless optimism.

We zigzag between the ridges, giving precedence to the highest waves and traversing their hollows amid splashes of foam and gusts to the transom.

We arrive in Arcoudi and everything calms down as if by magic.

We anchor in two metres of water and surprise opens the mouths of those who have decided to have a wonderful day with me, the wind is there but it passes over us, deflected by the low island.

The sea is motionless.

This is where I competed in the Southern Ionian Regatta with my Nitroglycerin in 2019, this is where we flew over the water with one hull cutting through the surface and the other through the air passing over the shallows at 13 knots under sail with my small, rabid catamaran.

But today we are taking it easy.

There is Claudio anchored further along with Liliana and Isabel, Katia will arrive in a few days.

We meet often and it is like family.

Then at a signal from the unconscious you raise the anchors and return. Some in one bay, some in another, but it is the course to Dessimi that puts the sea at your back for easier navigation,

and you return protected by the gods and the beautiful green bay, with Spiros waiting for you with open arms at the end of the pier.

"Great Captain!"

But it doesn't always go like this...

Sometimes as soon as you come out of the protection of Itaka, Aeolus and Neptune bar your way and no, you cannot pass, and the message of Spiros is another:

"Fabio all right? Wouldn't it be better to stretch and protect you behind Atokos?"

"And I guess so..."

Customers look at the wind-swept wall of water and then everyone, even the dog, looks at you.

"Don't worry, have you ever ridden a wave?"

You choose one, the highest, get on it and adjust your speed to match it.

The wind zeroes in, it goes at the same pace as you, perhaps a little stronger but nothing more than a gentle breeze in your hair.

You are high up and enjoy a view of a couple of metres and a half on the surface, which becomes even four up to the hollow.

And then you go like this, totally relaxed to Atokos and then on to Kalamos and Kastos, you circle around among forgotten coves and find yourself facing Mitikas, on dry land.

Spiros knows, he knows you made the right choice, he knows you will be late and he knows it's OK.

'Well done Captain' is his message that punctually arrives when the wind starts to die down.

And then begins one of the most beautiful water rides the Ionian Sea can give you.

It is almost sunset, the light is red.

The sun is a glowing disc in front of you as you run fast with Meganissi on your port side and its three beautiful bays, Homer's Beach and its sulphurous lake, the fronds of the umbrellas dancing to the Jamaican, Scorpio to starboard and Dessimi there, hidden to the west of the cape.

And here you enter the bay whose beach is already in the shade.

One glance at the grotto of St Nicholas, who smiled at us again today, and there he is, Spiros, at the end of the pier welcoming you with open arms, with Malu wagging his tail beside him.

"Great Captain!" he shouts smilingly.

And another beautiful day in paradise comes to an end... is there anything more beautiful in life?

There after reading this article, Dan called me and asked me to do the exact same tour.

That was an unforgettable moment of the season.

The night before, I had met a wonderful Dutch family who had left the comfort of their yacht from Syvota to go up to Vafkeri to taste my wines with the excellent Italian-Greek pairings prepared by Alina.

A tasting that gave us five new friends and at the end of which it felt like we had known each other all our lives.

The next morning, however, we spent a day at sea between Ithaca, Atokos and Arkoudi with Dan and his family, who absolutely wanted to sail the exact same route as narrated in the article.

It was really surreal to receive that request.

A request which I was more than happy to fulfil.

As soon as we left, they asked me if the one barking was really Cody, how and how much longer the little tree that had grown upside down would live, whether Aeolus and Neptune would let us pass through the canal.

It is always splendid to sail on that course.

In the morning the Cavalieri d'Italia (the Knights of Italy) accompany you at twenty knots skimming the water with their wings, the air is thick and pure and Atokos stands out in the background.

The sapling is always there, a bit bigger and closer to the water, a bit too close to the water, each year more and more.

And then Ithaca... its colours, its smells, its magic.

They made us spend that day, and the last dive was at the Arkoudi pools.

Returning to Dessimi I felt that wonderful feeling of gratitude for doing what I love in the place I love.

"No Malou with Spiros today, who is that guy?" Dan asks me.

"This is Kostas"

"But does he always laugh?"

"Yes he always laughs."

"It will be this place that brings you happiness."

And yes, Dan had it all figured out.

Kostas was there waiting for us, a big smiling face with two big blue eyes bursting with joy.

I played the horn given to me by him and he laughed even more, shaking his head.

"Great Captain!" He shouted from the dock.

And another day in paradise came to an end...

ALINA GOES, SPINAZZ COMES

The time for departure arrived.

It was always sad to part.

There was a time when I would fly off to California for months at a time , feeling free and knowing we would come back together, but after a few years being separated even for a week started to become burdensome.

Ali had not seen her parents for over two years, so it was a trip that had to be made.

So much had changed over there.

Her parents had sold the little house on the riverside where Alina and her siblings had grown up. They had finally finished the farm in the country and help was more than welcome.

There were Alina's nieces who had now become almost teenagers; in short, a trip that had to be made.

We hugged each other tightly and parted for a while.

That evening I went to dinner alone in the tavern and when I got home the doggies greeted me as always and then looked first at the door then at me.

They understood that someone was missing... especially Pepi.

I had lived alone for so long, I didn't mind that newfound tranquillity, even if only for a short while. Not that I wasn't at ease with Ali, on the contrary, but it was a feeling I hadn't had for a long time.

A sensation pleasantly forgotten the day after the arrival of the intrepid Capitain Spinazz.

The kind you never tire of.

We had met several times in Apulia with both him and his brother Luciano, but meeting again in Lefkada always had its effect.

He came climbing through the mountains with his car overloaded with wine.

I saw him coming up the driveway and stood outside.

"Well if you didn't send me the location, I'd be able to get lost up here in the mountains!"

"Mythical Spinaz! How are you?" I replied, smiling.

"All right, all right. Crazy, thirteen years I've been coming to this island and I've never seen this place, if I wake up here suddenly I don't know I'm in Lefkada," he said, looking around.

"Eh, you will see some beautiful and hidden places this summer."

"*See* this summer, two weeks I have to stay."

"Yes yes, that's what they all say... park up we'll have a nice coffee."

"Oh by the way..."

Spinaz sells coffee, and every time we meet he hands me those three or four kilos of good beans to grind.

For the occasion I bought myself an electric grinder, the manual one I had in Cassano was a tad too anachronistic.

Grinding coffee is wonderful, the aromas expand around the house and the craving for caffeine increases.

"Have you ever tried press coffee?"

"What?"

"Instead of doing it with the mocha you put it in this press, then you filter it. It's English let's say."

Spinaz's face became a whole programme.

"OK I'll make the moka..."

"No no go easy, I'll prove it to you."

"Yes but I also make moka, just in case."

After the customary coffee we started to unload the wine. As many as twenty-two cases.

"They all got into it in the end, eh?" I said.

"*Mado* what do you know..."

"What else happened?"

"I arrive at your father's farm, and a worker approaches the machine with a forklift, he wanted to load the platform and everything!"

"Yes my father's workers are quite rustic."

"Then as you predicted your father had fun playing tetris with the crates, eventually more would come in."

"Eh I told you, he's a biker: he could fit a wardrobe into a couple of briefcases."

The day went by chatting away until Spinaz said, "Let me lie down for a moment. In the best moment of sleep those people turned on the lights on the ferry... it was still over an hour before docking."

"Don't worry, I'm busy here anyway, I have to send some emails for the app and website renewals."

That evening we went to the Platanos.

I was not in the best of health, I felt weak and feverish, perhaps the hot day on the small island of St Nicholas followed by the motorbike ride up in the cool air had debilitated me.

"Don't worry Fabio, these two weeks I'll give you some food education."

Spinaz is someone who cares a lot about physical fitness. A great runner, he had recently taken up cycling.

We ordered a couple of Greek salads, *tiroV afkeri* and toasted bread.

"No beer Maria, just water."

Maria looked at us in terror.

"Fabio... Ola kala?"

"Eh not really I'm a bit down, better to avoid alcohol."

She raised her hands as she gave an incredulous look.

For a couple of days I was not great company, it was still cool in the evenings and a blanket was needed, but I did not sleep well, I alternated between moments of excessive heat and shivering.

Spinaz took the opportunity to go for a run in the surrounding area to discover the Lefkadian mountains while I worked on the computer between website and customer renewals.

"*Mo* Fabio beautiful, today I took the first right turn and went all the way up to Eglouvi!"

"So you came to Eglouvi by running?"

"Yeah... it's a slog up that hill."

"But you're sick *ualiò*! I just started it and came right back."

"Eh I had the same thought myself, then I always thought that the one in front was the last hill, until I got to the village."

He had run a goat course...

After a few days I started to feel better.

"Today we are going to Agio Ioannis, I have to meet a client. Or rather, a would-be one."

"Do you want me to go with you or would you rather go alone?"

"No don't worry, come, then we'll go for a bite to eat in town."

As we drove through the mountains, passing intrepid old men on motorbikes occupying the entire carriageway in the middle of Pigadisani, I noticed that Spinaz was looking at the island with different eyes.

"All right?"

"Yes yes everything is OK, it's that I had never even been here."

"Don't worry, take time to recover and we'll go by bike, it's the best way to discover the island."

"Do you have another bike?"

"No even the one I use is not mine actually, it's Andrew's, an Australian friend of mine."

"And where do we get the other one?"

"Dave..."

"Does he have a bike shop?"

"No he has a collection."

"Ah, passionate?"

"No, really sick."

We arrived at Agios Ioannis at the splendid *Lyogerma* restaurant.

The owners are not from Lefkada but descendants of exiles from Paralia.

Two brothers, two exquisite people.

While waiting, we had some marinated anchovies and a beer.

A Victoria, made in the northern mountains.

Once the brothers were reunited and seated at the same table, it only took a few minutes to close the deal.

We understood each other and liked each other instantly, and with a handshake and an intense look, the splendid Lyogerma also became my client.

"That's satisfaction Spinaz, when you close deals with people who sign with a handshake... nice restaurant huh?"

"*Mo* what a marinated anchovy show."

"Yes, fantastic."

"Only that they made me hungry."

"Gyros?"

"*Eh...*" Which in Bari pronounced the way it should be pronounced could mean *yes*, or *why not*, or even *great idea*. Between Spinaz and me, it was always a game of pun.

We ate the most typical Greek street food and returned to the cool of the mountains.

Feeling better, the next day we went to Dessimi, home of the Spiros nautical base.

"*Hellla Fabioooo great!*" greeted me as soon as I arrived.

"Hi Spiros everything OK?"

"Always OK file."

"Spiros this is my friend Marco Spinazzola, also a captain."

"*Hella capitagno!*"

"Eh *see* captain, not really, let's say apprentice."

"But what, this year we will work together, when you have numerous trips there are two of us OK?"

"Perfect Fabio, beer?"

"Ook."

Spiros disappeared into the back of his splendid wooden and palm frond office on the beach.

He came out with three ice-cold beers, while kittens played between his legs.

"And who are these now?"

"Eh new entry Fabio!"

Four beautiful kittens played happily under the watchful eyes of their mother.

Spinaz wasted no time and dived into the water, then Spiros asked, "Fabio are you busy?"

"Not really, total relaxation today."

"Could you help me get a boat from Geni?"

"Sure file let's go. Spinaz! *Mo veng!* (I'll be right back)."

I jumped into the car with Spiros, a brand new 4x4, and we drove to his winter base in the bay of Geni.

"Have you seen the new forecourt?"

"Yes I saw it while I was going to rest at Kiriaka."

"Ah bravo, I like that little church too."

"You know I used to live around here, right around the time of the pandemic."

"Yes?"

"Yes down in Geni, by the sea, I had the boat exactly fourteen steps from the front door."

"Really?"

"Yes, but then I ran away."

"And why?"

"The house was a hovel and when it rained from the north-west the door let water seep in, then the neighbourhood was not as quiet and welcoming as I imagined."

"Hella file now on the mountains you are in heaven, I also live on a hillside. Oh, look at this... you can't imagine how much I work."

We arrived at an area where all the vegetation had been cut down to make way for a large concrete yard full of small boats.

Spiros turned the van around and reversed into a boat on a trolley.

I went down and hooked it, then we went to the slide and pushed it into the sea.

"Perfect Fabio thank you, see you in Dessimi."

I started the engine and drove off slow and quiet.

I waved goodbye to the church of Agio Kiriaka, passed through the channel between Scorpio and Lefkada with Frixia bay to starboard.

Then I arrived at Glimaki and saw the beautiful Odysseia moored while the guests were enjoying the bbq.

Dimitris was at the stern, I greeted him, he sharpened his eyesight and returned the greeting.

It is always nice to return to Dessimi by boat, to feel that feeling of protection that the bay offers you with the shady cave of St Nicholas on the starboard side and the jetty in front, where I moor quietly.

"Thank you *morè* says Kostas to me."

Spiros waves thanking me.

I sat in the shade, Spinaz instead was lying in the sun, the lizard tattoo he wears with pride is no accident.

"Nice to work like this, eh?" I tell him.

"I would move right away..."

"Eh siga siga, let's see if there are any customers."

"But you say it would work out?"

"Why not? At the end the island is getting more and more expensive and people want quality services, different from the trip you took last year with *eighty euro skippers...*"

"*Mado hey* don't talk to me about it."

The previous season, Spinazz and family were on holiday with friends who were on a money-saving trip, and they went on a tour with local-improvised-skippers of whom they still have very bad memories.

"If you know where to take people and make them feel good on board you create your clientele and that's it. At the first opportunity we'll take a ride and I'll show you some little places."

The first opportunity materialised several weeks later in the middle of the season, when Spinaz's brother-in-law took the family on a holiday to the island and we took a splendid tour around Meganissi: its turquoise waters, the solitude of places that few people know about because they are accustomed to the more familiar routes – that feeling of being in paradise that pervades you whenever the haunting beauty of a place overcomes rationality.

"It's not as easy as I thought," Spinaz said after that outing, "the anchorages, the tight manoeuvres, dosing the throttle."

"You learn Spinaz, I got lucky because I always found the right people who taught me the right things, so I owe a moral debt to good luck. Let's do a few outings together and you'll see that you'll do great."

The day began quiet, the dinghy was new and a pleasure to steer.

Little Alberto, whom I had also had as a customer on Nitroglicerina the year before, was happiness made flesh.

It didn't take us long to get to the famous Papanikolis cave.

A stop designed to show the gap between a tourist spot and the paradisiacal nothingness that would characterise the rest of the day. Beautiful; splendid; incredible; and other synonyms were the most common words on board.

I gave little Albert another indelible memory by putting him at the helm of the dinghy.

Then when the north easterly began to blow, I took refuge in Scorpio's bays, where I greeted Gaia and Filippo, the friendly crew of Marine Adventures and other friends who were there to shelter from the *Grecale* north-eats gusts.

That was also a tourist stop, but a necessary one, if only because it is the only place where you can anchor in Scorpio.

'There would be another little place to go and hide – the lonely, isolated kind.

"Come on Spinaz, your turn," I said, and handed him the helm.

I hoisted the anchor and steered it into a tiny cove that had a patch of sand under a white limestone rock.

He managed to make a great anchorage, considering it was his first one he did not to bad at all apart from a small slip.

We secured ourselves to the ground with a rope and enjoyed the peace of the place.

Just us and the birds, perhaps annoyed by our presence.

The water shimmered and reflected on the white wall. Intrepid vegetation climbed the crumbly rock.

A dream place, the kind you never want to leave.

Then a beautiful little cloud darkened the sun and we realised it was time to go back.

Spinaz gave a doubtful look when he saw me moored in millimetrical manner between two other boats. "Don't worry, a couple of berths you might miss, but all the others will be fine."

DRINKING & CYCLING

Spinaz was now an accomplished cyclist.

We had gotten the monkey from the last sector. We were basically using an app called Strava to record our times on the bike.

During an outing to the Karia Hills we began to take it quite seriously.

"Ehy Spinaz, Dave asked us to go out with him on the bike tomorrow."

"Ah nice are we going?"

"Yes we just have to go and get a bike for you."

We went to Dave's house in the afternoon.

"Ehy guys buongiorno!" said Dave in his uncertain Italian.

"Ehy mate everything OK?"

"Very good thank you."

"Perfect, do you have something for my friend? He has a beautiful Bottecchia with Campagnolo gearbox but I filled his car with wine and so..."

"You did very well Fabio, there is no shortage of bicycles here, but good wine..."

We walked into the garage, the gorgeous, brand new carbon Cannondale Synapse was pulled out to a shine, it was a pain to see the White he had been riding since London relegated to second place. Then there were various mountain bikes and at the back a black bike: a Specialized with internal wiring.

"Isn't that one of Pete's bikes?"

"Yes it is."

"Maybe we use that one."

"We don't use it often, it's not very well put together."

It was sad Pete's bike, great frame, gravel tyres, triple Shimano gearbox, treated as the last wheel of the wagon: it was a great bike.

"I'll take her to Vassilis and get her fixed up," I said.

We did so, Vassilis is a former professional cyclist who has a nice bicycle shop in Lefkada.

After passing through his hands the black bike came back to life – the next day we did the Karia Hills.

From Platystoma to Vafkeri, the last stretch of our tour, Strava created three kilometres of sprints where we had to give it our all.

Dave and I slaughtered each other and finished the ride in a very close sprint, lowering our personal bests by several tens of seconds.

We stopped the hand just after eight minutes thirty.

Spinaz would later shatter those times by clocking on several occasions first eight minutes, then seven and a half minutes, then seven and fifteen and finally seven minutes and eight seconds! Pushing Vassilis back by more than thirty seconds and becoming the fastest cyclist ever to have raced on that sector.

Who knows, if he had started as a child, Puglia would have had its own Pantani.

Dave was shocked by those times to the point of suspecting that we had done them on motorbikes.

On another occasion we took a trip out of town, or rather, off the island, cycling to Mitikas – one of the most characteristic towns just outside Lefkada.

The coastline from Paleiros to Mitikas is something poignant, like something out of a movie.

Suddenly, and without warning, beautiful beaches with turquoise waters appear after a hairpin bend, gentle green hills can be climbed with pleasure, and finally Mitikas welcomes you with its colours and scents.

And in that village where time has stood still, you happen to see an old man pedalling on his ancient bicycle with rod brakes and a bag of fish attached to the handlebars, a barber still using sharp free-hand razors, a little shop where things are piled up in a bazaar-like order and where, if you know where to look, you can find everything from hydraulic hoses to fish hooks.

Stood in the shade of a few umbrellas on the beach, sipping coffee and orange juice, we rested and admired the view.

An old man sitting on a bucket was casting his line into the water with movements dictated by the time, a frame of cats around him waited patiently for perhaps a few too small fish to be offered to repay their company.

"What island is that?" asked Spinaz.

"The one on the right is Kalamos, the green island, on the left is Kastos.

"Ah OK, I have been there, but I had never seen them from this perspective."

"Yes they are beautiful, even more so in the evening."

"Are there hotels?"

"Yes there is something, if you don't go by boat there is a small ferry that leaves from right here."

"From Mitikas?"

"Yes from over there."

"Spectacular..."

"Eh... nice little place. In Kastos I tasted roast Serra fish for the first time: a delicacy. If you get the right exit you take customers there, there's an abandoned barge at the far end of the harbour, you can moor next to it and go ashore by crossing it."

"Isn't it dangerous?"

"Not unless you have the bad luck that it sinks right as you walk over it, but it's been there for several years so you would have to have a lot of bad luck."

"It's just that you never know..."

The evenings in the Taverna changed pace and Spinaz's dietary education went out the window. The Greek salad was replaced by roasted delicacies and the beer flowed.

A typical exchange was:

"*Mado...* I feel overstuffed."

"Don't worry, we'll go cycling tomorrow."

One of those evenings Spinaz looked worried at the four half-litre bottles of Mamoz lying empty on the table.

"Did we really drink two litres of beer?"

"No, two and a half, an empty bottle took Maria away."

"Ah..."

"Come on, Alina will be here in a while and then she will cook us something green."

"Eh... thank goodness."

Alina was our salvation, at least the salvation of our crushed livers.

As a wonderful and good lover of herbs, she brought us remedies for our internal organs battered by alcohol and animal proteins.

Let's say it was more of a slowdown than a stop because in Vafkeri every opportunity was good to celebrate.

Like: Alina back? Big party at Platanos.

Spinaz makes the sector record? Big party at Dave's house.

Pete gets a new titanium knee? Colossal drink.

Andrew returns from the desert? Party at Villa Dessimi.

It was always like that, but one episode surpassed them all.

Alina had just returned.

"So did you have fun without me?"

"Well let's say we didn't get bored, we just overdid it a bit with the meat."

"Yeah I guess..."

Then Spinaz asked me a strange question.

"Do you happen to have a rope?"

"A rope? A few kilometres maybe, what do you need it for?"

"I broke some grommets supporting the exhaust pipe, the muffler hangs a bit."

"Eh... welcome to Lefkada and its billiard-ball streets," I sang to him.

The muffler wasn't in bad shape, but it needed a temporary fix, perhaps fixing it with something less incendiary than a rope.

"I have steel line, or wire," I said.

"OK let's try."

"Wait I found it," I said.

I returned with ten metres of four-millimetre stainless steel chain and a shackle (the nautical kind, not the singing kind).

"E la catàin a ma mmètt?" Spinaz asked in Barlettano (and the chain we have to put on him?).

"And we try."

"And what do we do with the other nine metres and ninety centimetres?"

"We pass them around the tree so they don't steal your car." It was parked under the tree in front of the house.

"Naaa come on really."

"Dave has a nice big cutter."

The chain did its job, and apart from the fact that several metres of it dangled, it was perfect.

Then things went downhill from there.

We went to Dave to ask him for the cutter, in the meantime Ann had called him to put a bottle of white on ice because he had had a tiring day.

At the same time Alina told us to be back by 6.30 p.m. because she was hungry.

"No let's just go get the cutter." I said. She in response looked at us, arching her eyebrows.

"Hey Dave!"

"Hi Fabio, hi Spinaz, glass of wine?"

"No Dave thanks, we just wanted to ask if we could borrow the cutters for a moment."

"Yes of course, I have them in the garage, in the meantime have a drink."

"No really we would like to go to the tavern, Alina is waiting for us."

"And call her too."

"OK but first we should finish the job with the cutter, we'll let you know and bring it back."

"OK," he said, smiling as he poured us drinks.

We went back to the car, cut the chain and said to Alina, "Ali we're going to take the cutters to Dave, do you want to come for a drink?"

"No because I know how it ends."

"OK one glass and we come back."

Again that look with raised eyebrows softened this time by a half smile.

"Ehy welcome back."

"Hi Dave thank you very much."

"Have another glass."

"Yes only one though that Alina is waiting for us."

"But make her come," Ann said, smiling as she brought out wine and olives.

After a few drinks I called Alina.

"Ali couldn't you bring a bottle of Fiano with some eighty-four month aged Parmesan?"

"And at Platanos?"

"And we'll go later with Ann and Dave."

Alina came with a couple of bottles and parmesan cheese, Ann took some English cheese and more bottles.

Spinaz admired the beautiful sunset with a view of Scorpio and Meganissi from Dave's terrace, a first for him.

As soon as the sun went down, we went to Platanos, which has a cool cellar where I kept most of my wines for ageing...

In short, it was a pleasant evening, but Spinaz drew the conclusion.

"That is, whereas over there if you go to someone's house they ask if you want a coffee, over here..."

"Do we ask for white, red or beer here?" Dave finished for him.

"Basically, if I hadn't broken the muffler supports, all this would never have happened," Spinaz concluded to general laughter.

Another epic evening was when Alan and Dave (regatta) drove up to Vafkeri on a 50cc two-stroke scooter.

A premise must be made: Alan and Dave are great friends.

Alan is a distinguished British pensioner, ex-special forces with high-risk roles; Dave is my Scottish friend whose boat I rescued, a former Hebrides fisherman who can do anything in a boat. But really anything.

Smile eternally plastered on their faces, we did the Southern Ionian regatta with them in 2019.

An unforgettable experience that needs to be recounted to understand the guys I had to deal with.

* * *

Which in the end was not just the race, which was completed in less than two hours by the way, but it was the practice run, the tuning of Nitroglicerina, Dave's knots, who as a good ex-Scottish fisherman makes splices that hold tighter than steel shackles, the run to Syvota, the mega drink at Pirates, the night dinghy race with water balloons and annexed fights, the full English breakfast at the Family tavern with eggs, bacon, beans, mushrooms, sausages, tomatoes, orange juice and.... English tea with milk of course, the transfer to Vassiliki, the night wandering from one boat to another because everyone is a friend afterwards, the return in a downpour, the Friday wandering between Vliho and Nydri which began with happy hour at Vliho's yacht club followed by Mad Rob's alcoholic roulette at the Tree bar and the grand finale at the Road House until dawn with Heather dancing *Tequila* on the bar with two bottles in her hand giving drinks to the thirsty.

The pre-race charged us up, and the post-race made us forget the shit we had done in the race...

So:

Dave's starting tactic was practically perfect, but since we are three dickheads and we were not a little slowed down from the night before, we still screwed it up and were thirty seconds behind the line...

There were only three boats behind us, forty-five in front.

We also risked ramming the jury boat, which was the Ionian Spirit, my friend Francesco Giordano's splendid wooden sailing ship from 1956.

But, you know, every cloud has a silver lining and to overtake thirty-seven times in less than half an hour was a crazy piss, especially the one on the frenchman who tried hard to penalise us while we were stealing the wind under the gennaker, the bastard tried to the last but in the end he had to cross our trajectory not even half a metre from my windward rudder.

The ninth position lasted for quite a while and while the others chose a more conservative course off the shoals of Arkoudi we passed over it on the strength of Nitro's shallow draught and before the change of tack we were in fifth position.

We gybed almost perfectly, we overtook another one a couple of metres from us passing upwind between him and the island, he tried to close in and send us into a penalty, but the flat sea thanks to the island's back not even twenty metres away assisted by the sixteen to seventeen knot breeze made his manoeuvre completely useless – we were flying!

We did not even realise we had passed another boat and found ourselves third with only the two very fast X-Yachts ahead of us, an X4 in second and an XP55 in first.

We could have settled for third place, after all it would not have been so bad being Nitroglicerina the smallest boat in the race, but it is always easy to judge afterwards.

To be fair, when Alan saw the spinnaker flexing he suggested that perhaps the gennaker should be lowered, but when you smell blood it closes your vein so with the wind at the crosswind and the gennaker hoisted we continued.

Dave, who has not two hands but two tongs, did his utmost to steer the headsail and Nitro lifted a hull out of the water as if it were a *Formula 18*.

The X4 in front of us went into a strafing run, gennaker in the water, we avoided it by a few metres becoming seconds.

The Xp 55 however was flying, it was very fast, bowed with its white gennaker skimming the water. He was less than 30 seconds behind us (damn start!), we could have settled for second place, but since seconds are the first of the last, with the forestay bent in an arc we kept flying over the water. Then, of course, the big deal.

The Xp 55 lowered the gennaker, too much wind, ungovernable, we couldn't steer it any more either, we lowered it, everything was perfect, it was almost on board, then the bastard went under the hull.

We were stationary... in twenty to twenty-five seconds we managed to free the daggerboard from the gennaker (holy moving dinghies), the sail was back on board, we opened the jib and set off again.

Only Nitro wasn't going... I mean, he wasn't faster than the others.

The jib halyard had stretched slightly and wasn't working properly, Dave and Alan couldn't sort it out, it blew the top of the trampoline and we couldn't even go to the bow anymore.

It was over.

But since it's not over until the line is cut...

I handed the tiller over to Dave, balanced on the spinnaker and aimed the bow spreader without touching the now unusable trampoline, untied the skein of lines that had been created, cocked the stroppetto and gave the jib furler a couple of turns: perfect trim!

We picked up speed again, passed one that was quite far from us as the crow flies and came back fourth.

We engaged in a splendid duel with a Grand Soleil 50: it was huge, it was fast, we gained a couple of knots as soon as we got rid of its wind rubbish and distanced it by becoming third again.

The X4 was ten to fifteen seconds behind, but the bay of Syvota was very close, in the distance the XP55 bowed to the wind and lowered its sails, he had won.

Not long to go, then came a wind hole!

I opened the whole jib, but the X4 had the genoa up and was stretching, after a few minutes we saw him cross the finish line.

We were going slowly and there was little we could do, I remember that I proposed hoisting the gennaker as the Gran Soleil was not far away and with its immense genoa it was approaching but Alan told me "no way Faab, forget it" – too risky without a trampoline.

Dave was still at the tiller cursing in tight Scots, very close... and the Grand Soleil was inexorably gaining metres.

But he didn't make it.

We finished third, ahead of a fifteen-metre boat and behind two very fast racing boats of twelve and sixteen metres respectively.

My little one is only 7 metres long and she made it big among the giants, earned her category jump, did the impossible... I love her very, very much.

It was nice to meet all three of us again.

I got a message: *"We're at the yacht club, will you come for a beer with Alan and me?"*

"Spinaz, today you will meet two madmen."

"Alan and Dave?" asked Alina.

"*hee hee...*"

"*Ciao belli!*"

"Ehy Fabio how are you?"

"Well Alan, what have you done to your head?"

"Oh... I thought a porthole was open and instead..." he said in his English accent as I admired the cut on his scalp.

After a couple of beers, Spinaz and Alina took our leave for a wonderful fish dinner at Elena's, on the other side of the bay.

During the digestive stroll to Nydri we met them again sitting at a bar.

And that's when the idea came to me: "you should come up to Vafkeri one evening, you have never eaten meat like this on the whole island".

"Yes, we were just thinking about that."

"On Friday we are coming, then I have to go back to Scotland because I haven't got my residency yet."

"OK then, Friday at Platanos around eight, eight-thirty?"

"OK."

"Do you know where it is?"

"Of course I know..." replied Alan. "The tavern by the church."

Obviously on that Friday at half past eight they were not there.

I called them and Dave answered, "we are here, when are you coming?"

"We are here too, where are you?"

"Close to the entrance"

"Yes, so are we."

Alan didn't understand shit as usual and went to another tavern.

"OK I'll send you the location on the GPS, you can find two coordinates yes?"

"Aye," replied Dave in Scottish as he cracked up with laughter.

"We ordered two beers, we'll finish them and be on our way."

Around 9.30, when I had already given up hope, Maria said to me, "Fabio there are two people looking for you."

"Yes yes, let them in."

Dave laughed as always, Alan on the other hand was pissed "You didn't tell me it was on the other fucking side of the island!"

"In fact we are in the middle of the island Alan not on the other side, I told you Platanos Vafkeri and you told me yes the one near the church, and if you look out there is a beautiful church as you can see."

He realised that trying to shift the blame onto me was not working so he changed tactics.

"It's cold up here, I felt cold on the way up."

"You're British, you're a former special forces soldier to boot, and you're telling me it's cold in the in Greece at night in the middle of June?"

Dave was dying of laughter.

"OK, let's go eat," he finally decided to say.

Now when four sailors meet in the tavern it would be better not to transcribe word for word what they said to each other, inevitably the talk fell over Dave's latest girlfriend – just landed, then over wine, boats, that one and that one, we remembered the time in Syvota, the night before the race, when Alan picked us up from the Pirates wearing a cook's apron over a pair of shorts and threatening us with a wooden spoon to go back to the boat because dinner was ready, things like that...

I was just worried that they would have to go all the way down to Nydri with Alan driving, the two of them had been able to fall over in front of the yacht club because Alan had forgotten to put his feet on the ground – and as they fell Dave was laughing as usual.

"Why didn't you put your feet on the ground Alan?" asked Dave.

"Because I thought you put them on Dave." Laurel and Hardy stuff.

There was a solution, like any self-respecting tavern the Platanos had rooms on the first floor, so we asked Maria if my friends could use one but she said it was not possible because there was someone who was jealous...

"OK guys come on I'll take you," I proposed.

"No c'mon no need Fabio I can drive, just lend me a torch."

"A torch?"

"Yes you know... The lights don't work."

Bundled up in my mid-season clothes, with a torch in hand, they decided to try their luck and go down to Nydri, with the right-hand carriageway full of stones after the last Mistral blast.

"A pleasure: I know I shouldn't really be the one to ask this since I never did it when my mother asked me but... Give me a ring when you get downstairs OK?"

"Oook ook," they replied as they laughed out loud.

I never saw them again...

Lie... they called me 27 minutes later, from Nydri... safe and sound.

ALINA'S BAR

Summer proceeded as swift as the wind that swells Nitro's sails in the channel between Lefkada and Meganissi.

Many things happened that summer, but the most beautiful was the most unexpected.

Spinaz wanted to open a bar with friends and we visited several: in Lefkada town, in Nydri and one in particular near Egremni.

"Spinaz this guy is to be taken a bit with a grain of salt."

"You mean he's a nervous type?"

"No no in fact he is even too calm, he just lives in a world of his own.

Fanatical about Japan, even though there is nothing Japanese about him except the stamps in his passport. He is a strange guy, but a very good person."

We motored up to the pass that separates the east and west coasts.

We descended and fold after fold we arrived in Chortata and then continued downhill in a southerly direction.

We passed Athani and at the junction for Egremni a beautiful tavern full of flowers stood before us.

I parked in the shade of some trees and Nikos' blue eyes greeted us framed by his smiling face.

"Yasu Nik."

"Yasu Fabio, ti kani? Ola kala?"

"Eh... File gesti... poly gesti."

It was ridiculously hot.

"This is my friend Spinaz, a great coffee expert."

"Ah pleasure."

"How are you doing Nikos, did you manage to sell?"

"Not the tavern, but the land up there on the hill," he said, pointing to an amphitheatre overlooking the sea.

"Ah well."

"Eh... Israel... they come and they pay."

"Good for you Nikos, and didn't they also want the tavern?"

"Yes, but they wanted to make a house instead of a tavern."

"*Emmè?*" which translates as "What about this??" from the Bari dialect.

"No Fabio no, I don't want the Taverna to close."

"Sorry how much did they offer you?"

"Two hundred thousand for the land and seven hundred and fifty thousand for the tavern."

"*Waliò ma tu allor si trmon adaver Nikos!*" (untranslatable)

"Eh I no understand."

"Eh better... listen my friend would like to open an ice cream bar here in Lefkada, have you completed the first floor?"

"Almost, the land money I'm putting there, come let's go and see."

We climbed the stairs without railings to the roof of the tavern.

There was a beautiful view of the Ionian Sea from up there, a wooden structure was topped with shady bamboo, concrete seats that rose up to become flower holders wound around that beautiful Japanese-style terrace.

It looked as if it had been designed by a modern design office when in all likelihood it had been created by some improvised local bricklayer who had only followed the eclectic instructions of Nikos, who himself must have seen that garden somewhere in the Land of the Rising Sun.

A masonry bar counter was just waiting to be equipped.

"But this one has this facility here and doesn't use it?"

"What your friend says?."

"He wonders why you don't use this good thing."

"No people to work."

"That is, lack of personnel?" Spinaz asked.

"Yes, understand why you have to move?"

Spinaz called his associates or would-be associates several times, but as always there is a sea between saying and doing, even if in this case it was only a little over forty nautical miles.

Nothing came of it and that summer the tavern was sold.

We returned to Vafkeri and Spinaz was sad, if it were up to him he would have started the same day.

We were at Platanos, in front of the beautiful structure that was to serve as a bar.

A small brick and wooden house with a stone patio shaded by some trees.

Beautiful.

Closed.

Used as a depot, even more humiliating.

"It's fashionable here not to use bars eh?" asked Spinaz dejected.

"Eh... A few weeks ago Costantinos asked me to help him on opening day, making a few spritzes and serving a few glasses of wine."

"And then what?"

'No staff,' I replied, imitating Nikos.

It seemed incredible but no workers could be found on the island. On the one hand because the Greeks pay a pittance, on the other because many of them are too lazy to work.

There we were, with Constantinos and Maria sitting at the neighbouring table waiting for evening customers.

I don't know what set off the spark, but that night Alina was pissed off.

"But it is not possible for a facility like this to remain closed! Look how beautiful it is!

A lot of cyclists, hikers, not to mention those who venture inside on quad bikes, pass by in the morning. And you keep it closed!"

"Alina no staff."

"Of course you can't find staff! You pay a pittance!"

"It is the youth of today who do not want to work!" replied Constantinos.

"It's true..." Maria echoed, not too convinced.

"Oh, yeah? Hand it over to me! I'm not afraid to get my hands dirty."

"You?" said Constantinos with a scowl.

Now: never challenge a Transylvanian... ever.

Ali has the sweetest face with a sprinkling of freckles on her baby cheeks, her green eyes are as deep as I have ever seen in my life.

When you provoke her, and when she gets pissed off, those same eyes flare up and her gaze becomes of incinerating a vampire slayer.

Alina looked at Constantinos with that look.

He picked up a set of keys, slamming it on the table, "Go on, open up!"

Alina accepted the challenge...

"Tell me what I owe you for the rent," he said as he took the keys.

"For now open it... I really want to see if you can do it," replied Constantinos with a dangling cigar.

"In two days you will see the village bar open," Alina said with her teal eyes sending flashes.

It was only a few months later that we found out that the agreement between him and the owner of the building did not include the nice little bar. And that was very fortunate.

Thus Alina's Bar, as it was christened by the foreign community in Vafkeri, was born.

The locals continued to call it the Platanos bar café and came in the mornings to order their hellenicos and that horrible frappe coffee, while in the evenings it turned into *The Wine Tasting Guild,* the venue for my wine tastings that saw people disembarking from their yachts moored at Syvota and Nydri go up to the mountains to drink great wines.

But the officially accepted name was *Alina's Bar.*

It became a point of reference for cyclists and hikers, Welsh and English alcoholics anonymous naturalised Vafkerians, devourers of croissants filled with ice cream, drinkers of semifreddo cappuccino and habitual holidaymakers who came just to admire Alina's smile and those eyes that once seen you're fucked for life... I know something about that.

A CLASSIC SUMMER DAY

It often happened that Spinaz and I were working on the same day on different boats.

We would go down to the café early in the morning, have a double Neapolitan espresso each, then a cappuccino, various croissants, another double espresso and off with the Ninja down the Lefkadian hills.

Which in the morning are a unique sight.

The view you can admire coming down from Vafkeri towards Nydri early in the morning is something that must be seen once in a lifetime.

Even more than once because it varies depending on the weather, the season, the incidence of light, the angle of the sun.

After the first few hairpin bends, the figure of Iannis crouching by the side of the road invites you to slow down.

Before long, in fact, the village goats will appear on the asphalt ribbon, crossing the road again and again and disgorging shrubs here and there.

Once past the mountainous part, a breathtaking view always manages to take your breath away.

The bay of Vliho shines in all its stillness, dotted with dozens of small sailing dots.

Behind the pass that gives access to the bay of Dessimi stands Atokos: a rock in the middle of the sea, a piece of rock among the rocks of that pass that is shaped like a chalice.

A unique view.

Keep going downhill and after the first hairpin bend they appear, the pearls of the Heptanese:

Scorpio and Scorpidi, Kalamoos and Kastos, Meganissi, Madouri, Keloni, and at the end, if the view permits, the Dragonera.

You have to be careful because this view bewitches you like a siren's song, but the asphalt doesn't think so and besides the hairpin bends it is full of potholes and fallen stones.

Once you get down to sea level, the temperature rises a lot and you begin to miss the coolness of the Lefkadian mountains.

I accompany Spinaz to Perigiali, today he will be on the Ionian Spirit as one can guess from the T-shirt he is wearing: grenade with the boat's logo, a beautiful anchor framed by the tops.

My logo, however, says something else, as does the colour white. My destination is Dessimi.

Another wonderful ride among those wonderful little islands that I admired on the way down.

Once relieved of Spinaz, the Ninja's rear end becomes lighter and with every touch of the accelerator I am reminded of how qualitatively useless the asphalt is on the island.

It's a continuous wag, even when I'm not in the rain.

I arrive in Dessimi and enter the car park of the very nice Fani.

There is also his daughter, the beautiful Susanna, who always greets me with that Lefkada blue-eyed smile of hers.

I park the Ninja under a tree and go down two steps, I am on the beach.

"Hella Fabio" Spiros calls to me from the kantina next to the car park, hidden by bamboo.

"How are you doing captain all right?"

"Ne '*re*," I answer him.

A little chat in the shade and then we go to the office.

A litter of all-black kittens is lovingly nursed by their mother, who is obviously the same colour.

I take a bottle of ice water and relax under the dry palm fronds.

"Who are today's Spiros customers?"

"I don't remember it *file*... but they are from the agency that likes you so much."

"So quiet people"

"Ne '*reee*."

The water is wonderful in Dessimi, in the early morning even more so.

I take the opportunity for a swim, the air is salty and the sight soothes your soul.

I see the beautiful Wallaby at anchor, floating regally in the shadow of the hill.

"Nice huh?" I hear behind my back.

I turn around and its owner, that Tuscan Claudio Selmi is there, with his two beautiful Border Collies.

"Hey Claudio hello."

"Hello captain, where are you off to today?

"I think Kalamos and surroundings."

"Dude, no Ithaca?"

"I was there a few days ago, always splendid... think an American family reading the blog contacted me and wanted to do the exact same tour."

"And I believe it, the way you write makes everyone dream of coming here."

"You think so? I should stop then, I like peace and quiet."

"Eh who are you telling... are you coming on board when you get back?"

"Sure, of course."

"Come on, if you come back from Ithaca, go get that ancestral wine I told you about," he tells me, walking away. His Tuscan accent is a hoot.

The two gorgeous big dogs make it clear that they want to walk, so we say goodbye.

I dry off and go to have a look at the boat.

Today I am on Cleopatra: a twin-engine Master 7.80.

The customers arrive and Spiros points at me.

"We are relying on you," three English ladies, who chose the most comfortable boat in the fleet to experience a relaxing day, tell me.

They will not be disappointed, the beautiful bays of the wild side of Meganissi first, the immaculate Formikula later, where the monk seal pup greeted us with a funny look. For lunch we stop on the green and beautiful Kalamos.

"Hela Christos."

"Hi Fabio."

We are at Varka Family Tavern, a magical place where the food is great.

You arrive and moor at their jetty or if there is no room you squeeze between a couple of boats at the fishermen's pier.

A tavern on the white pebbles of one of the most beautiful islands in the Ionian Sea.

You choose a table and the view captivates you.

If the Malavoglia's Medlar House had ever existed, this would have been its perfect copy.

White lime paint with the ever-present light blue on the windows and door.

The quality repays the wait and after one of the best lunches one could wish for in these parts, we board the boat and anchor not far away – on an idyllic little beach that can only be reached by boat.

The colour of the sea changes from midnight blue to emerald green to transparent.

The beach is thin and topped by a steep hillside thick with majestic maritime pines that seem to glow with their own light.

The scents are unforgettable, the afternoon breeze pampers you with the gentleness with which a mother would caress her newborn baby.

At the far end is the mainland, Meganissi and the mountain of Lefkada: the mystical Mount Skaros: a mushroom imploded on itself that resembles a volcano, a reference impossible to ignore if you go by sea in these parts.

The clients are dozing on the boat, I am on the beach on the foreshore with the water lapping against my body and I think how lucky I am to be doing what I do, and to know how to do it well, since there are those who seek and demand me as captain for a certain type of clientele.

I touch the rope crucifix that Alina gave me after my last visit to the monastery of St Nicholas, smile, and see a shape on the water that turns my gaze.

234

A very small sailing catamaran with a familiar shape and colourful sails.

He comes up on the breeze and passes us. I don't believe it: an Hc 17 – my first boat.

On the trampolines used in the regatta to balance the buoyancy of the wind are fixed camping tents and other objects, the crew consists of a young couple. They stop a little further on.

They anchor and secure the boat on land.

They will sleep here tonight, be alone, make love and feel like the happiest people in the world.

This place is pure magic and attracts like a magnet free spirits who can feel its soul.

I see me twenty years younger, and the me of twenty years earlier would have wanted to be alone.

I get on board and slowly walk away from the beach, the two smile at me and I smile back, an understanding of those who can communicate without speaking.

That 20-year younger me was thinking: *how I would love to do that job*.

The present me watching him drowned in memories.

A passing of the baton dictated by time and the absence of regrets between those who possess the art and courage to live life to the full.

We return, skimming the northwest side of Meganissi and floating on its shallows.

Dessimi welcomes you with open arms, customers say goodbye, thanking you for a wonderful day.

"Ola kala?" asks Spiros with that half-smile he always does when he's taking the piss.

"Do you have doubts re-malakka?"

"You take more in tips than all the waiters in Nydri put together."

"It must be that they never smile."

Spiros shakes his head as he strokes T.C. a cute red and white kitten he is carrying.

I take one last swim, go aboard Wallaby and Claudio as always uncorks something unforgettable. After a few good stories we say goodbye and I swim quietly ashore.

The petrol station's tank enters the car park, refuels all the boats' tanks and last of all that of my Ninja.

Time to dry off, then I start the bike, say goodbye to Fani and his beautiful smile, go to Perigiali to pick up Spinaz, and fold after fold we go up into the mountains.

The beautiful Alina is there waiting for us at *Alina's bar.*

As soon as she sees us, she smiles, tilts her head to the side, puts his hands on her hips and says to the laughter of Dave and the other patrons: "Does this look like it's time to go home?"

How I love her... I look around and I know I am home, there is already a bottle of *Sellato* uncorked on a table to oxygenate and dinner is there, on the grill.

And another beautiful day in paradise comes to an end... is there anything more beautiful in life?

BAR LIFE

Autumn arrived in a blaze of orange-red colours.

Vafkeri's mountainous morning sees me open the door of the cottage, inhale puffs of pure air, and walk across the white pavement that paves the village towards the café square.

The view is stunning, a touch of antiquity in the middle of the Lefkadian forest.

A medieval hamlet of wood and stone.

I pass the monumental old grape press, the mechanic's house with the vat full of freshly made must, and take the shortcut.

A few steps and I am in front of the beautiful and cosy *Alina's Bar*, a balcony overlooking the Vafkeri valley.

This vision is always beautiful.

The bar is a delightful mountain hut.

I open the wooden door, greet her and glance towards the coffee machine.

"Will you be good today yes?" Sometimes she's mischievous....

Espresso ristretto, cappuccino and spectacular views.

I am almost always alone early in the morning.

Zaza wakes up with ease if he has no work to do, he has litres of tzipuro to digest.

I tried to keep up with him once, just once – and I won't try it again, as the floor just outside the door of the Platanos still remembers my exorcist-style vomiting.

Never drink with a Georgian. Or rather, drink with one, but not at his pace.

After a good handful of minutes, *Lagos comes* up from lower Vafkeri.

"Kalimaera Fabio"

"Kalimera Lagos ti kanis?"

"Ola kala nasta kala."

"Ena Ellenico ne?"

"Ne parakalò"

I will never understand why people continue to drink that slop inherited from Turkish rule when we have one of the best if not the best espresso on the island at the bar.

Machines set by Spinaz, Borbone Blue blend coffee, Dios back-loaded water chosen after countless trials.

Nothing...

Then comes Kostas, the shepherd.

He does worse: he drinks *caffèfrappè*.

That I do not even have the decency or the will to write down what it is made of.

Kostas comes down the alley like a ghost, you never hear him when he arrives. But you sense him.

Or rather, I learned to perceive it after a while.

One morning I was there enjoying my cappuccino, it was still summer.

I hear a dry clap of hands, turn around and see Kostas.

The dull, watery blue eyes, the dishevelled white hair, the lurid shirt unbuttoned on his chest. He simulates bringing a cup to his mouth with his empty hand a couple of times.

His elegant way of asking for coffee.

I do not move, I do not get up from my chair, I continue to enjoy my morning cappuccino.

He sits at the end of the last table.

I can only see the blue eyes hidden by the white hair that is beginning to flare.

He gets up and approaches almost floating.

"Ena café."

I look at him, square him from head to toe and say:

"*Delete kalimera sto orios re malakka?*" which means: have they deleted good morning from your village *********?

At which point his beard ripples into a half-expression of surprise followed by a sarcastic smirk.

"*Buongiorno,*" (Good morning) he says to me in Italian.

"Can I have a *caffèfrappè* with a drop of milk?"

I tilt my head to the side in affirmative.

He sits nearby and when I bring him coffee I tell him "I didn't know you spoke Italian".

He looks at me with those spectral eyes and says, "We speak many languages."

I look around and ask "We who?"

And in response as he sips his horrendous frappe coffee his blue eyes take on colour as if backlit.

"I'll pay for his coffee Fabio."

I had not noticed Lagos and his terrified look in all this.

"No problem," says Kostas, turning towards him.

"You will offer it to me tomorrow."

Lagos is a well-dressed gentleman, a former owner of a profitable business in Athens who comes here to Vafkeri to keep an eye on his son, a nice boy who wanted nothing to do with his father's business and who works as a courier with a half-ruined van.

"I don't understand what he does with that van," he told me one day like any other.

"How does he support himself!"

That time, however, I could not resist and asked: "Lagos, but what were you doing in Athens?"

"Funeral home... yes I know, but it was paying well, very well. Now I've sold everything."

"Well maybe he didn't want to deal with the dead."

"Ah! And he's staying here? Even worse..." he said, turning dark in the face.

"What do you mean?"

"Nothing nothing..." he replied, trying to change the subject.

"I don't think more people die in Lefkada than in Athens," I said, insisting.

Lagos stared me straight in the eye "Dead people are not the problem Fabio."

"Ah well of course the living are much more annoying."

"Yeah," he replied, smiling.

Then he looked at me as if he wanted to tell me something but he shut up.

The bar is located on the western slope of the Vafkeri hill.

This means that before a certain hour the sun does not come and you stay cool, even too cool for Alina who is a cold-blooded creature.

That is why she always arrives at the bar an hour or so after me and every time she makes her entrance the atmosphere changes.

Maybe it is the sunlight that begins to kiss the wood of the chairs and tables, maybe it is that where she comes she always brings cheerfulness, but from the moment she sets foot in the bar everything becomes more relaxed and soothing.

"Hi there, are you OK?" She asks.

"Yes everything as usual, the early risers."

Alina's arrival is announced by Bibi and Pepi, who arrive a handful of seconds earlier trotting and wagging their tails.

Then Neo, her beautiful black kitten who came from nowhere, also turns up.

One evening after a boat trip my clients asked me to meet them again, so I invited them to the mountains.

It was a beautiful evening, they tasted the different wines I proposed and delighted in the typical specialities baked in the kitchen.

Then before they left their car started meowing.

A tiny black kitten all skin and bone was hiding in the engine compartment.

After several attempts they managed to get him to leave and he came to hide behind the bar.

He was really skeletal and it was clear that he was not one of the village cats.

Those of the last litter must have been a couple of months old while he was smaller.

Alina was very worried because living out there without a mother he could become prey to foxes or hawks.

We did not see him again for a couple of days, then he turned up. He was hungry.

Ali started to prepare some puppy milk for him and tried to leave it where he could see it but we didn't know if it was him or the other cats eating.

The fact is that we began to see him more and more often even though the other felines in the colony chased him away.

One image will remain with us for life: one day there was a mother cat suckling *Macchia* in front of the bar, her kitten.

Little Neo tried to approach to eat him too, but she pushed him away viciously.

From that moment on, Ali decided to take care of him at all costs.

She started spending more time with him, trying to approach it and when she gained its trust by even managing to touch it, he decided that it had become her cat.

Black, tiny, with two green eyes very close together.

The name lottery among the British neighbours began, and in the end Ali chose Neo – a very apt name.

Today *Neo* & *Macchia* are inseparable. They sleep clinging together and fight most of the time. They eat and drink from the same bowl and are the bar's main entertainment.

Even Lakis comes to play with the cat, preparing some sticks tied to strings by his own hand.

It takes little to change even the oldest spirits, not all of them perhaps, but for some it is enough to make them see things from a different perspective.

"Three dogs, two cats, something else?" I say to Alina.

She smiles, "with cats it's easier, once they are adults they are very independent, then there's Ann."

"What if we have to move somewhere one day?"

"*Bo?* We can take them with us, or let them decide. But I don't think Bibi and Pepi want to travel any more."

"A long stop in Lefkada is expected then..."

"The island will decide."

FORTY

Ann Mystico's unmistakable laugh spread cheerfully across the patio of Alina's Bar.

Every time she returned to Vafkeri, the entire village was seized with an irrepressible contagious glee.

I was on my way back from Karia for some shopping and found her sitting with Sue and Alina laughing it up.

"Hey you're back!" I told her.

"Ehy Fabio how are you? Yeah we're back for a few weeks, John's home and going crazy with work, I'm here catching up on the latest island news."

"Ah, and where are you at?"

"Ah well... I know about the new little dog that has now become a big dog, I know that Maria unfortunately left, I know that the tasting in Syvota with Karen went great..."

"Yes, the tavern will never be the same without Maria, what an absurd decision to send her away.

Sometimes I don't understand local people... Anyway, thank you so much for introducing me to Karen! Despite the fact that the conditions were not the easiest for a tasting and not even the time of day, it ended up going very well, the customers were delighted."

"Yes, she told me."

"Has Alina told you about her birthday party yet?"

"What???"

"Ehm... not yet..." shyly said Alina.

"You know I turn forty in a few days and I don't know maybe it would have been a good idea to celebrate all together here at the bar."

"We will talk about it tonight, we can also organise something at Villa Mystico."

"What's going on tonight?" I asked.

"You don't know yet?" replied Ann with her sardonic smile.

"Tonight is *Pink ladies Vafkerian night!*"

"It sounds scary..."

"Women only."

"There, now that sounds even scarier."

"Alina should be with us if *someone else* offers to take over the bar in the evening..."

Ali looked at me with that typical little girl's face asking grandpa for ice cream.

"OK OK I'll stay no problem, the alternative would have been to accompany you or pick you up so I'm more than OK with that."

"Ah don't worry about that, John will drive us and Dave will pick us up."

"Is Boring Dave still alcohol free this week?" I asked.

"Yes..." replied his wife sadly. "He's terribly boring when he's always sober, now I'm not saying he has to get drunk but a couple of beers never killed anyone did they?"

"But aren't you finished with the triathlon?" I asked.

"Yes, but he feels very fit now and wants to keep it."

"How I understand it... look at me for example: I can't drink more than four tsipuros a night these days. I have to get in shape too you know, winter is approaching and wood is expensive this year so alternative heating systems are needed."

"By the way, how much do you pay for the wood?"

"Zaza increased by 30 per cent"

"Meaning?"

"One hundred to one hundred and thirty per van load," I replied.

"In Karia they asked us for one hundred and sixty and the van was loaded up to the banks, no more."

"Yes that's a thief I always told Dave."

"Yassu Vafkerit."

Lakis' deep voice greeted us from above from the alley overlooking the patio.

"Ehy Lakis. Ena portokalada?" said Ann, offering him an orangeade. The Lefkadian elder tilted his head to the side in the affirmative.

He represented the cheerful, old-fashioned image of the village, always dressed like a tramp despite having land worth hundreds of thousands.

He lived off his pension and the few eggs he sold to me and the other inhabitants of Vafkeri.

Lakis is one of the good ones, Lagos once told me.

With time he has found a kind of inner peace. You always see him smiling even though he is now alone.

In fact, I often saw him sitting under the century-old plane tree enjoying the afternoon coolness, talking to himself in an incomprehensible language, with those dull watery eyes that seemed to come alive when he was there, under that century-old tree - guardian of the island's secrets.

"I had never seen Lakis play with a cat!" burst out Ann Mystico.

He had tied a broken twig to a string and was playing with Neo.

"Yes, he does that a lot lately: he comes here, always sits at the same chair and plays with the kittens," Alina said.

"Amazing... maybe we'll save one," replied Ann Mystico referring to the fact that the locals saw animals in a different way to us, or at least I thought she was referring to that.

But seeing Lakis smiling in bliss when Neo did his stunts was a novelty.

His nephew had forbidden him to come to the bar, we still didn't know for what reason: whether it was because Lakis didn't shine very well at personal cleanliness or something else. In the end he didn't bother, he was harmless and even though he didn't show up for a few days we invited him for an orange soda and he came back to play with the kittens.

"Why do you think Vassilis told him not to come?"

"I have no idea," Alina replied.

"Maybe he realised that we were the ones who freed Pea from the chain," I said.

Vassilis was the oldest of the sons of Theodoric, Lakis' brother and my neighbour.

The youngest, Alekis, often came to the bar and was always smiling like his uncle.

Vassilis, on the other hand, was perpetually pissed off.

Years ago he brought Atina and put her there on the chain. A splendid little dog that had never been taken hunting.

This winter brought a two-month-old puppy descended from a famous breed of hunting dogs from the Ionian Islands dating back as far as Argos, the dog of Odysseus.

It was clear that Alina and I were raising the puppy and that he no longer recognised Vassilis as his master by not responding to her calls.

Only after six months he managed to catch him and put him on the chain.

'They took Sweet Pea," Alina told me tearful over the phone.

"OK quiet tonight I'll take care of it."

I was in Perigiali fixing things on Nitroglicerina.

As soon as I returned I passed by the bar.

"Hey, what happened?"

"I went upstairs for a moment to change my dress and saw him at the chain, he's been crying since this afternoon."

We closed the bar, went up to the house and without even opening the door I climbed over the low wall dividing the two properties and cleared it, taking advantage of the darkness.

He, amidst much celebration, followed me into the house.

"And now what do we do?" asked Ali worried, "we can't keep it a secret."

"No, I'll make something up."

I called Andrew and he immediately made himself available to keep him for a while.

After a few days, however, he asked me to take him back because he ate whatever was within reach of his teeth and did not get along well with his other three dogs.

I managed to keep him hidden for almost a week then I had to release him into the village.

He had become bigger, faster and a bit smarter.

"You'll see he won't get caught again," I told Alina, "in the end he's happiest when he runs free in the woods, we could even find him a family but look at him... he'll never be that happy living in a flat. He needs so much space."

"Yes, that is true," agreed Alina. "maybe with a little patience the right family will come for him too."

"Yeah, Vassilis is getting on my dick anyway," I concluded.

In fact he never came to the bar, if he had something to say he would tell Lakis who would then report back.

Instead of being grateful that we looked after the dogs he abandoned in the grounds behind his 90-year-old father's house... Strange people.

The *Pink ladies'* evening was a huge success.

"Did you have fun?"

"Yes, a lot, but the most hilarious thing was John to Dave..."

"Meaning?"

"John was so serious when he dropped us off like we were at a funeral, but Dave... He looked like a whipped dog when he arrived."

"Come on, why?"

"Ann asked him how he had spent the evening and he all mopey *I reheated what you left me to eat, watched some TV, that was it.*"

Just imagining it made me burst out laughing.

"What about you?"

"I was on video call with Spinaz drinking whisky."

"What about the Italians who had booked in the tavern?"

"Nothing showed up. Constantinos closed and went drinking in Karia."

"Is he pissed off?"

"No he didn't care, he was smiling when he left."

"What assholes though."

"I don't know, I think he made up that *pappara* there in the end.... The number we were trying to call was non-existent."

"Yes it can be, what a moron."

Since the tavern had changed management, many things had changed.

Alina ran the bar perfectly and Maria in the kitchen was a fantastic cook, but the jealousy and envy typical of some islanders ruined the environment.

Maria was dismissed for no reason whatsoever, which in the long run would have condemned the new management to leave the tavern, good thing the bar was safe.

It is amazing how much things change when you start experiencing them from the inside.

During the summer at one of the private tastings held at the bar, a kind of audience was created.

A VIP transfer brought a Dutch family up from Syvota: father, mother and three beautiful girls.

They sat down on the sofa and the tasting went great.

I didn't notice it at the time, but among the astonished and delighted eyes of the local holidaymakers who return to Vafkeri every year for their holidays, there were also little eyes looking with growing envy at what I was doing amidst the jubilant laughter of the Dutch girls and the smug ones of the family members of Angelo, the owner of the building that includes the Taverna and Bar.

At the end of the evening his son-in-law complimented me.

"You know Fabio I was just telling a friend of mine on the phone if he remembered the bar back in the days when we were kids and the people who ran it used to lock themselves in there drinking Jack Daniels. And look what it is now. Your wine expertise is outstanding and the fact that there are people coming all the way to Vafkeri for these tastings of yours is really great for the village."

"I thank you, you know Vafkeri is the wine village and it is good that tourists learn about the essence of Lefkada, which is not only sea and beaches."

'The essence of Lefkada..." said Angelo's daughter, leaning her head back and closing her eyes.

"You know they were all shepherds here, some are still here, some are gone, some will stay forever," he continued almost in a whisper.

She was beautiful, a sweet look and two eyes changing from brown to blue, almost chameleon-like.

"Yes, sometimes they tell me about it."

"Who?" she asked, staring at me. His gaze was magnetic.

"A little bit of everyone, but the longest chats I had were with Sotiris Santas, who I think is your cousin."

"Yes, indeed he knows a lot about Lefkada."

"True, in winter we used to spend hours in the tavern chatting, he told me many things, but over time I realised that he didn't really tell me everything..."

"And what did he tell you?"

"I remember him telling me about old stories, about the real Ithaca and the ancient forest."

"What did he tell you about the ancient forest" she asked without asking.

"Not to go there."

"And he did well," she replied in a silky, sensual voice as she sipped some excellent Primitivo.

"Yes but it is beautiful, I realised there are also truffles."

"Who told you about the truffles?" she asked almost nervous.

"Iannis of Karia, you know of the bar Pablos."

"Iannis..." she said contemptuous shaking his head.

"Wasn't he supposed to?"

"Young people today have no respect any more," he continued.

"And they waste their gifts..."

"What's wrong with that forest? I was there once and it was incredible. It breathes and lives a life of its own."

"Indeed... not everyone is welcome."

At that statement I was reminded of the sense of unease I felt walking among those ancient trees.

"Never in a forest have I felt... too much like that time."

He looked me straight in the eyes and I could clearly see the light in them.

"There are things that are difficult to explain, some people call them magnetic fields, some call them time holes, some call them energy zones. You seem to be an intelligent person and I think you have already noticed certain things. Maybe the forest wanted to protect you or maybe it was your sixth sense that did it, the fact is that my cousin gave you good advice. You should not go wandering in that forest, much less scouting for truffles."

A gust of wind blew in from the back of the bar tousling her hair, she nodded to turn around, and in the semi-darkness the embers of Kostas the shepherd's cigarette glowed far away in the shade of the last tree on the patio. Two bright blue eyes stared at us.

"There are things that never die," she said again.

Then she finished her wine, raised his cup and said. "Great, can I have some more?"

"Of course," I replied, and when I returned with the bottle of Sellato I noticed that everything was different and in a different light.

As if that conversation never happened.

SPEAKING DIVINE

I have always had the idea of doing wine tastings.

Ever since I became a sommelier I wanted to do it.

But an idea remains a smokescreen until it is put into practice, and Ann gave the decisive push with the tasting at Platanos.

That was not the first tasting done in Vafkeri if we want to be picky.

In fact, to be fair, the first tasting in Vafkeri was not even of wine, but of whisky.

Organised by a former yacht club waitress, it was an online tasting.

That is, we had samples of fine whisky in front of us and connected via streaming with the producer we could interact both with him and with other tasters around the world.

It ended up as expected.

That tasting, however, gave us the idea to do another live one while preserving the friendly environment that had been created.

After giving my British friends a taste of the Apulian wines, they began to drink nothing else, and since their and my cellar were pretty well stocked, we decided to get rid of a few bottles all at once.

All in one evening.

I drew up a wine list and everyone brought a few bottles, minus Dave who only opened a couple of his but hosted us at his house.

It was an evening to remember, the forerunner of The Wine Tasting Guild.

We enjoyed ourselves as never before and on that occasion Vafkeri's superstar, the 2016 Primitivo Sellato, saw its supremacy falter as we compared it in the same tasting with its older brother: the Marpione, of which we had a 2017 but especially a 2011... one of the best vintages ever in Puglia.

The Marpione is an old-school Primitivo, with important tannins and old-fashioned wine scents.

Sellato is a new interpretation of Primitivo where glycerine and those modern scents that the market demands blend in a superlative way with the DNA of the grape variety.

It was not easy to explain the differences to my friends, but the sense of the evening was a glimpse into the future.

From there we organised the spring tavern tasting I have already written about, but above all the tasting that will remain in the history of the Vafkeri Wine Society.

Which ironically was not in Vafkeri.

I was about to go out on my bike, as is often the case around here, when Dave's voice distracted me from my thoughts about the millimetres I would have to file down the position of the saddle in relation to the vertical axis of the —

"Ehy Fabio, good morning neighbour."

"Ehy mate how are you?"

"All good all good, what are you doing?"

"Ah I think if I could move the seat forward a few millimetres I would have a better push on the pedals."

"Oh my God Fabio, I have created a monster."

"Eh, it happens when I get fixated on something, you should have seen me on go karts..."

"Did you drive go-karts?"

"Yes a lifetime ago."

"Interesting. Fabio, I was thinking: my family will come to visit me for a few weeks, they will stay at Villa Dessimi."

"Oh... and does Andrew know?"

"Yes, I think so." He replied, laughing.

"Do you need a skipper?"

"Maybe that too, but I was thinking more about your true vocation: I need a sommelier."

"My true calling eh? That's because we've never been on a boat together Dave... even though I think being a sommelier on board a boat is my absolute peak."

"That is also an idea, but how do you see the tasting we did at the Platanos relived at Villa Dessimi?"

"I see it well, I think that if the weather is like today, and it certainly will be, we will be able to use the terrace."

"That's exactly what I thought."

"That can be done, in fact I can't wait... how many wines do you want on the list?"

"Six or seven."

"How many people?"

"I think about fifteen but not everyone drinks."

"Doesn't everyone drink? In your family? Are you shitting me Dave?"

"No Fab in the sense that there are a couple of children..."

"Ah in that sense there... come on it's never too late."

"OK then, shall we put the idea in the pipeline?"

"Sure, consider it done! I'll draw up a wine list right away, do you want just Puglia?"

"Of course mate."

"You are home then."

The tasting was something memorable.

To date, the best ever.

The pairings were not perfection but I have never seen people having so much fun during a wine tasting.

It started off very seriously, with Dave introducing me to the audience, who turned out to be very interested in the different types of glasses, the tastevin and its ancient function, and Murgian wines.

It ended with dancing and wild dances of which we still retain indelible memories today.

The setting certainly helped, a villa perched on the hill of Dessimi with a view of the bay and the sea there that you could almost reach out and touch.

The colours became bright and vivid once the sun greeted us as it went behind the hill.

'I'd say it went well,' said Alina once the tasting phase was over.

"Yes, I would say so."

"You should really think about doing it as a job, your eyes sparkle when you talk about wine, a bit like when you go boating."

"Yeah..." I said as I lowered my gaze, thinking of my grandfather and the early wine-tasting lessons he used to give me as a child.

"Now do you mind if I have some fun too?" said Ali, bringing a glass of Fiano to her mouth as she gave me a funny smile with those now green now light grey eyes.

"And you need to ask?"

She and Dave's daughter Jo were the entertainers of the evening.

An instant chemistry had been created between them and they were having the time of their lives in more or less silly dances while the level of alcoholic beverages dropped irretrievably.

I think we also hit Andrew's cellar that night.

The next day Alina had hurt her neck, Jo didn't leave the house, and Dave couldn't stop thanking me for how well we had made his family feel.

"Really Fabio we had a great time, we should do it again by the end of the season."

"Is everyone OK?"

"Yes except Jo still sleeping, Alina?"

"Yes, she is more or less in the same condition, plus she has neck pain."

"It must have been some fresh air after sunset."

"Yes maybe that's it."

We found out the truth by watching the videos of the evening.

At one point to the tune of Tina Turner's Proud Marie, Alina can be seen twirling her head in metal style, making blonde circles with her hair.

Those videos are top secret as you can well guess.

I remember that during the evening Dave was watching Alina jump like a cricket, whereupon he took me aside and asked, "Fabio, seriously... what did you give Alina?"

I couldn't stop laughing. "What do you mean?"

"No no really, I have the triathlon in two months... if it's something legal I would like it too."

"It's called wine Dave – the nectar of the gods – it does that to Alina."

From there it all began.

I explained my idea to Mariangela, my sister.

As I expected she praised it and as a great former art director in a few days he came up with a logo of *his own* that is now the official logo of my tastings and can be found on every photo of mine related to the theme.

Afterwards I organised with Francesco Giordano, the owner of Ionian Spirit, the tasting on board his beautiful boat that I have already written about.

That too was a huge success, it was very different from the one in Villa Dessimi, more formal and relaxed but with the same professional content.

The idea was to make it a weekly appointment, which we failed to do in the first season.

In fact, the thing that caught on was hillside tastings.

That break from the routine of the normal boat or coastal holiday became something much appreciated.

It is no coincidence that my slogan reads something like this:

In your villa, on your yacht, on our yacht, in our guild...

Now: our guild was the one that went the most.

And indeed, looking at them, the tavern and bar of Vafkeri are indeed a guild, a medieval synonym for the word club or even coven, lair.

When you climb those hills you get the distinct impression that you are somewhere that has nothing to do with the island we are all used to seeing in pictures.

You enter an exclusive club that brings you closer to the heart of the island, to its soul.

This is also why my tastings in the mountains involve a marriage between Apulian wines and typical island foods and between Greek wines and Apulian foods.

This wonderful combination has a name – and it is called Magna Graecia.

People also appreciate the historical factor, in fact just a few years ago, before the Roman civilisation, southern Italy was a Greek colony called Magna Graecia.

Calabria, Sicily and Apulia were part of the grandiose Hellenic empire.

And this tasting of mine is a tribute to those times, those flavours and traditions, which at the time must have seemed like innovations to us Italians.

The olive trees, the vine saplings, everything we have now in Italy comes from here.

From Greece.

What are now our traditions, such as our wine and oil, are qualities inherited from that ancient period when our land experienced one of its greatest moments of splendour.

In Calabria, a very sweet wine is still produced from Malvasia grapes that was used during the Olympics; the similarity between this wine and the one produced in Ithaca by farmers following the ancestral method is incredible.

We will see how this new adventure turns out. I am very confident.

After all, in Vafkeri the tradition of wine is deeply rooted, they just can't make it cleanly.

I am completely convinced that a winemaker worthy of the name would be able to create an amazing wine from these blends.

Scattered throughout the valley are vines cultivated in the form of saplings, on the south-facing slopes, on the hilltops, ancient and untamed vines take root even in the karstic strata where the island has its reservoirs of pure spring water.

A bit like Acquaviva delle Fonti on my Murge.

Their fruits are sweet berries with thick, colourful skins. What a great wine would come out of them.

The must I have had the pleasure of tasting is a divine nectar.

Only the next step is missing. The wine.

During the season I used the Platanos cellar to store my wines.

It was too hot both at home and in the bar, while in the cellar the temperature remained fairly constant.

I think for the first time bottled wines went in there.

There were huge glass barrels used for fermentation and from which the local wine was transferred without further steps directly into the jugs that ended up on the tables.

No clarification, no refinement, except in the stomachs of patrons.

A scent of fermented must pervades every single wooden plank.

At first, I was almost tempted to take the bottles out and lay them on their side, letting the wine breathe through the cork that so typical scent.

But in the end I gave up.

Especially during the summer season there is too much traffic in there.

One of those evenings I walked in and found myself in a lake of wine.

About fifty litres of *typical* wine produced by Zaza, the Georgian, sought their way out of the cellar.

Luckily the step at the entrance was a few centimetres high, I dread to think what would have happened to the wooden floorboards if there had not been that barrier put there by accident, mistake or divine will.

I took a couple of photos and sent them to my friends at the Vafkeri *wine* society: *'the end of Zaza's wine'* I wrote at the bottom.

It is a pity that such splendid grapes are vinified so sloppily.

THE ANCIENT FOREST

In the end the rains came.

A perpetual cycle that you cannot control and for which the island is grateful.

Only the day before we were in the green waters of Kalamos and Kastos, sure they were cool and we needed a light sweatshirt when we were moving at twenty knots running on the water, but it was late October and one morning like any other the humid air filtered through the half-open window.

Then the gentle drumming of the drops on the tiles, those gusts of thick, heavy wind, the different light filtering through the doorways.

A thick, woolly nembrous mantle enveloped the hills.

The island breathed. A low, guttural sound – like the sigh that follows taking a sip of water after a long hot summer day.

The morning sunlight backlit the clouds, giving the whole thing a mystical and surreal aspect.

The temperature had dropped a few degrees and the distinct and instantaneous feeling that summer was over suddenly entered my head.

It was over.

It had been beautiful, unforgettable, unique.

But it was over.

I felt a heaviness in my soul that also meant something else.

It was as if a cycle had closed.

Yes, now was the time for wood-burning stoves, winter dishes and their scents wafting slowly through the houses, short, quiet days, walks in the woods.

But something else had also ended.

I could not explain what, nor how.

Something had changed in an instant, my life, my habits, my thinking and even my future.

I felt that horrible and thrilling feeling at the same time of having lost something, like having closed a door having forgotten the keys behind it.

A door full of memories, good times, good things.

Now there was a blank sheet of paper in front of me, as there had been several other times in my life.

I just no longer had that youthful exuberance and energy that would suggest what to write.

I felt a certain sadness, a summer where the green waters and beauty had pervaded my senses had come to an end.

Re-entering the grey, albeit intense, winter was something I thought I was ready and waiting for.

But with the summer, a piece of something else had also gone that had accompanied me for so many years and was now part of me. Yes, I would have survived without that baggage of life, but how? Better? Or worse?

It mattered little because I could not go back.

When a deep wound opens, stitches and the steady hand of the best surgeon are not enough to heal it, a gaping scar will always be there, reminding you of what it was.

Even if your life changes for the better, that memory, that scent, that infinite beauty will always be there.

I read somewhere that the world is like a chocolate in a wrapper. You have to unwrap it and admire it little by little.

Now this simile really sucks, and then comparing the world to a chocolate is complete bullshit.

The world is a mysterious set of sensations.

You have to be trained to fully discover and appreciate every single inch of it otherwise you risk losing something beautiful just because you were distracted on that stretch of road, or you were asleep, and perhaps a beautiful landscape that could have been just a gateway to something more magnificent runs away and is lost forever.

How many times has this happened to me? Of course I don't know...

But I know what I lost when the first rains began to fall like tears on the cottage.

The same tears that a place I loved and still love cried when I left it for another adventure, which I still carry in my heart. And which is also over.

Places are imbued with the spirit of those who lived them.

You can't just walk away and forget them.

Every corner of matter is full of energy and trees are its custodians, those who bring it to the surface from the depths of the earth.

Have you ever tried hugging a tree? To feel that ancient energy flowing through you?

On the bar square, the centuries-old plane tree is an inexhaustible source of it.

Just by sitting in its shadow you feel better, just by touching its trunk you enter another sensory dimension. It is no coincidence that it is Lakis's favourite spot, if he is not out and about in the woods he is almost always sitting there.

The lives of those who walked and lived the places, of every single living thing and those immortal plants are there.

A valley unknown to most, who only stay on the island for the beautiful beaches, which in summer close like a hedgehog as if to protect themselves from the encroaching humanity that tramples them without restraint.

The spirit of places lives deep within them, in their silences, colours and smells.

It is something that goes beyond any religion.

It is something primordial that goes back to the creation of the universe itself.

And we are part of it, of this immense energy flywheel. We can fight it and crash into it, we can surrender to events, we can hide from it, or we can explore it, like a windsurfer running on a wave choosing the best trajectory.

But like on a wave you cannot turn back. Because if you just think it, you fall and go under.

It was over. The island was no longer the same.

In my eyes at least, and I was no longer the same in his.

What to do now? What trajectory to follow?

To continue doing what I have always done since I discovered the beauty of discovery and travel?

Or stay, slow down and let the wave of life go. That beautiful wave full of energy, now blue, now green, now grey. Get out of the surf and admire it as it goes.

I don't know, I have always ridden the wave when in doubt. I always drank my fill of it while being aware that so much water was lost.

Only something had changed forever. And there was no way to get it back.

A little ring lost in the depths of the sea while I was on that very thin board that separates adrenalin from static survival.

She was gone, her perfumes, the depth of that iridescent green that was the mirror of her soul, her bewitching tenderness.

Now it was just a wrapper without those feelings. A beautiful wrapping, to be fair.

Perhaps I should leave it to someone else to explore it as deeply as I have had the honour to do.

Maybe I should let go and go too.

Maybe I really should leave the island.

We had lost Sweet Pea.

The madman had been missing for days.

I went out to look for him and also unleashed Atina and Bella.

After hours spent in the valley and from the Australian's peak down to the monastery, nothing.

Even the dogs were not looking for him with too much conviction.

I had become attached to that big dog, I had watched him grow since he was only two months old.

I asked in the tavern if Vassilis had taken him away but nothing, not even the one who was supposed to be its owner knew anything about it.

Then Kostas the pastor told me that he had been spotted in the Ancient Forest, near the Red Church.

He told me this with an air of defiance, as if to emphasise that once I went there I would never find him again, if only because up there the dogs go wild, like any other animal that enters the bowels of that mountain.

Not even hunters go there anymore.

There is no point wasting time there, the dogs do not respond to orders and this is at best; they have even turned on their owners.

On one occasion, an old hunter was attacked by his dog.

He managed to free himself and shot him.

He told everyone that he had killed the dog, even though he knew inside himself that he was lying.

It had struck him true, the yelps of distress as he ran away frightened had tormented him for long sleepless nights.

Until the dog was spotted in perfect health drinking from the spring on a long, hot summer's day.

The hunter did not even go looking for him, refusing to believe his friends. He had changed, by all accounts he had aged a few years in a few months. He died the winter following the opening of the hunt, falling into a cliff and becoming trapped there.

They searched for him for weeks but no one heard his cries.

He died of thirst, after two days of excruciating suffering in which he could not move a limb without experiencing excruciating pain in his broken bones.

The Forest is revengeful, ancient spirits inhabit those places.

I took courage and went in search of Sweet Pee, taking only Bibi with me. The other dogs in the troop refused to get into the car, perhaps sensing my intentions.

Bibi never liked *Pisellino*, but he never left me alone and accompanied me on this latest crazy adventure.

Years ago he did the same thing in another forest where I grew up.

A beautiful Argentine dogo jumped a fence and came to see what we were doing there, in his territory.

The only one of my dogs who was stupid enough to challenge him, a cross between a dachshund and a foxhound who in another life would have been a Rottweiler did: he challenged him.

The dogo grabbed him by the throat and dragged him away, running like a lion does with a baby gazelle.

I was running as fast as I could trying to keep up with the dogo but nothing, he was distancing me.

Then I saw Bibi, who certainly does not have the looks to frighten even a cat, overtake me and reach the dogo biting him in the genitals.

I have never seen an Argentine dogo run away yelping like that.

Tarallo was safe, that was the name my sister chose for that dumb dog given to us by Michele, the tractor driver who worked for my grandfather Tonino.

Bibi was with me that afternoon.

We passed Platystoma and reached the Red Church.

I parked Gypsy nearby and opened the tailgate to let him out.

He calmly trotted along waiting for what to do.

That forest is dense, there are no paths.

You have to wander into nowhere hoping not to lose your bearings.

They said that compasses were of no use because some magnetic field deflected the needle.

As a good sailor, I had two with me.

I went into the forest among those majestic trees.

Bibi became silent, serious and guarded, advancing at a leisure pace.

I should have called Peewee, or at least tried to make him understand that we were there.

But a deep respect for the place made me advance in silence.

If he is here he will hear me, if he wants to come back he will come to me.

I had never seen such strange trees, the shade was everywhere and visibility very low despite the hour.

It is difficult to walk around there, you grope around using your hands to keep your balance.

We started climbing up a hillside, diagonally to the east, or what I thought was the east.

I turned around to look for the reference of the church but I could see nothing, just trees, moss and dry leaves.

Bibi looked around, careful choosing where to place her paws with each step.

Then we came out into a tiny clearing with trees enclosing it in a semicircle, like an amphitheatre.

We continued the search but without much hope, we started to descend the other side, deviating to the north east, or what I thought was the north east.

We skirted a small spring pond full of water lilies, although the summer season had been short on rain that pond did not seem to suffer.

We made a wide loop with the intention of returning to the church by hugging the forest and passed a tall, bare rock.

A surreal silence permeated the air.

Bibi approached her, sniffed her and then walked a few steps away and peed on a nearby tree.

"Come on Bibi, according to my calculations we should have the church on the left; so, let's continue north for a bit more and then turn west."

Bibi looked at me like someone who knows you're just talking bullshit, in fact after three hours of walking we were lost.

He too looked around bewildered not knowing which direction to take.

I was no better off, the sunset was approaching and the light of twilight in the west signalled it, only the compasses towards what should have been the west pointed south-east.

"Very good Bibi... I think we fucked up, but don't worry, it's an island, let's follow a direction and sooner or later we'll pop out to sea."

Instead, to pop up it was Pisellino.

In his usual way, like a wild horse, he threw himself at Bibi to shower him with feasts.

Bibi growled as always to be left alone.

"Hound dog shithead where have you been?"

He wanted to play, he wagged his tail and provoked Bibi.

I took a collar from my pocket and tried to approach him but he recoiled just enough to not let me touch him, I tried to approach him again but nothing.

It was starting to get really dark and having no other viable solution I started to follow him.

"Hopefully he's going towards the car, the direction seems right," I said to Bibi.

After a half-hour or so of medium-fast descent we emerged back into the tiny clearing – and there he crouched.

"Hey wait a minute... we've already passed this clearing and it was upstream as we came down. How the f—"

Two tiny blue eyes appeared in the trees, Bibi approached me, backing away and growling as if to protect me.

Two watery lamps in the dark illuminated an albino face.

She was the lady from the tea bar, seen a year ago.

She looked at me with an indecipherable gaze, curious I would say, but stern, almost mean.

With all the calmness of the world, Peewee lay down and went to sleep.

The lady was dressed in a dark cloak and advanced a few centimetres.

She emanated a faint light of her own from her face.

Then I heard Bibi growl again and Pea raised his head looking to his left.

Two more little eyes in the trees, this time shining on the face of an old man dressed in a shepherd's coat: it was the shepherd I saw at the lighthouse near the monastery of St Nicholas.

I started not feeling well at all, I didn't know whether I was dreaming or not.

I turned around realising that I was surrounded.

Some of those faces I had never seen, some were familiar.

There was Iannis from Karia and also Kostas, the shepherd from Vafkeri, with a worn-out old shirt unbuttoned on his chest: he had a devilish smile.

Bibi was close to me and was shaking like a leaf while continuing to growl softly.

Peewee didn't give a shit and was there, in the middle of the clearing, scratching his back belly in the air, moving around as if to create a bed for the night.

"It must be a dream, I'm waking up now."

Except that in dreams you don't feel that icy sensation that paralyses even your back.

Then Lakis appeared at my side.

He looked at me smiling and as always greeted me with a "kalispera Vafkerit."

At these words a deep murmur invaded the place, like the sound of an earthquake tremor in slow motion.

Those things in front assumed an astonished and frowning expression.

I turned again to Lakis who made a grimace as if to say "*don't worry, they are just kids.*"

His blue eyes were alive and alight, only they emanated a less strong light but also much more intense, deeper, like the pallor of his face.

Kostas the shepherd approached in a less than friendly manner and said something to Lakis in an ancient, incomprehensible language – I could hear the sounds without him moving his mouth.

Lakis made a simple expression with his face as if to say he did not agree.

Kostas then pointed his stick at me, continuing to look at Lakis even more fiercely.

Lakis did not even reply and Kostas smiled as he softened, looked at me shaking his head and stood by Lakis' side.

The others in the group began to move as if floating, pointing their twisted sticks at me, curving and moving like wiggly cats; there was no wind but their cloaks floated as if they were underwater.

Then a deep, guttural sound silenced them.

Lakis, who had remained with his hands crossed behind his back the whole time, took his stick and placed it on my chest and said:

"Ine Vafkerit."

And then I woke up.

It was late in the evening, Sweet Pea was licking my face and Bibi was growling at him.

"What the fuck happened."

The moon shone in the sky illuminating the clearing, I saw the stone hidden by leaves and covered with moss on which I had slipped, my head hurt like crazy.

Bibi guided me to the Red Church, which shone alive under the full moon.

Gypsy was there, I opened the hatch and the dogs jumped in.

"Hey you found him!" Alina said to me as soon as I got home.

"Yeah... a mess... I even slipped, see anything here?" I asked pointing to my head.

"Yes you have a bump," she replied, shaking her head and doing that irresistible half-smile of hers. Then she changed her expression.

"Are you OK there?" She asked looking at me in a strange, almost frightened way.

"Yes, why?"

"No nothing, for a moment I thought your eyes had turned blue."

Fabio
Vafkeri 11/10/2022 09:34

EPILOGUE

The highlight of the evening was the dialogue between myself, Kostas and the online translator.

Kostas is a shepherd who comes from a family of shepherds with roots in days gone by.

He also has those icy eyes that change expression depending on the mood.

His white hair tousled by the wind as he follows with his eyes every abnormal movement among the bush branches, every sound that makes him realise where his goats are.

You see him in summer leaning on his curved stick, old Methuselah of incalculable age.

No matter what one says, he speaks English much better than many islanders, which is not taken for granted for a shepherd, the island's primordial profession.

Only the evening's conversation was too specific for me to understand with my very limited Greek vocabulary accompanied by his worthy English.

So I resorted to the translator.

"Perimene" (wait a minute) I said.

I pick up the phone, open the application and say in Italian: "the red and white kitten was locked in the tavern all night, I think he hid to sleep in the warmth."

And away goes the translation fired by the translator's melodious voice.

He nods, then looks at me questioningly and says, "Alina?"

I don't understand at first, then I tell the translator "no it's not Alina it's an automatic translator".

After listening to the Greek translation he says to me "Automatic? Who is it!" he says seriously "Who's on the phone!"

"No Kostas there is no one on the phone, it is an automatic translator and the voice is not a person's, try speaking."

"Oki oki oki..." (no Mickey no...) he does shaking his head.

I can hardly contain my laughter.

"Look let's give it a try...

"Tomorrow do you think it will rain?" I say.

And he, after listening to the translation, shoots out something in Greek translated as "who xxxxx is on the phone?".

Nothing...

"Kostas... every phone has this automatic translator, you just need to be connected to the internet," I tell him in English.

A breach in the wall.

"Try if you want."

"And how much does it cost?"

"But even a cheap phone, not even a hundred euros, is enough for this."

"Wow," he says in amazement.

Then he adds in English: "I didn't know Alina spoke Greek so well."

And nothing... Lefkadian life pills.

Ciao Belli!

SUMMARY

Printed in Great Britain
by Amazon